CURVES FOR DAYS

LAURA MOHER

Published by Sourcebooks Casablanca, an imprint of Sourcebooks
P.O. Box 4410, Naperville, Illinois 60567-4410
(630) 961-3900
sourcebooks.com

Cataloging-in-Publication Data is on file with the Library of Congress.

Printed and bound in the United States of America.
LSC 10 9 8 7 6 5 4 3 2

To my quirky, brilliant, bookish dad, who
believed in my writing before I did;

And to my mom, aunt, and grandma whose
beautiful names appear in this book;

And to Mrs. Bemiss, whose Friday free-write
period was the best part of elementary school;

And to my quirky, brilliant, bookish son, the
best part of my life, forever, period.

CHAPTER 1

Alice Rose

THE WORLD GREW COLDER WHEN Mr. Brown died. That was obvious to me.

What I hadn't realized, when I was cradling his head on that hard sidewalk and he'd shoved the little bag with his weekly Altoids-and-lottery-ticket purchase at me, was that my world was about to implode.

I'm not saying all this money doesn't rock. Hypothetically, it *could*, I guess. But not at this particular moment, as I'm elbow-deep in my ripe kitchen trash, trying to bury three hundred tiny pieces of a note from Timmy Johnson.

I'd waited till three a.m. to check my mail, to avoid my neighbors. I'd turned the key, eased open the box, and...another flood of letters and cards, from strangers, acquaintances, and people who were my friends in high school before the bullying started and they'd backed off to save their own asses.

I tucked it all into the folded-up hem of my sweatshirt and shuffled back to my apartment.

The eighteenth card I opened was the worst. I literally gagged when I saw Timmy Johnson's signature. "Just wanted to say congratulations," he'd written. "We had some good times in high school, didn't we?" *Uh, no, Timmy, that night might've been fun for you—your sadistic friends certainly enjoyed the story later—but not for me.* "Give me a call if you'd like to get together and catch up."

Reading that shit must've burst some dam of rage and revulsion inside me. Growling and panting, I tore that sucker into tiny pieces and jammed them deep into the trash bag, under the slimy salad remnants now sticking to my elbow.

And isn't this just a perfect metaphor for what my life has become: bits of terrible, mashed in with the regular unpleasant stuff?

No, that's not right. I'm *fortunate.* Winning the lottery was *lucky.* I'm being ungrateful.

I ease my arms out of the stinky mess and wash my hands three times because I'd touched something *he'd* touched.

There's still a sizeable pile of unread mail, but the next card is almost as bad. Another former classmate writing to say he'd heard about my winnings, always thought I was nice, etc., etc., and to look him up if I want to go out some time. Pretty sure he's the one who drew the caricature of me as a cow with a huge swollen udder on the board in homeroom.

I mean, it's not like I don't have a fucking mirror. No guy my age has ever shown interest in me without having plans to do something rotten. I wasn't as big then as I am now, but I was never the pretty, popular type. Eighty million dollars may make *them* forget what really happened, but the money hasn't damaged *my* memory or made *me* stupid.

I can't make myself read any more of this stuff. Can't even make myself drop it into the trash. I'm also out of food, haven't had dinner, and can't stomach the idea of seeing anybody, not even a delivery driver, if there's even anything available at this hour. So after checking all my locks again and pushing a chair up against the door, I crawl between the sheets on my lumpy old couch, starving, drift off to sleep...and promptly have my *Jesus Christ Superstar* nightmare for the sixth night in a row.

In the dream, I'm outside surrounded by people, some familiar, many not, and they're all reaching out, trying to touch me, asking, begging for stuff. Like the crowds around Jesus in the movie, everybody wants something, and they turn loud and grabby and angry and scary when I don't immediately respond. I try to get away but two of them seize my arm and tear it off. A third trips me and they push me down. They rip me to shreds and run off with the pieces, all except my eyes.

As always, I bolt upright, frantic, my heart thudding in the silence.

I can't take another day in this place—or anywhere else in Indy—hiding from all the people who want a piece of me. The media's pretty much given up, but hopeful-looking strangers still drift by out front and neighbors hang out in the hall, ready to pounce if I so much as crack open my door. I'm trapped.

The people at the firm I hired for accounting and legal advice had suggested I look into a bodyguard service. Riiight. Where the hell would I put a bodyguard in my studio apartment?

I guess they didn't expect me to stay here. And it's true, the building is dingy and leaky and smelly, but it's familiar. Every other option I've considered—a hotel, a new apartment, a house, a cruise—involves doing things I have no experience with, dealing with a million new people in strange places, at a time when everybody looks at me with, like, hunger. Or jealousy, or anger. I'm alone. I don't trust anyone now, and *certainly* not anybody who knows about the money.

But this place has become a prison. I've got to break out.

So. Four thirty in the morning and I'm tiptoeing around this old place for the last time, looking for things I care enough about to take with me. Not the cast-off furniture and worn-out kitchenware Mom scrounged before I was born. Not the clothing and shoes I can't get the restaurant smell out of.

I shove my Important Papers folder, the Yeats poetry book Mr. Brown gave me, a toothbrush and comb, and my two photos of Mom into her old sewing bag with a pair of jeans, a sweatshirt, and all my underwear. No way am I leaving my undies behind for people to paw through. Then I creep out the back entrance to walk to the bus station, slipping a check and a "Fuck this dump, sell all my shit, I'm moving to Hawaii, Sincerely, Alice" note under the landlord's door on my way out.

'Course, I'm not going to Hawaii. And I'm not going by Alice anymore. From now on I'll be Rose. Always liked that part of my name better anyway. Roses don't take any shit. Gotta be careful grabbing a Rose. Might get a handful of thorns.

A Rose wouldn't let herself be all alone at age thirty-two because of something mean kids did when she was sixteen.

A Rose wouldn't have spent the last two and a half weeks cowering in her apartment as people tried to get at her.

A Rose would bust herself out and go after whatever she wanted.

So a Rose climbs off a Greyhound bus four hours later, halfway between Indianapolis and St. Louis, after spying a pockmarked Honda in a used car lot. She dusts off her driver's license, changes direction to fool any would-be followers, and heads vaguely southeast, without a single soul giving her a second look.

I'll call my Hail Damage Special Lillian. Rose and Lillian sound like gutsy characters from a classic buddy movie, and I'm ready for an adventure. And a buddy.

She smells like dust and fake pine but Lillian has a valiant heart. Barely pausing at the interstate entrance ramp yield sign, she bursts into traffic with a squeal of tires and a tiny fishtail and begins to build speed. She's just a little four-cylinder, so it takes a bit to catch up to the car in front of us, but we've done it! The Alice part of me reacquaints herself with oxygen, breathing deeper than I have in weeks, and we settle in to flow with the traffic until I've got some reason to stop.

Goals:

1. *Find a hideout for a while, maybe near the ocean. I've always wanted to see an ocean.*
2. *Find a new home where nobody knows about this goddamn money. Is ungratefulness a sin?*
3. *Decide what to do with all this goddamn money.*
4. *Buy a bigger Cuss Jar.*

Angus

When the burst of pain and the urge to maim and destroy passes, I set aside the hammer, fetch the ice pack from my cooler, and stand in the Wheelers' front yard holding it to my smashed thumb.

That's what I get for breaking Rule Number One of working with tools that can do a body harm: Never, ever think about your other job, especially if it involves helping troubled veterans with all the shit they've been dealt.

I'd been hammering down a replacement porch board, my mind on my newest client. Young army vet, recently discharged, wrestling hypervigilance, insomnia, rage, depression. "Man, I fucking *hate* people who think life is just fine, who don't realize the world's full of shit people doing shit things and you can't let down your guard for a single goddamn minute," he'd said in our second session.

Sounded just like me when I got out.

Made me realize how far I've come. Made me wonder if I might be ready for a life with more than just work in it. Question is, have I *earned* more?

Life would be a lot easier if there was a big scoreboard in the sky to let you know how much good you'd put into the world versus how much you'd sucked out of it. How the hell am I supposed to know how many therapy clients I need to help to make up for killing my marriage, watching the light in a good woman's eyes die out day by day? Or how my pitiful counseling efforts stack up against the worry I've caused—worry that carved years off the lives of the two best people I know?

I must've been feeling too cocky after surviving another set of winter holidays and Valentine's, that three-month stretch of frigid hell designed to really rub in aloneness.

Used to love holidays. Grandma'd fill the house with every lonely, hungry person she could find. My buddy Lenny was always there. Some of the other kids with screwed-up families. Neighbors, single people, anybody down on their luck. No telling who'd show up. Grandma'd load 'em up with good feelings and good food. Anybody shy, she'd hand 'em a paring knife and some potatoes to peel. Talk their ear off, making up crazy stories about me or Grandpa. Have them howling with laughter inside of five minutes. Grandpa and I'd be on our way through the kitchen to get more chairs, and he'd give Grandma a wink so quick you'd think you imagined it.

Been four years since Grandpa died. Two since Grandma followed, and now I pretty much hate holidays.

I miss 'em.

And sometimes I miss being married. Having somebody to belong to. Miss the part of me that was husband material.

Couple of weeks ago on Valentine's night, I cooked up a pot of chili for my clients and friends who had nowhere else they wanted to go. We played cards and ping-pong. Talked trash, watched sports. Normal and happy as we could manage. Afterwards, I bagged up our garbage and took it to the bear-proof bin in the cold backyard. Night leached the colors out of everything. Reminded me no one was waiting for me inside. The weeds rattling against the fence looked as desolate as I felt. But I'd made it through another wasteland of holidays, dammit, and dragged some other guys with me. That seemed important.

The next weekend, I let Lenny talk me into going out to hear his band play. I sat with James's and Rashad's wives, watching the Blue Shoes work their magic on the crowd at Lindon's. Tisha and Shay started in with their matchmaking bullshit. I shut them down quick, like always, but I guess they got me wishing.

So a minute ago, I was hammering that porch board,

batshit-hopeful thoughts flapping around in my head, feeling like I might be close to ready for…something.

Then a car backfired out on the highway and I brought that hammer straight down on my thumb. That's what I get for hoping.

I flex my injured hand. Big blood blister, some swelling, but nothing's broken.

That blister's the universe's big loud *no* to my unspoken question about whether I've built enough karma or grace or whatever to start looking for something for myself. Message received, universe.

It's coming down awful hard for March. Been sleeting and snowing all morning, especially the past couple hours. Thick white flakes. I eye the Wheelers' house. Next job is to climb up and replace rotted trim around the dormers.

Nope. Not in this weather.

I toss the ice pack back in the cooler. Gather up my tools, dry 'em off, load up the van. I'll get carryout and take the afternoon off for once. Watch *Die Hard* again. Maybe even take a nap. I scrape my windshield and head for home.

At the stoplight just inside the *Welcome to Galway, NC* sign, a little Honda is sideways in a plowed heap of icy snow. Tires spin, slinging dirty slush as the driver tries to get unstuck. Nothing happens. The engine whines and the wheels spin faster. Still no traction.

I pull over, put on my flashers, and climb out. The driver lowers her window as I come near. I'm surprised she can see over the steering wheel, she's so short. Thought at first she was a kid, but close up she looks maybe thirty. Messy brown hair, big brown eyes, zero makeup. Kinda cute.

"Need some help?" I add a few more points to the karma board.

She leans out her window to look me up and down. Waves her hand at the driving lane. "Yeah, could you just, like, pick the car up and set it down over there, please?"

Alright, so *not* cute. Thinks she's funny. Thinks I haven't already heard every giant, lumberjack, yeti, Hulk joke in the world.

I point to her trunk. "Lemme get in position. When I nod, give it gas real gentle." Can't help but notice the pockmarked roof and trunk lid as I walk around the car. "Geez, poor li'l thing." I don't expect her to hear me.

She does. Snaps, "Hey! Lillian's sensitive about her complexion."

O-kaaay. I brace my hands well above her temporary plate. God forbid I goose poor Lillian. I give the signal and push.

She eases the car out of the snow and into the lane. Squeals, "Oh, man, thank you so much!" Totally different tone than before.

I head back to the van. "No problem." Wave without turning around.

I'm dripping ice, looking forward to cranking up the heat. Almost to my driver's door when something small and hard smashes into the back of my skull. "What the—" I spin around, slip on the ice, and almost go down.

The Honda driver's eyes are huge, her hands up over her mouth. "Oh shit! I'm so sorry! Thank-you Snickers."

What'd she call me?

She points at my feet. "Thank-you Snickers."

There's a candy bar in the slush. Brown Eyes beaned me with it.

Just help the lady, my scoreboard had whispered. *Have a few laughs. It'll be fun.* No, that last bit might've been Bruce Willis. *Yippee-ki-yay.*

I rub my head and fish the candy out of the mess. Couple of cars maneuver slowly around us as I open my door and drop the Snickers into my trash bag.

"Sorry! Thank you! Really!" She's waving both hands now, silly grin on her face.

I shake my head. Climb in. Raise my hand, willing her to move on.

Instead she hollers, "Hey, is there a motel around here? I think I should get off the road."

Got *that* right. "B and B, two blocks up." Sabina'll take pity on her being out in this mess if she's not full up. I slam my door. Enough conversation.

Hell of an arm, but the woman's a menace.

Glad she's just passing through.

CHAPTER 2

Rose

THAT WAS THE SINGLE LARGEST human I have ever seen. A skyscraper, with shoulders like boulders. A curlier-haired Jason Momoa if Jason weren't such a delicate little fella.

But somehow not scary, despite his size and his wild ice-crusted beard and his crankiness.

I probably should've made sure he heard me holler before I threw candy at him.

Too late now. I need shelter from this weather, preferably somewhere where I can think and plan. Last week was pretty much a bust in that regard.

The bed and breakfast Mountain Man had mentioned is lovely, loaded with pastel gingerbread trim and quirky décor. I can see through the window that somebody likes lizards. They're painted, sketched, stitched onto pillows, blown from glass... They're everywhere, in colors probably not seen in nature.

A tiny woman with a silvery-white pixie cut answers the door, sees my flimsy hoodie, and hustles me into a warm kitchen. Once I'm seated at the table, she pours me a steaming mug of cocoa from a pan at the back of the stove.

"Now. I'm Sabina. What can I do for you?" She surveys me through bright blue eyes, and I imagine she's seeing my baggy jeans and cheap sneakers and thinking I'm here to apply for a janitorial position. A month ago she might've been right.

Sitting in her bright kitchen, surrounded by scents of cinnamon and chocolate and fresh-baked bread, I make a snap decision. "Do you have a room available for a couple of weeks?"

Her eyes widen a fraction. "Let me check." She fetches a laptop from what was probably once a butler's pantry. "You know, if money's an issue at all," she says, not looking at me as she clicks through a few screens, "it would be cheaper to get a room in one of those motels out on the highway..." She trails off and meets my eye.

I see only kindness there, but no way am I telling her about the money. "It'll be okay. I've never taken a vacation before, so I'm, uh, splurging."

She nods and quotes me a price roughly equal to three months' rent at my old apartment.

The thought of freely spending that much makes me feel giddy and wasteful at the same time. I manage to say okay without blinking or stuttering.

"How do you feel about stairs? The attic room is open. Some of the others are available part of the time, but I'd have to move you between them once or twice."

People usually assume that fat women are out of shape, but I've been a waitress my entire adult life. I can run rings around most people. While carrying two coffee pots and an armload of heavy dishes. "Stairs are fine."

"Let me show you, then." She leads me through the dining room to the foyer with its wide wooden staircase. Everything is bright and homey. Spotless. Reptilian.

Two flights up, she opens a door. Daylight streams through three dormer windows in the slanted ceiling. The walls are a pale warm apricot with crisp white woodwork. Bright accent colors pop from framed prints and cushions. I smell lemon furniture polish and clean linen.

It's like a room in a magazine. It's the prettiest place I've ever been.

"This is lovely." I finger the soft cotton quilt on the bed and watch snowflakes dance against the windowpanes. "I want this room." *I could live in a place like this.*

We take care of paperwork down in her office, and I retrieve my stuff from an already-snow-covered Lillian. I've got a small suitcase now in addition to Mom's old sewing bag. The clothes in it are better suited to the South Carolina beach where I'd spent last week than to this Christmas-looking mountain town. Maybe I'll shop for warmer things tomorrow.

Upstairs, I unpack my clothing and one delicate whelk shell. My beach stay hadn't provided any big *aha!* moments about where to live or what to do with the money, but at least I'd relaxed and stopped looking over my shoulder expecting to see Timmy Johnson or paparazzi or a frenzied hoard all wanting a piece of me.

The ocean itself had been amazing: an endless heavy roaring mass that threw light back differently every hour of every day; the unfamiliar smells of salt and fish and fresh air and seaweed and creosote and other things I can't name but will never forget; the cries of the shore birds circling overhead and skittering along the water's edge; the constant grit of sand under my feet in the weathered little cottage I'd rented.

I'd taken long meandering walks along the shore. Spent rainy evenings in a rocker on the screened-in porch, just thinking and listening and smelling the ocean and marsh. Read a few books. Wondered what to do with the money. Keep it secret, obviously, so I can have some kind of private, normal-ish life. But what else? I'm pretty sure other people with eighty million have a plan. I've got more than I could ever need, nothing big I particularly want to buy, and nobody to share it with. Nobody to leave it to. Nobody I love. Hell, I don't even have anybody I trust. And let's be honest: nobody needs that much money. Nobody.

One thing sticks in my mind. My last day there was too stormy to spend on the beach. I'd driven downtown for lunch instead. From a corner booth, I watched my sweet and hugely pregnant waitress bustle around keeping the noon rush customers happy, carrying heavy trays, delivering food and refills with a kind word, and smiling. Always smiling. But whenever she had the chance, she'd roll silverware in napkins or do some other task that involved sitting for a minute. I know that trick. Her feet were killing her. Her back too, probably.

When I'd finished eating, I dug into the hidden pocket of my purse and pulled out my emergency cash. Five hundred. Just a drop in the bucket now, but when I was waitressing it was a fortune. I wrote *For you and Baby* on a clean napkin, tucked the money under it, and hustled out to the parking lot, where I could watch through rainy windows to make sure she got it.

She did. She stood at my table, head bent, one hand holding

my note and the money, her other hand pressed to her mouth. As I drove away, I saw her touch the apron where it stretched tight across her belly.

I'm still picturing her face as I settle into a big comfy chair with a mystery novel. My gut tells me I did something right in that restaurant. That's gotta be a clue.

I read until three, do some extra stretches to loosen the muscles that had tensed up during my icy drive, and then head downstairs for tea in the parlor.

Sabina's just placed a plate of tiny sandwiches on a sideboard, next to one of homemade cookies. No one else is here.

She turns to me with a smile. "Come help yourself. Are you enjoying the attic?"

"Oh, yes. I *love* that overstuffed chair. You might have trouble getting rid of me." I fill a plate with goodies and pour myself some ice water from a heavy cut-glass pitcher.

"It's good that you got in when you did." She selects a few things for her own plate and sits down on the love seat opposite mine, moving a bright pillow out of her way. "I just got two cancellations for tonight, and another couple called to say they'd be a few hours later than expected *if* they can make it at all. On the radio they're advising people to stay off the roads."

"Wow, I *was* lucky!" I nibble a triangle of buttery shortbread heaven. "What's Galway like? Is there somewhere I can buy warmer clothes when it's safe to drive?"

"I love it here. It's small enough that it's easy to learn your way around and meet people, but big enough to have most of what you need." She picks up a sandwich. "Unless you want big-city noise and bustle. We don't have that. But you'll have no problem clothes-shopping."

Well, someone her size might not have trouble. We'll see if anybody carries my size.

She tells me about the heart of town, the old public square a few blocks away. "There's a library at one end, across from the courthouse, and a grandstand at the other end. Outdoor concerts in nice weather." She gets up to refill our drinks and moves the water pitcher to the coffee table between us. "The streets around the square are off-limits to cars. The businesses have outdoor seating and pretty flowers most of the year. Lots of twinkle lights in the evenings. It's lovely."

It grows dark and we're still talking. We share a love of houses built before the 1950s. We both like mysteries and documentaries and cooking shows. Neither of us can fathom the popularity of okra.

I ask about the lizards, and she tells me it started on her honeymoon when her husband snapped photos of one that always hung out near the ceiling of their hotel bedroom in Mexico. "Howard called him Tom. Peeping Tom."

I laugh, and she does too.

"After that, he gave me something lizardy for every anniversary until he died." She gives a lopsided smile to her glass. "I've still got those honeymoon photos in our room. My room."

We're quiet for a moment. I can't fill the space in the conversation or in her heart where her love still lives.

She examines a chocolate chip cookie as if to ensure it meets her roundness standards. "So, what brings you to Galway?"

I can't tell the whole truth, but she just shared something personal and I don't want to lie to her. Don't want to seem mysterious or make her curious about me. "I...want to relocate, but I don't know where yet. Spent a week at the beach, but now I'm just wandering, looking. I stayed in Greenville, South Carolina, last night and decided to turn north this morning. The weather stopped me here."

She smiles. "I'm glad it did. What's your accent? Midwest?"

I nod. "Indiana." That much should be safe to share. "I want a change. You know?"

"I do. Especially if there's nothing much keeping you there."

Nail, meet head. Now the achy space is in *my* heart. Sabina, too, knows better than to rush to fill the hole.

This is the longest, nicest, most personal conversation I've ever had as an adult. Mr. Brown and I had mostly talked books.

Is this what women's friendships are like?

"It's supposed to warm up fast tomorrow." Sabina adjusts the little napkin under her teacup. "If the roads are okay, I'll go to the grocery and run errands after breakfast. I can drop you at the town square if you'd like. You can do some shopping. My friend has a restaurant—July's—on one corner. I could meet you there after you're done."

That becomes our plan.

My attic bed is wonderfully comfy and I wake up refreshed.

Snow blankets everything, but plows have been through and the glistening icicles on the eaves are dripping furiously as I eat breakfast with the couple who did make it in last night.

Sabina's helpers arrive and she hands over the reins for a few hours. "They'll clean up, do laundry, bake something for tea, field calls," she tells me as she turns her car toward downtown. "I'm free until about one thirty."

Like she said, it's only a few blocks, lined with big trees

and nicely kept old houses. I could easily walk it in good weather. The square is as lovely as she described. She drops me at a snowy evergreen-filled concrete planter marking off the pedestrian-only area and points me to a long-windowed brick building on one corner.

"That's July's. Meet you there at noon? We can have lunch if you'd like." She waves and drives off.

I already love this town. A city worker nods and smiles at me as he clears plowed snow from a crosswalk. An Asian man outside a spice shop leans on his shovel and talks to a woman in a bright sari. She's sprinkling salt on the steps of a tiny bakery. The library, newer than the surrounding buildings, beckons, its tall windows revealing well-stocked shelves, but I resist, exploring the stores instead, trying to imagine living here. Having friends. Shopping for gifts for people I care about.

A self-proclaimed general store yields a heavy canvas barn jacket in dark taupe—thank heavens the only 2X fits—and a pair of jaunty red rubber boots polka-dotted in orange and hot pink. "Sure, honey," the elderly clerk says when I ask if I can put them on right there. I snag a matching scarf and gloves from a display near the cash register before venturing back outside.

From a fancy chocolatier I buy a box of mixed truffles for me, because I've heard so much about truffles, and some pecan turtles for Sabina. They didn't have lizards. An indie bookstore lures me in and spits me back out with three new novels and a box of poetry magnets. For the refrigerator I don't have. In the home I also lack.

I've never bought so much damn stuff at one time.

Hm. First time I've thought-cussed all day. In fact, I've

cussed less and less each day, without even really trying. Good. I'd hate to let rip a blue streak and offend Sabina.

A window display catches my eye as I head to the restaurant to meet her. Feminine mannequins, having a party amid cut paper hearts, glittering white faux snow in drifts around their bare feet, cocktail glasses in beringed hands. They're wearing feather boas and very little else. I stand and gape at the sexiest, fanciest underwear I have ever seen. *Ever.* Wisps of silk and satin and lace, tiny straps and see-through panels, and cups that lift breasts like offerings.

Not a price tag in sight. Meaning each set probably costs more than Lillian did.

I tear my eyes away and continue on to the restaurant, picturing the shabby, shapeless, faded, holey cotton garments in my drawer at the B and B, little end pieces of worn-out elastic escaping from frayed seams.

What would it be like not to purchase underpants in multipacks from discount stores? Not to buy giant ugly bras in cheap cardboard boxes? To wear pretty, soft, well-sewn undies against my skin all day, like a special secret beneath my clothing?

It never even occurred to me to use some of the money to buy nice underwear. Not that a shop like that would carry such pretty stuff in my size...would it?

I push through July's glass door and pause. It's almost full, with enough lively conversation that I can barely hear the bluesy music playing in the background. The furniture is eclectic, sturdy and mismatched, bohemian-looking tablecloths over black-painted wood, a single bold flower in a bud vase on each table. A friendly waitress with *Sonya* on her name tag and *I can dance if I want to* tattooed on her left arm leads me to a roomy booth near a side window.

I'm studying the menu, trying to decide which delicious-looking thing to order, when I feel eyes on me. It's a little old lady with a too-big pearl necklace, staring at me from the next booth. She rakes me up and down with a disdainful look. Then she sniffs, raises her eyebrows, and turns her attention to her salad.

Sabina arrives as I'm wondering whether a Rose would let such rudeness pass the way Alice always had.

"Miz Ames." Sabina nods politely to Pearl Necklace before sliding in across from me. "You had some luck, I see!" She nudges my rubber-booted toe and nods toward the new jacket and scarf folded over my bags on the bench beside me.

"I did. And it was fun!" I push the other menu toward her. "Everything looks yummy. What do you recommend?"

She pulls out a pair of reading glasses and perches them on the end of her nose, eyebrows raised as she considers *Today's Specials*. "I always order something different from what I serve at the B and B. So no quiche or baked goods for me." She nods at a table full of women dressed in purple and red. "I'd forgotten it was the Red Hat Society's day to come in. They've probably gobbled up all the quiche anyway. But the soups here are fabulous. And the pastas. And salads. Hot sandwiches."

"Sabina. That is not very helpful." I focus on my menu again as she grins.

We decide to split a grilled cheese and tomato soup combo and a roasted beet, goat cheese, and arugula salad. I've never tasted beets, arugula, or goat cheese, but I'm game for whatever she wants.

The waitress who takes our order obviously knows Sabina, and a few minutes later, July herself brings out our food. She's maybe mid-thirties, her streaky, shiny blond hair pulled back in a ponytail. Her smile is as wide as her shoulders. With her impressive biceps and sturdy build, she looks like she could move mountains. Now I understand why I could fit in this booth. This is a woman familiar with a need for room.

Sabina waves a hand in my direction. "July Tate, meet Rose Barnes. She's new to town, looking for a good place to relocate, and I think she should move here. Convince her."

I sit blinking in surprise at both of them, warmth spreading through my chest.

July laughs, slides our food and an extra bowl and plate in front of us, and shakes my hand.

"Welcome, Rose. Nice to meet you. Move here." Her voice is like smooth dark honey.

"It's tempting." My heart sure feels warmer here, except where Pearl Necklace over there is concerned.

Sabina divides up the soup and salad and hands half of each to me. "You can use the next couple of weeks to explore. July knows everything and everybody if you have questions I can't answer."

"Be happy to help, anytime. Enjoy." July nods at me, then heads back to the kitchen, exchanging greetings with people at every table she passes, calling them all by name.

Sabina tells me tidbits of Galway history and funny stories about the shops around the square as we eat. Everything's delicious, even the beets, which, contrary to what I'd heard, don't taste much like dirt at all. When we finish, we squabble over who'll pay, and finally flag down the waitress to ask her to split the check. She says, "Nope. July says it's on her today."

I fucking *love* this town. Oops.

Ten days later I'm coming through the door to July's again, as is my habit now. Over the past week and a half, I've explored the whole town, setting out from Sabina's B and B and walking a different route every day. I've found the fanciest grocery—a big new Ingles out near the highway—and another I like better: a shabby but clean market about a mile from the town square where the owner and his kids and grandkids treat the customers like old friends.

I've smiled and said hi to probably a hundred people, and most have responded in kind. I've never had so many doors held open for me in my life—men, women, children, everybody wants to help. A twinkly eyed librarian offered me a temporary library card and showed me all the best nooks and crannies for reading.

I've waited without success for inspiration regarding the money.

I've tried other restaurants, some really good, but I still end up eating lunch at July's most days. If I'm here when it's not a rush, the employees sit with me on their breaks. I know everyone's name now. My favorites, besides July and Sonya, are two women I'm pretty sure are July's right and left hands. And I'm pretty sure they're partners. They couldn't look much less alike, with Donna so tall and dark and Tina petite and pale, but their glances at each other contain love and devotion a person could see from across the room.

I recognize a lot of the regular customers now, too, including Pearl Necklace Ames. Nobody except her ever seems to have an unpleasant thought in their heads. They tease and laugh and seem to truly enjoy each other.

Amazing.

I still love my attic at the B and B, though Sabina never lets me help, even when it's busy. My favorite days are when there's no one there for tea but me and her. Then we eat in the kitchen and laugh and talk and build what I'm hoping is a real friendship. That's what private jokes and kindhearted teasing and shared stories mean, right? It's ridiculous that I don't know for sure, and the Rose part of me feels pissed at the Alice part every time I think about it. Yeah, I had to leave high school for my own survival, but I absolutely did not have to isolate myself for the next sixteen fucking years. So here in Galway, I've been trying to do better.

One day I bought a laptop, and Sabina helped me set it up with virus protection and office software. When I told her I was thinking about taking some classes, she sent me to talk to a friend of hers in the admissions office at little Galway College, which nestles against the biggest of the surrounding mountains. I'd always wanted to go to university but dropping out of school killed that dream. It's scary to think of starting at age thirty-two, but dammit, I want to know things. I want to learn stuff. *Like what to do with a buttload of money.*

I'd headed to July's that day too, and she'd seemed as tickled for me as Sabina had. "I took some business and culinary courses, but you'll be so much better at studying than I ever was." She'd grinned as she stood to go back to the kitchen, admitting, "I kind of have trouble sitting still."

I'd laughed and straightened the salt and pepper shakers and sweetener packets she'd been fiddling with.

But today I have *really* big news, news I can hardly believe myself, and I'm dying to share it with someone. Sabina's got a full house at the B and B and I don't want to bother her, so that leaves July and her staff.

I've found it. My new home. It's exactly three and a half blocks from July's in the opposite direction from the B and B, in one of those older neighborhoods where each house is unique. Mine is a smallish Victorian that needs some love. I wandered through it with the Realtor, asking questions and taking notes and pictures. There's a lovely front porch, perfect for a couple of rockers. The first floor has four rooms: a dining room and a living room with a big bay window in the front, and a kitchen and bonus room in the back. The only bathroom's upstairs with three bedrooms.

My need-to-do list was two pages long by the time I was done, but I knew it was The One. Every room has big, graceful windows filled with natural light. The high ceilings and beautiful woodwork and floors far outweigh the need for updates. There's potential everywhere.

I'd told the Realtor I'd pay full price, cash, if we can close before my time is up at Sabina's. Then I came straight to July's to babble incoherently at whoever will listen.

It's busy, as usual. However, for once, it seems chaotic. I stand inside the door, seeing no clean, empty tables and only Sonya covering the dining room. I catch her eye and she pauses with her tray full of dirty dishes and a near-empty pitcher of tea. "Tina cut her finger," she whispers. "Donna took her to the hospital. Bonita's home sick. July's alone in the kitchen."

"Give me that. I'll bus." I take the tray to the kitchen, toss my purse into July's office, and scrub my hands at the sink near the hallway door before grabbing an apron from a hook.

July glances up from warp-speed order-plating as I pass her with a clean bus pan. "Bless you, Rose."

"Anytime." I clean the tables in a flash and then find an order pad and pen behind the counter.

Sonya's brows raise as she comes from the kitchen after dropping off new tickets.

"Assign me some tables, Sonya. I've got a lot of experience, I know the menu, and I figured out the table numbering days ago. Just not Miz Ames, please." Because of course that pearl-encrusted little biddy is here again, and of course she's giving me a good long up-and-down, her eyes lingering on my midsection. You'd think she'd be happy to witness me getting exercise. I'm sure she doesn't believe fatties like me ever do such a thing.

Sonya looks relieved and gives me some tables near one wall. 'Bout time somebody lets me help. Being useless is no fun at all.

CHAPTER 3

Angus

"NEED A FEW MORE MINUTES to look?"

The waitress's voice is familiar, smooth, and friendly, but I don't remember any of July's servers filling out the top of an apron quite so spectacularly.

Oh shit, I'm staring at her chest. What am I, twelve? I yank my gaze up. "Sorry."

Her smile is polite. Her big brown eyes are dead serious.

Oh, shit, *again.* I know this woman. I sigh. "Snickers."

"We don't have—" She stops and cocks her head. Squints at me and my beard. Measures my shoulders with a look.

Lenny sets aside his menu, his attention ping-ponging between the waitress and me. No sign of the finger-tapping he usually does whenever he's away from his keyboards.

Snickers nods, slowly. "Cranky Samaritan." Her tone is dry as dust. "So we're on a nickname basis. *Awesome.* What can I get you fellas?" All brisk and professional now. She takes our orders and bustles away.

Lenny watches her go too. "Who's she? What's with the names?"

She hadn't batted an eye when we substituted soup for salad and barbecue sauce for mustard and jalapenos for pickles. Just said, "Gotcha," and made straight for the kitchen.

I shake my head. "She's a mess. I pushed her car out of the snow awhile back. She said thanks by beaning me with a candy bar."

Lenny's brows raise. He tilts his head back and laughs, making his reddish curls bounce. "You know, when a girl picks on you, it's a sign she *likes* you."

God help me. "That's a *terrible* message." I change the subject to the Blue Shoes' Easter gig.

He shrugs. "We'll be playing here in town. The guys want to be near family."

I know Lenny feels different. "You got plans or you wanna come over?"

"I'll bring over some Chinese takeout. Kick your ass at your stupid racing game. The guys invited me, but..." He shudders. He loves his bandmates' wives and kids and parents, but the whole family holiday thing is hard on him. He always used to end up at Grandma and Grandpa's house. Usually with bruises dotting his pale skin.

We talk basketball until Snickers brings our food. It's perfect, exactly what we ordered. She's even got extra bread, warm from the oven.

I have to say *some*thing to her. It'd seem weird not to. "Didn't know you work here."

"I don't." She refills our tea. Her hands look soft and strong. She smells good. Soap and oranges. "Just helping out today."

"You're good at it," Lenny offers. Normally he goes for taller, thinner women, but for Snickers he's all puppy-dog eyes.

She gives him a real smile. A sweet one. Doesn't say anything smart-ass or throw anything at *him*. "Lots of experience. Everything look okay? Can I get you guys anything else right now?"

I want her away from the table. "Thanks. We're good."

Lenny watches her all the way back to the kitchen. "She seems nice."

Like I said, holiday weeks are tough for a lonely single guy.

Don't know why I hate the idea of Lenny taking up with Snickers. She's wacky, but he needs somebody. And *I* sure don't want her. No matter how soft she looks or how good she smells.

Not that she seems interested in either one of us. Just doing her job.

When it comes time for us to pay, she waves us off. "On me," she says, looking me in the eye. "Thanks for helping me. Sorry about the—" She gestures at the back of her head.

And refuses to take my money.

I fucking *hate* that. I stuff it in the tip jar on the counter as she walks away, that damn mental scoreboard weighing on me.

"Real gracious, man," Lenny says as we leave, and I realize I'm growling under my breath.

I tone it down to a mutter. "I can pay my own damn way."

Lenny nudges me with one big shoulder. "You know she's just trying to make things even. Like somebody else I know."

I snarl, and he laughs and drops it.

A few nights later—Easter night—I stand on the porch and wave him and a handful of other guys on their way. Been a decent day. That's a victory. Lenny's drummer, Chris, came over, quiet and lost like he always is after taking his kids back to their mom. Some of my vet clients dropped by, knowing the door would be open. I gave three of them a hard time about being Duke fans. Heard 'em later making plans to watch a game together. Score. Knew another guy liked the blues. Got him talking to Lenny and Chris. Double score.

The guys brought Chinese carryout, hot sausages, and bratwurst. Queso and chips. Pizza. We wolfed it all down. Held a racing video game tournament. Played poker for pennies until after midnight. Now it's almost one and I'm looking up at the cold stars, wishing I had a warm, sweet woman waiting inside for me.

Snickers's face flickers through my mind, shocking the hell out of me. Not her. Definitely not her. She'd be soft and warm, but no telling what wild-ass things she'd do. Probably tie me up and pelt me with candy. Do god knows what with licorice whips.

That mental image has a shocking effect on me too, so I shove it away.

Don't have any business thinking about a woman. Tonight's all I'd have for her. Be pretty shitty to kick her out first thing in the morning.

Snickers'd probably spend the whole night mocking me anyway.

Sure wouldn't have time to feel sorry for myself with her around to irritate the piss out of me.

I'm looking forward to the new job.

July'd caught me a few days back, said she'd given somebody my number. "Friend of mine's buying an old house that needs a lot of work. She asked me to recommend somebody. She'll probably call you soon. Do a good job for her, okay?"

"Always do." Long projects are the best. I can look back on them and see I really made a difference.

"I know." She gave me one of her July smiles that make it seem like summer. "I like this woman. She's good people. Don't scare her off."

Please. Not my fault if people judge this book by its big hairy cover. I just shook my head and July laughed.

Sure enough, her friend called that night. Introduced herself as Rose Barnes, told me there's a lot she'd like done. We arranged to meet at the property today right after she closes on it.

But I'm running later than I'd like. Got a crisis call from one of my vets. He's trying to learn to walk with only part of a foot. In a lot of pain. Had a big argument with his wife. It took me a while to talk him down, make sure he'd be okay, help him make a plan for the day.

So I pull up to the house at the agreed-on time instead of early.

Nice old place. Good location, good bones. I let myself in the squeaky iron gate and follow the buckling brick walk up to the porch. *Note: Oil hinges. Level path.*

Front door's open an inch or two. I give it a push and let my eyes adjust to the dimmer foyer. I'm blocking most of the light from the doorway, but the stained-glass transom above me bounces colors off the shiny dark hair of a woman in the hallway. "Ms. Barnes?"

She spins around to face me and...*shit.*

It's Snickers. Because of course it is.

And she's got tears in her wide eyes.

Goddammit. Just when I'd decided she was only annoying, not unhinged.

Past experience has taught me this can go one of two ways, and she's already proven she's not in the oh-no-he's-an-axe-murderer! camp. That leaves the giant-teddy-bear camp. Gonna launch herself at me any second now. Expect me to hold her while she cries all over my shirt. In five—four—three—

"You have *got* to be fucking kidding me." She tilts her head, plants her fists on her hips.

What? Wait, what?

"No way is my Cranky Samaritan July's friend Angus Drummond." She's shaking her head, all traces of tears gone.

I'm not anybody's anything. I *am* instantly defensive. "It's a small town." I head back out to the porch.

She follows. "Where are you going?"

I eye her from halfway down the steps. "Leaving. Pretty clear you don't want me here."

"I didn't say that." In the weak sunlight, her skin looks like it would be smooth as a baby's if I trailed my fingertips over it. She frowns. "I was just surprised it was you. I pictured some little old hermit guy."

My turn to frown. "Why?"

She shrugs. "July said you work alone and you hardly ever talk."

"That a problem?"

Again with the shrug. "I just want somebody good and trustworthy. July says that's you."

I want the job. But she's…weird. Unpredictable. Can I work with somebody like that?

Dude, you work with people with more serious problems than that all the time.

She's watching me.

I sigh. "Why were you crying in there?"

"What?" Her brows furrow for a sec, then her expression clears. "Oh. I wasn't really crying. Just a little overwhelmed for a minute. This is a big deal for me."

I wait.

"I've never lived in a house, okay? Just apartments." She picks at a curl of peeling paint on the railing, then stops and smooths it back down, pats it with gentle fingers. "I was thinking how excited my mom would be. Wishing she could enjoy it with me."

That's…not weird. "Your mom not alive anymore?"

She shakes her head. There's sadness in her eyes, but not fresh grief. No tears.

I suck in a big breath and blow it out. Might be about to make a mistake. "Want me to look the place over? Then we can talk about what you want done."

"That'd be great."

I check the cramped attic. The roof. Under the house. Furnace, water heater. Walls and ceilings and floors and wiring. Plumbing and windows and doors.

I find her in the back hall, staring across the yard toward the garage off the alley. "Structure's sound," I tell her. "Roof's got another year, maybe two. Wiring should be brought up to code."

"July said you can do pretty much everything, right? The wiring and the roof, plus other stuff?" She scoops a notebook and pen off the cracked kitchen countertop. Hugs it to her chest.

"Most stuff, yeah." I take my own notebook from my back pocket. "Let's do a walk-through and you tell me what you'd like for each area."

She goes straight to the broom closet under the stairs, near the back door. "Can you turn this into a half bath, so nobody has to go upstairs for that?"

I nod. Measure the space. Start my list.

She wants to make one of the upstairs rooms into a laundry/bathroom/closet adjoining the bedroom with the bow window. Turn the room across from the kitchen into a library with built-in shelves. Refinish the floors and existing kitchen cabinets. Paint. Make sure all the windows are operable, with new screens. Replace any bad wood. Do some hardscaping outside. Gonna have somebody else put in a pool.

We end up out front on the porch. I scrawl the last of my notes and look over at her.

Her eyes are calm. She's been practical and efficient telling me what she wants done. I've got no good reason to turn the job down, even if I wanted to.

I sigh. "Long list."

She nods. "Can you do all that stuff?"

"Yeah, but it'll take time." Grandpa and the army gave me a unique set of skills, but I've still only got two hands.

"Can I live here while you do it?" She gives me a sweet, crooked half smile. "I like the B and B, but I'm really excited about moving in."

"Some days I'll have to shut off the power or the water for a few hours. But mostly you'd be okay. I can keep my mess contained."

A full smile breaks over her face like sunrise. "You willing to do this, then?"

I hold up a hand. Don't wanna give in too easy. "Ground rules. No calling me 'Cranky Samaritan.' Just Angus."

She smirks. "Not 'Mr. Drummond, sir'? Okay, then, no calling me 'Snickers.' And no 'Ms. Barnes,' either. I'm Rose."

I grunt. Fair. "No throwing stuff at me."

"Completely unreasonable." She heaves a giant sigh. "But I guess a wee fella such as yourself can't be too careful."

God, she's a mouthy little thing. Never met such a smart-ass in my life.

"Alright." I stuff the notebook in my pocket and head for the door. "I'll work up an estimate. You got time to go over it with me tomorrow afternoon?"

She trails behind me to the gate. We reach for it at the same time and my hand closes over hers, giving me a jolt of... something I don't need right now. I step back fast.

Her eyes widen like she felt it too, but if so, she recovers instantly. "Yep. I'll be here cleaning all day. Got people delivering my new fridge and some furniture."

I'm back in my van driving away when doubt hits. At a stop sign, I pull out my phone and call July. First try goes to voicemail.

Second try, she answers. "Angus?" There's a clatter of pots in the background.

"Sorry, I'll make this quick. How well you know this Rose Barnes? You sure she's okay?"

She laughs in my ear. "Geez, Angus, you two... I *just* got off the phone with her. She asked me the same thing about you."

Well, that's just not right. *I'm* the normal one in this business arrangement. "What the hell? What'd you tell her?"

"Told her I've known you forever. That if you're a serial

killer, you've been very discreet." At my snort she adds, "I told her you do all my building work. That you pretty much saved my life in high school, and that I'd trust you with anything, anytime."

Jesus. What am I supposed to say to that?

"Then reassure me about her."

"I haven't known her real long, Angus. She's new to town. But Sabina at the B and B is crazy about her, and so's everybody here. She's kind. Funny. Great tipper. She helped out here one day without being asked when Tina cut her finger. Worked her ass off, did a great job, and then wouldn't take any money. Told me to give it to Tina for her medical bills. Sonya saw her stuff a couple extra bills in the tip jar too."

I mull that over until I remember July's trying to work. "You don't think she's flaky? You think she'll be okay to work with?"

"Angus, from what I've seen, she'll be fair and reasonable. And fun."

I don't need no stinkin' fun.

I tell July thanks and hang up feeling like an ass for calling. Still uneasy. My instincts are pinging about...something. Something besides that unfortunate touch at the gate. If she can ignore that, I can too.

God help me, I want this job. Even more now than before. Makes no damn sense.

CHAPTER 4

Rose

THE DUSTY FLOOR MAKES ME sneeze as I lie in the foyer a foot from the staircase, admiring the lovely high ceiling two stories up. I let my phone hand flop back onto the notepad beside my face and watch the sunlight pour in colored streams through the transom. I should put a couch right here.

Don't know why I bothered July at work. She already vouched for the guy. That's good enough. And I got no sense of threat or danger from him, except for a split second there when I realized someone was blocking the door, his shoulders as wide as the opening. And that fear wasn't about Angus Drummond.

It's just—well, two things, really.

First, his eyes. Jesus, those eyes.

When I saw him in the restaurant, I didn't recognize him right away. I hadn't seen his face clearly the day he pushed me and Lillian out of the snow, with his hat brim pulled low against the weather. So at July's when he trained those eyes on me, that's all I noticed.

I've seen that color before in photos of the Caribbean. Too green to be called blue, too blue to be called green. Just bright and *stunning*. Breath-stealing. I don't know what the rest of his face looks like under that curly beard and mustache, but Christ, what does it matter, when he's got those eyes?

The last time I admired a guy's eyes, the guy was Timmy Johnson. I learned a tough lesson about not judging a guy by his eyes. Doesn't matter how many stupid sparks flew when Angus's big rough hand closed over mine.

So, that's problem number one. Problem two is that he clearly detests me.

I'm used to being invisible. Of course I am, after sixteen years of waitressing and purposely keeping a low profile. And I've never been considered attractive. But most people don't seem to find me actively irritating like Cranky, er, Angus Drummond does. Do I want that attitude every day in my own home?

I sit up and brush dust off my shirt. On the other hand, if he doesn't like me, he won't be chatty. Won't ask questions I don't want to answer. My money secret will be safer that way.

And he said he "contains" his mess. I can probably just avoid whatever area of the house he's containing.

This will be fine. I'll be fine. I'll just stay away from him and his stupefying eyes.

Anyway, I've got work to do.

By midafternoon, I've bought cleaning supplies, towels, bedding, and a sturdy ladder and dropped them off at my house. I head back to the B and B for my last night under Sabina's roof. The occasion calls for something special, so I stop at the town square and pick up—what else?—bittersweet chocolate for us to share.

The closest parking I could find was near the lingerie store. Today the mannequins are naughty glasses-and-negligee-wearing librarians. Wispy translucent nighties slip off their smooth plastic shoulders as they bend to pick up magazines, ride up their hard-curved little butts as they reach for top-shelf books. I pause, chocolate forgotten on the passenger seat beside me, my key hand hovering near the ignition. What would it be like to be a person who wears stuff like that?

Really, I should have some special little solo celebration for this new home milestone. Something to mark this enormous step and make up for all the steps I've missed over the years.

My hand tugs at the car door handle and my legs haul me out.

On the sidewalk in front of the shop, I try to summon a *Pretty Woman* "big mistake" attitude, sure that when I go in, they'll look me up and down and say they don't carry anything in my size. Sure that their voices and gazes will drip disdain. But when I finally push through the door, the auburn-haired salesclerk glances up from behind the counter, gives me a beaming smile, and asks how she can help, and she is no slender twig herself.

"I have terrible underwear," I blurt, and a blush burns its way across my face. "Do you carry these pretty things in sizes that might fit me?"

She comes around the counter, leans back on it, and crosses her arms. "Honey, if I didn't, it would be a mighty bad business decision, considering two-thirds of the women in this country are not thin. I decided from the beginning not to even carry products by designers who won't do large sizes. If you see something you like, I'll have it."

What a novel experience it is to hear someone say such a thing. What a lovely, novel experience.

A display of floaty negligees with beaded bodices catches my eye and I touch one, rubbing the delicate fabric between my fingers. “I want nice undies. And maybe some of these.”

She laughs. “Great! We should start by measuring you. Have you ever been professionally fitted?” She ushers me to a roomy, comfy dressing room, asking a million questions about my favorite colors and fabrics and styles.

I’m pretty sure she’s talking to distract me from the embarrassing, too personal measurement process. And kudos to her. She’s brisk and quick and professional, and soon I’ve stopped blushing and she’s bringing me an assortment of impossibly beautiful stuff to try on.

Who knew a professional fitting could make such a difference? I knew my boobs were big—I mean, I wouldn’t have had to work so hard to disguise them all these years if they weren’t—but I had no idea how great they could look in a good-quality bra. Not that anybody’ll know. I’m still gonna tuck them away under my baggy shirts. But *I’ll* know they’re there, dressed up all pretty. My private secret.

I’m ridiculously giddy as I pay my favorite shopkeeper *ever.* I peer at her name tag. “Thank you, Naomi. I’m going home to burn all my old stuff.” *Again with the TMI. Get a grip, Rose.*

She just laughs, not seeming a bit surprised. “Good for you! Enjoy.”

Back at the B and B, I run upstairs, bag up all my old underwear, and stuff it in the dumpster out back before joining Sabina. She’s clearing away the remnants of afternoon tea.

“Hey, put that down. You know the rules. Guests can’t

help." She'd probably slap the sandwich tray out of my hands if her own hands weren't full.

"I'm not helping. I'm stealing." I lift a tiny fancy cucumber sandwich and pop it into my mouth as I follow her into the kitchen.

"Something came for you today." She sets down the three-tiered dessert dish and snags an envelope off the table, pushing it into my hand and relieving me of the sandwiches and the bag from the chocolatier's.

I'm aware of her pouring us glasses of ice water as I slide my finger under the flap to open the envelope from Galway College. It's a single sheet of paper. The first word I see when I open it is *Congratulations!*

I sink into a chair, big silly grin plastered across my face. "I got in."

She's smiling too. "A toast, then." She clinks her glass to mine. "To the best guest ever and one of my favorite people in the world. May college and your new house be everything you've dreamed."

"To my first friend in my new town." I'm teary. Maybe she is too, but I can't tell with my vision all blurry.

We eat chocolate and talk until well after sundown, and then she gives me a lovely lavender-scented hug—hers is fierce despite the fragile feel of her narrow shoulder blades under my hands—and sends me upstairs.

Not too much to pack, thank heavens. I keep out some sweats for tomorrow, since I'll be cleaning all day, and shove all my other clothes in my bags to take down to the car. Something crackles in the pocket of the suitcase, and I pull out the box of refrigerator magnets, with a sheet of paper wrapped around it. It's a list I'd made a few nights ago. It says:

buy house
start college
figure out $
get suntan, stop looking like a damn cave fish
learn another language
learn to cook
get passport, visit another country

I'm smiling as I fumble in my purse for a pen and cross off "buy house." Tomorrow when they deliver my new fridge, I'll post this list where I can see it every day until every single item is crossed off.

Angus

Glad it's a gym day. Found out years ago working out's therapeutic for mind *and* body, so now I do it informally with my vet clients. Eases the just-returned folks back into life at home, gives 'em a chance to meet people who understand what they're going through.

Helps with my own problems, too. Today as I spot one of my newer guys on bench press, I decide not to worry about Rose Barnes. July's probably right. It'll probably be fine. Maybe even a non-issue. It's a lot of work she's asking for. Lot of money involved. Maybe she'll take one look at my estimate today and say, "Nope, can't afford you." And I'll say, "Okay, see ya," and that'll be that.

I finish my workout, shower, grab breakfast, and hold a couple of individual sessions before the weekly morning therapy group. They're fired up today, all teasing Beau about finally proposing to his girlfriend last night. "Geez, finally, man!" "She said yes? Must not be as smart as I'd thought." "Aw, dude, you've gone and done it now..." I think some of them take her yes as reason for hope for themselves for a real life after the military.

So, anyway, we spill over our hour a little. It's worth it but leaves me only a few minutes to look over the Barnes paperwork once more before I head to her place.

She answers the door with a scrubbing pad in her hand. Her pink sweats are a couple sizes too big. Her face is flushed and there's a streak of dirt across one cheek and a dust bunny in her hair. I have the damnedest urge to pluck it out, see if her hair's as soft as it looks. If it were anybody else, I'd think she looked cute.

The house smells of lemon cleaning soap. The bonus room in the back is spotless, ceiling to floor. New heavy library table with four sturdy chairs in there. Looks like she's almost done with the kitchen too. A sudsy bucket and kneeling pad mark a clear line between freshly scrubbed and still-unwashed floor. Everything else looks clean. The battered old round-topped fridge that was here yesterday has been replaced by a gleaming stainless steel one.

July was right. Girl's a worker.

She sees me looking at the new refrigerator. "Pretty, huh? Deliveries came already." She waves me to a chair at the library table and goes to wash up at the kitchen sink, dropping the scrubbing pad in the bucket as she passes.

I set my paperwork on the table and sort it into two stacks, one for her, one for me.

She comes over with a roll of paper towels and a steaming

pizza box she's pulled from the oven. "I was starving, so I had pizza delivered. Don't have dishes or silverware yet. Sorry." She plops the box down and heads back to the fridge. "Coke okay?"

"Nothing for me, thanks." It's not a damn date.

She pauses, eyeing me over the open refrigerator door. "You sure?"

At my nod, she shrugs and comes back to the table with a single red can. Pops it open, takes a drink, and shoves the pizza box aside. "Okay." Her stomach growls loud enough for me to hear it, but she focuses on the paperwork I've put in front of her.

"Go ahead and eat. I don't mind."

"That's okay. Let's do this." She frames the papers with her hands.

"Your lunch'll get cold."

She blinks up at me slowly, brown eyes wide. "Gosh, if only there were some mechanism by which a person could reheat cold food."

Christ. Smart-ass. "I don't want to wreck your lunch. Go ahead and eat."

"And *I* don't want to eat in front of you. It's rude." She scans the top page of the estimate and lifts it to peer at the second.

"And *I* don't want your food. I'm not hungry, okay?" Not true. Garlic and tomato and sausage scents rise from the box, and my stomach growls louder than hers, just to amplify my lie.

Her mouth quirks up at one corner. "Right." She eases up the box lid and the aroma washes over me. There's the perfect amount of melty cheese, and they've been generous with the toppings. "Just in case you change your mind..." She lifts out a piece, cheese stretching, sets it on a doubled paper towel, and slides it toward me.

I stare down at it, wishing breakfast hadn't been quite so long ago. My stomach growls again and I sigh. "Okay, but only if you let me pay for it."

She's taken a slice for herself. Her eyes roll as she bites into it. "That's okay, I've got it."

"No, it's *not* okay. If I'm going to eat part of your pizza, I'm going to pay for it."

She stares at me as she chews. "You're a strange man. Who turns down free pizza?"

"I do." God help me.

She shakes her head and huffs out a breath. "Fine. You can pay half. It was fifteen and I tipped five." She takes another bite.

I fish a ten out of my wallet and slap it down on the table. Grandma'd be shocked by my rudeness.

"Coke's in the fridge." She tips her head in that direction.

"I'm not drinking your damn Coke." Ah, lordy, now Grandma's rolling over in her grave.

Rose Barnes raises her brows and opens her mouth to say something.

I head her off. "I'm sorry. That was rude. Don't know why I'm so irritable." *Irritated. By you.*

Her pretty smile is nowhere in sight. "Maybe get a handle on that? So you don't keep being a jackass to somebody who never did anything to you?" One side of her mouth quirks up and she gestures at the back of her head. "Except for the near-concussion." Then she frowns. "For which I have apologized. Sincerely. Multiple times."

She's…not wrong.

I nod. "Fair enough. Sorry."

Takes us five mostly silent minutes to demolish two-thirds

of the pizza. I'm so thirsty I almost wish I'd accepted her drink offer, scoreboard or no. Almost.

She clears away our mess, washes her hands again at the sink, and resumes her seat, looking at me expectantly.

I guide her through my timetable and cost estimates. "This is the order I suggest we do the work in." I flip pages. "Itemized list for each job. Projected overall total. Red asterisks mean you'll have to pick something out or make some kind of decision."

She takes her time paging through, reading everything, asking an occasional question. She must be overwhelmed. It's a big project with a bottom line that's almost certainly higher than she expected. She's probably trying to figure out what she can afford and what she'll need to cut off her list.

I aim for gentle. "It's okay. You don't have to consider everything at once. I should rewire first and then start on plumbing. We can adjust other stuff if you need to."

She nods slowly, her eyes on the pages in front of her. "Lots of decisions." She gives her head a little shake. The dust bunny comes loose and drifts to the table and she frowns at it. "Okay, then. Baby steps. I can do that."

Huh. No mention of money. I point to the overall total to give her another chance. "Estimate's not perfect. They never are. Best I can do at this stage until I get into the work."

She plucks the dust bunny from the table and rolls it between her fingers. Looks me in the eye. "It's fine."

Well, I tried. "Okay. If you find you can't afford everything on your list, let me know as soon as possible so we can reprioritize, okay?"

She nods.

"Generally I ask for half up front and the other half on

completion, but with this, let's take it task by task." I show her the wiring estimate again and she whips out a checkbook.

"My first check from my new Galway bank account." She fills it out and hands it to me with a private little smile.

I fold it into my wallet. "Got any questions for me at this point?"

She laughs. "I'm sure I'll be full of them as soon as you leave, but I'll just start a list so I can ask you later."

We shake hands as I leave. I'm surprised at how small hers feels in mine. Her personality's so big sometimes I forget she's a shrimp. That *zing* I get from touching her, though? *That's* outsized.

Ridiculous. I gotta put a lid on that.

CHAPTER 5

Rose

WELL, YAY ME, FOR STANDING up for myself to a man.

I've only ever done that twice. The first time blew up in my face—I knew it would; you just can't get away with calling your boss a greedy, heartless, soulless motherfucker in front of a dining room full of customers, no matter how big a jerk he's being—but this one worked out okay. Angus Drummond might hate my guts, but he checked himself. And actually apologized.

After he leaves, I finish scrubbing the kitchen floor, and then clean the bathroom upstairs and take a quick bath so I can do a shopping run for basic dishes and cutlery and groceries. A hostess should at least be able to offer guests plates and glasses for their delivery pizza and canned soda. Classy all the way, that's me.

Tomorrow I'll run to campus to buy books for my classes and then clean some more.

When I think about starting school next week, I can't decide whether I feel more like victory-dancing or puking. Most classes were already full, but apparently 8 a.m. is not a popular time slot, because I was able to get a Monday-Wednesday-Friday Intro to Sociology and a Tuesday-Thursday Algebra I.

Please, powers that be, let college be better than high school. I'm sure there are bullies everywhere, but please let me be invisible to the college variety.

"Hey, hey, hey! You get your hand out of that purse!"

The man's voice startles me and I jump back, crashing into my own cart.

Shit! "I didn't—I wasn't—"

But it's the owner of the family market and he doesn't want to hear from me.

I can feel the flush creeping over my neck and face. I'm every bit as embarrassed as if I were guilty of what he thinks I was doing.

I'd been wandering the aisles in a happy mood, filling my cart with basic kitchen staples, when I'd noticed the woman. She'd put two cans of name-brand tuna in her nearly empty cart, then peered at the price card on the shelf and frowned before putting the cans back and turning to look at the price cards for the off-brands.

So I'd paused, scrabbling in my purse for the emergency money at the bottom, and when she'd bent down to squint at something on one of the lower shelves, I'd dropped five folded twenties into her purse.

And promptly gotten caught. And now I have no idea what to say that won't give away my secret. Maybe jail won't be as bad as they say...

The market owner glares daggers at me. "Miz Fleming,"

he says gently to the old woman without taking his eyes off me, "would you check your purse, please, to see if anything is missing? I need to know whether to call the police or just kick this person out." His voice is low and deadly, his dark face set in lines I'd never noticed before.

Because he thinks I was stealing from his customer.

Fair enough. Good for him.

The woman's expression changes from outrage to bewilderment as she reaches into her purse and pulls out the folded bills. "What—?"

And then I know what to say. "I'm sorry to cause a fuss. I didn't mean to upset anybody. It's my birthday and my grandpa gave me a nice present, but he also gave me that," I nod at the money, "and told me to do something good with it."

They both stare at me. Her fingers tighten on the cash.

"I didn't know anybody to do anything good for. I'm new here. Please accept it so I can tell Grandpa I did what he asked." It's Mr. Brown's face I imagine when I say *Grandpa*. I send up a brief prayer that Mr. Brown'll put in a word for me, to keep me from going to hell for lying.

The owner's name tag says "Mr. Ahmed." He can tell I'm lying. He can also see as well as I can that the woman needs that money. "Miz Fleming?" he says, finally, as if deciding to leave the decision to her.

She nods primly. "Tell your Grandpa I said thank you."

"I will." My hands are shaking. There's a possibility my knees are going to give out.

With a last glare at me, Mr. Ahmed nods at the old lady and heads back to where he'd abandoned a stock cart. I give the Fleming woman a weak smile and push my cart in the opposite direction. I go on about my shopping as normally as I can, feeling like all eyes are on me. When I go up to check out, Mr. Ahmed himself comes over to relieve a girl I've thought must be his granddaughter.

"Today is not your birthday," he says, ringing up my items, not looking at me.

"No." Not sure how he knew that, but I don't feel like lying again.

"We take care of our own here." His voice is too low for anyone but me to hear.

I nod and dig in my purse for my credit card. "I figured you did. I've noticed how kind your family is to the customers." I hand him the card and meet his eye. "Miz Fleming was going to put back the tuna she wanted. I just… I hadn't planned it. I just wanted her to have that tuna."

He looks at me another long minute before swiping my card. "One hundred dollars is a lot of tuna."

"Yes."

He doesn't say a word as I leave.

Takes me five minutes of eyes-closed deep-breathing in the car before I can drive home.

It's a relief to let myself back in my house. I'm learning the smell of the place—old wood and dust and sunshine—and adding my own scents to it. I put away my purchases, and then I'm ready to crawl into bed with a book. I wish I'd been able to wash my new sheets and blankets before using them, but it's still the laundromat for me until Angus Drummond puts in my laundry room.

I only get a few pages read before I set aside the book to lie listening to branches scraping and floors popping, memorizing the night sounds of my new old home. My lovely home. Despite the fiasco at the market, I'm pretty sure I fall asleep smiling.

Angus shows up promptly at eight in the morning. I show him the alley parking next to my decrepit detached garage, ease my spare house key off my ring and hand it to him. "This is yours while you're working here. I'm taking classes and probably won't be home most mornings." I wave at the sagging privacy fence. "I don't have a real lock for the gate, so just come on in."

He nods and starts unloading tools from his van.

I'm just climbing in my car when he says, "I do some other work too. Won't be here on Wednesday mornings. Sometimes I might have to take a call. I'll make sure you get a full week's work from me."

Hmm. Mysterious. "Okay." I drive off imagining what his other work might be. Lumberjacking? Naw, nothing that stereotypical. Maybe people hire him to sit on their porch and shout, "Get off my lawn!" at neighbor kids.

My classes start off surprisingly well. I was afraid the desks would be those old-fashioned ones with the attached arm, and that I either wouldn't fit at all, or I'd be so squashed I'd be in too much pain to concentrate. But both of my classrooms have table-type desks with rolling chairs, some of them armless and not too flimsy, so I'm good.

I'd also been afraid my age would make me stand out. Given the nightmare high school was, with people scrutinizing my every move, waiting to pounce, I'm not going to beat myself up for fearing that. But again, I didn't need to be concerned. The other students straggle in wrapped up in their own thoughts, most of them clutching some form of liquid caffeine like a lifeline. Some appear to be at least my age. Maybe thirty-two is not as old as I'd thought.

My library-to-be, with its two walls of tall windows, is where I spend most of my at-home waking hours. Between classes and cleaning, I haven't bought any dining room or living room furniture yet, so I use the heavy library table as both an eating surface and a desk.

Angus and I mostly ignore each other, which works just fine. But today it's bitterly cold and sleeting icy needles, and when Angus grabs his lunch from the fridge to take it out to his van where he usually eats, I break the silence.

"Angus, if I promise not to talk to you, would you consider sitting in here to eat?" I wave at the three empty seats and long, mostly bare expanse of table. "There's plenty of room and it's horrible out there."

He pauses, his hand on the doorknob, and looks at my comfy, sturdy chairs.

"I *promise* I won't say a single word." I turn back to my laptop and my sandwich, to prove how disinterested I am.

A moment later he slides into a chair at the opposite corner of the table. "I'm not going to yell at you if you talk to me," he mutters. "I'm not a monster."

I raise my eyebrows and nod without looking up.

No, he's just a big warm fuzzy ball of fun.

Angus

The first day goes better than I expect. Rose Barnes is gone all morning, so I get everything set up the way I like it without her around to give me grief. I make some progress on the wiring before she gets home.

There's a giant jar half full of quarters on one end of her kitchen counter. A sticky note on the side reads *Cuss Jar.* A lot of damn quarters in there. Gonna take her forever to fill that sucker.

On the refrigerator is a list in small tidy handwriting. Little word magnets *seize*, *life*, *do*, and *this* hold down the four corners of the paper. How bad are her money troubles that she's got *figure out $* on the list?

I'm not usually so nosy. Her stuff is none of my business. I get back to work.

After a few days, we find a routine. She's okay with me arriving early, so on non-gym days I get there around seven thirty as she's on her way out the door.

She shows me how empty her fridge is. Says I should consider the middle shelf mine. I resist for a few days, but one day I forget the ice pack for my lunch bag. After that I take her up on her offer. Decent of her. Dammit.

The thing that bothers me is the coffee maker. She doesn't talk as much as I'd feared, but the woman's damn observant. Must've seen me come in juggling my tools and keys and my giant Dunkin' coffee a time too many, because one day she shows me a brand-new Mr. Coffee on the counter and a bag of Dunkin' Donuts ground coffee on my shelf of the fridge. She's brewed me a pot and the kitchen smells like heaven.

I stare at my boots, trying not to say anything rude, but I'm pissed. Unreasonably pissed.

Apparently, she can read me even when I'm not talking. "You hate that I did that." Her voice is flat. "Well, I won't make coffee for you anymore, then. And you don't have to use that bag. I'll stick it in the freezer." She does that as I watch. "I have friends now. I needed a coffeemaker in case I have them over. It's here if you want to use it. Feel free to bring your own beans." She grabs her purse and a notebook off the counter and heads out the back door.

I watch her go, hating her for giving me something thoughtful and unexpected. Hating myself for having such a strong reaction to such a little thing. A nice thing. Damn scoreboard.

She doesn't mention it when she comes home later, but I'm sure she noticed I didn't drink any. Next morning, the glass carafe is empty and clean, winking at me from the unplugged machine.

Not sure how it happened, but now more days than not, I eat lunch in her library. One weak moment on one nasty-weather day, and now we're sharing a table. Usually silently.

She doesn't bother me as much as she used to. Rarely even talks to me. She hasn't made me any more coffee or tried to feed me pizza or anything else. Mostly she sits and works at her laptop, algebra and sociology textbooks and notebooks scattered around her.

I can't figure out what she *does*. How she supports herself. If she's between jobs, that would explain why she's worried about money. Maybe she makes do with student loans, but that wouldn't cover house renovations... But it would explain why she's got basically no furniture. Probably can't afford anything else.

Maybe she's a young widow, living off life insurance. Or divorced, with alimony. But she doesn't seem sad or angry.

Maybe she hated the guy (or the woman?) and drove the poor soul to an early grave.

Nah, that's not fair. She's okay. Besides, her finger shows no sign of having had a ring on it. Doesn't matter, anyway, as long as her checks are good.

Maybe she does some kind of online work on that computer she likes so much.

One day after handling a call from a vet in crisis, I head toward the library room to ask Rose about fixtures for the half bath. She's been quiet all afternoon, but as I near the doorway I hear her talking to someone. She's not using her indoor voice and she does *not* sound happy.

"Goddamn son-of-a-bitching motherf—"

I come to a full stop. Whatever this is, I don't want in the middle of it.

"Fucky fuckle fuckerpants. *Come* on, you bloody piece of shit! Don't do this! No, don't—goddammit all to hell!"

Don't do this! No, don't? Does she need help? I peek around the corner.

The movement must catch her attention because her head comes up and her eyes find me. She's alone, talking to no one, hunched with her hands frozen like claws over her laptop.

Pink washes across her face as she stares back at me.

"Do you *miss* the sea, sailor?" It's out of my mouth before I think better of it.

She draws in a long slow breath and straightens her spine.

"Um, sorry. I forgot you were still here." Her voice is back in her normal low register, but just barely. "My first paper is due in"—she checks her phone—"thirty-eight minutes, and this mother—um—darn online course management system has f—um—eaten it." She unbends her fingers one by one. "I spent three days on this paper. I wanted it to be perfect. But I couldn't get it to upload, and now my laptop is frozen, and…" She sighs and shoves the laptop away. Lowers her forehead to the table with a faint thump. Whispers, "Worthless piece of shit."

I should be sympathetic. Helpful. Or maybe completely unmoved. Not my business or my problem. But there's an unfamiliar burning in my nose and a hitch in my chest, and I can't let it go.

I clear my throat. When she looks up, I tip my head toward the Cuss Jar on the counter a few feet away.

Her eyes narrow. Holding my gaze, she gropes for her purse on the chair beside her. Fumbles inside it, pulls out a roll of quarters, starts to break it open, and then says, "Goddammit all to hell. Catch," and tosses me the whole roll.

CHAPTER 6

Rose

THE GIANT SMART-ASS CATCHES THE paper tube of coins with one hand, drops it into my Cuss Jar, and exits through the back door.

I sigh. I can't claim to have fallen off the clean language wagon, as I can't ever quite seem to crawl fully up on it.

I'm pulling the laptop back over to me when I hear something in the backyard. A rusty, alarming sound. I turn just in time to see Angus doubled over, holding his gut, his big shoulders shaking.

The noise is laughter. Big butthead's laughing at me.

After a few seconds he straightens, turns, and heads back inside, his mouth twitching.

"Hey, I meant to ask if you've picked fixtures for the downstairs half bath. Wanna go with me to get those tomorrow after your class?" His damn ocean eyes are watery, and he brushes a hand over the lower part of his face. Probably hiding a grin. Jackass.

"That would be fine," I say with as much dignity as I can muster.

His eyes crinkle and he leaves fast, letting the back door slap shut behind him as he jogs across the backyard to his van, that rusty sound floating behind.

Dandy. Just dandy. *So* happy I can provide free entertainment for someone who despises me.

My laptop dings. I look down and see a message from the course management system: Your document has uploaded successfully.

Well, okay, then. I can bear this one indignity. Life is still good.

I've let my classes and the house distract me from what I should be doing. Moving and renovating and college are all huge milestones in my life, but on the grand scale of the planet, they're not even tiny blips.

Eighty million dollars is one enormous fucking blip.

It could be helping somebody. A whole lot of somebodies. And it's sitting there, doing nothing but growing, until I make some damn decisions. Helping the old Fleming woman and that pregnant waitress was just peanuts. I won't live long enough to do the money justice at that rate. I've done the basic math. Even if the safe investments I've made only earn two percent annually, that's an additional $1.6 million per year, piling up, replicating, bursting out of imaginary coffers in my mind, while people go hungry and do without housing and medical care. While I redecorate.

I'm an indecisive chickenshit.

I've tried asking the financial and legal guys in Indy what people do with such obscene amounts of money, but all they'd talked about was "diversifying my portfolio" and "ensuring maximum return on investment." They gave me a really depressing article on everyday (read: working class) people who'd won the lottery and then blown through the money so fast they'd ended up worse off than before. All very interesting—ah, who am I kidding? This stuff's either boring or heartbreaking. No help at all.

The first thing I thought, when the money dropped on me, was how sad it was that it came too late to help Mom. Just a tiny piece of it would have made her life *so* much easier... Maybe she'd still be with me today.

I've never had an if-I-win-the-lottery list. Survival was a full-time job, and it mostly involved keeping my head down at work and then going home to ramen and library books. So I'm not going shopping for a tropical island or a pile of diamonds. I want to do something good with the money. But what? The pressure to decide is crushing, whenever I let up on schoolwork or cleaning long enough to think.

Angus is waiting when I get home from class the next morning. He holds the passenger door for me as I climb into his van, and we go straight to the home improvements store.

Nine different people wave or call him by name. Men, women, old people, younger ones. Other contractors, store employees. He lifts his chin and grunts at them. Of course he does.

I pull out my list. We go to the bathroom fixtures section and find the toilet and sink I've chosen. "Will this one fit in there okay, do you think?"

He consults the dimensions listed on the boxes and then shows me a sketch he'd made in his own little notebook. "You're within the size limits for everything. These're fine."

Since it's a tiny windowless space, I'm going for white paint and glass tiles. I point to a mirrored medicine chest and he loads it onto our rolling pallet. We add a light for over the sink, and then we enter the checkout line on the contractor's side of the store.

"You were pretty speedy with all that. You always this decisive?"

He must be happy we finished quickly. His tone is barely surly at all.

I think about his question. "Don't know. Never been in this situation before." *It's the important stuff I'm wishy-washy on.*

He nods. We keep our usual silence on the way home. When we get there, he goes around to open the back doors of the van to unload the big items. I grab the bags with the hardware and other small things, partly because I want to help and partly because I want to poke the bear.

"I'll get that!" Yup, he's annoyed. Score.

"You've got the heavy stuff." I reach to unlatch the privacy fence gate and find that it's not hooked. We're going to have to be more careful about that. I pull open the gate and go in, leaving it open behind me for Angus.

Angus

I'm just lifting the new toilet out of the van when I hear running footsteps, a cry, then a thud and clatter. Then crinkling plastic bags and a *Whack! Whack! Whack!*

I set the toilet down none too gently and run for the gate.

Ten feet inside the backyard, there's a scrawny white dude on his belly on the ground, looking like a turtle trying to draw his head into his body. Got his arms covering his skull. Scattered around him are sections of copper pipe and wire I should've stashed in the garage.

Rose is circling him, cussing a blue streak, rooting in her purse as she moves, raising her shopping bags threateningly whenever the guy twitches. "Angus, get your ass in here and kill this guy!"

"What happened?" Pretty sure she's more dangerous than he is, but just in case, I step between them.

"The gate wasn't latched, and when I came in, he charged me!" She's nearly squeaking. "He almost impaled me on one of those pipes!"

"I wasn't charging you! I was trying to leave!" The guy shows his face for an instant.

"*With our copper!*" Rose is the picture of outrage, her curls standing on end, her scowl ferocious. She pulls out her phone and dials 9-1-1. Asks them to send officers. Keeps pacing, more agitated than I've ever seen her.

I reach out one arm and reel her in. Tuck her into my side, ignoring both the buzz that starts under my skin and the startled look she shoots me. She's trembling, from fear or excitement or rage. I can't tell which.

I pull her a little closer, watching the guy on the ground and trying not to laugh. "Turn loose that copper and just lie there, buddy. Not sure I can stop her if she wants to hit you again." I refocus on Rose's tense face and speak slow and easy, hoping to loosen her up. "So you want me to kill him, huh?"

She sighs and relaxes against me, all warm and soft and orange-scented. Still shaking. "No." She adjusts her purse strap on her shoulder. "I don't think he was really trying to hurt me—I think he was probably only trying to get out the gate with the stuff."

The guy on the ground holds his hands up in a see-I-told-you-so gesture, and I get a better look at his face.

"Jerry? What the hell, man?" Goddammit. Turtle Man is Jerry Hawes. Two years behind me in school.

He sighs. Stares at the dirt for a minute before meeting my eyes. "Hey, Angus. Sorry, man." He shifts his gaze to Rose. "Sorry, ma'am. Been a really bad day and I made a really bad decision. I'm sorry I scared you."

Rose has gone still at my side, looking from me to Jerry.

I give her another little squeeze, not because it feels so good but just to reassure her. "Sit up, Jerry. Just don't make me chase you." I'm bigger than he is, but I'm just as fast, and today he looks too hungry to outrun anybody.

He pushes himself to a sitting position, brushing grass and dirt from his face and clothes.

"What the hell were you thinking, Jerry?"

He shakes his head. "Not enough, obviously." He nods toward the alley. "I was taking a shortcut home. Walked downtown for a job interview this morning—we really needed me to get that job, and the truck's not running—but after me and some other guys had been waiting a couple hours, somebody came out of the office and said they'd hired as many as they needed." He shakes his head again. "I'd been planning to pick up a steak or something on the way home if I'd gotten the job. Get Lydia some red meat, you know? Help build her up some. But they sent us home. So I was walking slow, wondering what to tell her so she won't worry, and I saw this gate sagging open. Got nosy. Heard somebody'd bought the place, wanted to see what they'd done with it. Peeked in, saw the copper. Tried to tell myself nobody'd miss the leftover bits and pieces." He rolls his eyes, looking disgusted with himself. "Stupid. Stupid, stupid, stupid."

"Lydia not doing so well?" I'd heard his wife had cancer. Sweet woman. First grade teacher. Everybody loves her. This'll kill her if the cancer doesn't.

Jerry clears his throat. "She made it through the surgery okay, but the chemo and radiation are kicking her butt. She's so tired. So thin. Scares me to look at her sometimes, Angus."

"Money tight, huh?" I don't like asking him in front of Rose, but she shows no sign of going anywhere.

Jerry nods. "Family leave ran out a couple of weeks ago. Lydia was too sick for me to leave her alone. My boss held my job open as long as he could, but they finally had to hire somebody." He laughs but there's no humor in it. "Lydia wants to go back to work—misses the kids something terrible—but no way, right now. She wouldn't even be able to handle half days, till we get her built back up some."

"What kind of work do you do?" Rose's voice is quiet.

He meets her eye. "Been a delivery driver for the past twelve years, ma'am. Do some odd jobs here and there since Lydia's been sick—stuff that don't take me away from her long."

The police pull up in the alley before Rose can ask any more questions. She's up and away from me in a flash. I'm feeling disgusted at myself for missing the warmth of her when I hear her say, "I'm so sorry, officers. I should have checked with Angus here before I called you. I didn't know Jerry was doing him a favor."

Well, I'll be goddammed.

They turn to me. "Angus, y'all good here?"

That wacky, pain-in-the-ass woman. That kindhearted, wacky,

pain-in-the-ass woman. “Yeah, sorry, guys. Miscommunication. My bad.”

Rose and I wave the officers out the gate. Jerry slumps forward, arms on his knees, shaking his lowered head. “Ah, god,” he croaks, his shoulders shaking, when they’re gone.

Rose backs toward the house. “I need to wash up. Jerry, make sure Angus has your number. I heard about a job that might be right for you.” She turns and half trots toward the house, those deadly plastic bags of hers crackling and clanking.

Jerry raises his head to watch her go. Wipes one hand across his eyes, clears his throat. “Nice lady.”

“She’s all right.” Sweet as can be. And she smells good and feels damn good. Dammit.

I take out my wallet, peel off a couple of twenties, and haul Jerry to his feet. “Get Lydia that steak on your way home. And don’t pull this shit again. You can’t do her any good from jail.”

He sighs. “I know.” He stares at the money for a long minute before shoving it into his pocket. No way would he take it if it weren’t for Lydia. “Thanks, Angus.”

“I’ll keep my ear out for jobs. And I’ll be by later, look at your truck with you.”

“Thanks, man.” He pauses at the gate, glances back at the house. “Tell her I said thanks.”

“Will do.” I hook the gate behind him and go looking for Rose. She’s in the kitchen, head down, arms braced on the counter. “Come on.” I lead her outside, making sure to lock up and latch the gate behind us.

“Where are we going?” She climbs obediently into the van. Must be even more shook than I’d realized.

CHAPTER 7

Angus

"WE'RE GOING TO GET LUNCH and something hot to drink. Then we're going to go buy new locks for the gate and house. I'll put them on this afternoon."

I take her to July's, where I know everybody loves her. Well, except for Miz Ames, who, as Lenny puts it, "is the grouchiest person in town besides you, Angus." She and Rose engage in some kind of weird stare-down as Sonya waves us to a booth on the other side of the room. I could swear I see Rose stick her tongue out at the old lady as we slide into our seats, but surely that was my imagination.

After we order, Rose sighs, rubbing her temples. "I'm sorry I mentioned your ass."

I almost blow tea out my nose. "What?"

"I shouldn't have told you to get your ass in there and kill Jerry. Not just because you shouldn't kill Jerry, but because I shouldn't be telling you what to do with your ass. It's your ass. And it's completely inappropriate of me to mention it. Or even notice it. Much less boss it around." Her fingers rub tight little circles at her hairline. "I have a terrible cussing problem."

I clear my throat, trying to keep down the unfamiliar laughter that wants to burst out of me like it did in her yard yesterday. "Well, okay then. Apology accepted."

Our food arrives, and it's perfect, as always at July's.

We eat in silence for a few minutes before I look at her again. "What's your accent? Not North Carolina."

"Nah. Midwest. I wound up here by accident. The storm, actually. When you got my car unstuck? I hadn't planned on stopping in Galway."

"Huh."

"I'm glad I did, though. Obviously. I love it here." Her eyes fix on my forearms as I unscrew the lid of the hot sauce.

"You didn't come for a job, then? Or family?"

"Nooo... I'd been wanting to move someplace new, but I hadn't decided where. And I'd been wanting to start college but didn't have a school picked. Getting snowed in here made me realize Galway's what I was looking for."

Can't read her expression. I wait for her to say more.

She doesn't. "What about you? You grow up here?" She takes a big bite of pasta.

Huh. A deflection.

"Yeah. Couldn't wait to get out. Went straight to the army after high school. Then couldn't wait to get back."

Over the course of the meal, her shoulders lose tension, especially when July comes over to say hi. Still, she grips her hot chocolate mug tight enough that her knuckles whiten.

July notices. Lays a hand on Rose's arm, squeezing. "You okay?"

Rose glances over at me. "Yeah. I had a bad morning. Angus is babying me through it."

July nods. "Good." She touches my shoulder as she goes back to work.

Time to raise a sensitive issue. I put my napkin on the table. Lean back, trying for casual. "Nice thing you did for Jerry."

Her eyes dart to me, then back down into her cocoa. "Well. My mom had cancer."

I nod and wait but she doesn't say more. I try again. "He's a good guy. What you did was probably right, for him. But you gotta be careful, you know? Some guys'd play you with a sob story and come back later for more."

Now those big brown eyes come up to hold my gaze. "I'm aware of that, Angus. I just don't believe Jerry's one of them."

"I don't think so either." Obstinate woman. I let it drop. But if he or anybody else tries to pull any crap with her I'll...do what exactly? I'm no hero. Certainly not hers.

Rose is staring across the room again. Miz Ames is still there, giving us the evil eye.

I tip my head to her. "What is *with* you two?"

"You can see her too? I thought she was a demon."

I can't help it—I snort-laugh. Right out in public. "*What?*"

"She's acted like this, staring at me, since the first minute I laid eyes on her." Rose sounds downright grouchy—a real first. "I think she's my evil nemesis."

"You could ignore her." But that wouldn't be nearly so entertaining.

"I've tried. It only makes her stronger." She sighs. "Let's go buy some locks."

I wave Sonya down but she won't let us pay for our lunch. I hate that. I was going to treat.

Rose seems jumpy and off the rest of the afternoon. I stay a little late to try to catch up, and as I'm gathering my stuff to leave, I have to ask, "You doing okay?"

She's trailed me to the back door. There's anxiety in her big brown eyes as she glances at the darkness beyond the glass, but the stubborn woman won't ask for help. That's good because some dumbass part of me would probably offer to stay. Sleep on her floor, like a good guard dog.

"I imagine I'll be a little nervous tonight." She traces a crack in the countertop with her thumbnail. "But it'll be better tomorrow. And then better the next night."

She's close enough to touch, and before I realize it, she's put her hand on my arm, her fingers sending a zing along my skin. Her eyes fly up to mine. "Thanks for being so nice."

She moves away and I step out, waiting until she's locked all three locks before I head across the backyard to my van.

I'm stowing my lunch in the refrigerator when Rose comes downstairs the next day.

"Morning." She covers a yawn. Tosses a little spiral notebook on the counter. She's still wearing yesterday's clothes. From the creases, looks like she slept in them.

I take extra care closing the fridge. "Sleep okay?" Shit. Too personal. Not my business.

She waves a hand. "So-so." Slumps against the counter and watches me check the lid on my coffee cup. "Sometimes I wish I drank that stuff."

Usually her posture is military straight. Like a little tank.

"Want me to make a pot?" I'd even drink some if it'll help her feel better.

"Naw. I like the smell but I can't get past the taste." She rubs her hands over her eyes and then roots in the refrigerator. Comes out with a can of Coke, pops the top, and takes a long drink without bothering with her usual straw.

I get the damnedest impulse to lean in and press my face to her smooth pale throat, breathe in her scent. Taste her there.

Thank god she lowers the can. "I'll be late getting home today. Curtain shopping. I started feeling like I was in a fishbowl last night. Gotta nip that in the bud or I'll be nervous and paranoid all the time." She nods toward the notebook. "Just finished measuring the windows."

Smart girl. *Woman*. Brave.

I nod. "Probably be weird if you *didn't* feel nervous for a while. That was a violation of your private space yesterday."

She takes another long drink, eyeing me, and covers a cute tiny fizz burp with her fingertips. "You are surprisingly wise in the ways of these things, grasshopper."

I snort and turn away to get to work.

"Really, though, thank you for everything yesterday. I felt a lot better having you here." She touches my arm in passing as she heads back upstairs. There's that damn zing again.

I hear water running in the bathroom a minute later.

I shouldn't be standing here staring after her. I should be thinking about the day's work ahead of me, or where to get Jerry a new alternator, or whether my new client Bobby would be a good fit for the Saturday therapy group. Dammit.

Rose

I have to leave the kitchen fast. I can't stop thinking about that damn hug yesterday, and just now when I touched him, my whole body started buzzing. *Dammit!*

That hug was fucking a*ma*zing. Best thing ever on a cold scary day: to be wrapped in a solid, soap- and coffee- and man-scented hug, against a body so big and strong and warm I can still feel my own melting into it.

I have never. In my entire life. Had a comforting hug. From a man.

I have also never in my entire life wanted so much to cuddle up to someone. That's a ridiculous thing for me to want. The man doesn't even *like* me. He was just being kind yesterday because I was upset.

After Angus left last night, the house seemed huge and empty and eerily silent. Except for all the noises I'd never noticed it making before. Creaks, pops, scrapes, sighs. I went around the downstairs, double-checking locks on all the doors and windows, feeling like a fish in a clear glass bowl, sure somebody was watching me from the darkness.

I mean, not my neighbors. I'm starting to know who they are. The family on the kitchen side, who is always moving at warp speed, both dads carrying sports gear and lunch boxes and who knows what else, ushering their preteen kids ahead of them to the SUV. The middle-aged couple across the street, whose yard is so perfect it looks like a retouched photo. The lady who must run a daycare somewhere down the street and who always calls hello as she goes by with a full quad stroller, a baby carrier on her chest, and another child by the hand.

And the absent-minded professor lady with the cane who lives in the house to my right. I actually had a brief conversation with her when I took her some mail that was delivered to me by mistake. Then, leaving, I tripped on a loose board on her porch and almost fell down her stairs. Angus saw; he was coming around my house and picked up his pace when I stumbled. Didn't know the big guy could move so fast.

"You okay?" he'd called when I caught myself.

I said yeah and asked if I could borrow a hammer and nail to fix that board so my neighbor lady wouldn't break her neck on it.

But of course Angus had frowned ferociously, muttering and grumbling, "I can—not gonna let you—" as he came over and hammered it down himself.

So it wasn't my neighbors I feared last night as I made a second circuit and turned off all the lights. They're no more threat to me than I am to them.

And Jerry turned out to be okay, and I could probably have taken him in a fight anyway. No, it's just...he made me realize that although Galway has seemed like paradise to me, like a safe refuge, there are people I don't know out there, and not all of them mean well. And they could, like Jerry, come into my space or watch me when I'm alone at night.

Why haven't I taken time to get window coverings? I need them. I mean, my whole purpose in leaving Indianapolis was to find somewhere where I could have privacy and peace.

Last night I made my way up the stairs in the faint light from a streetlight half a block away. I brushed my teeth in the dark bathroom before going in to sit on my bed. Didn't want anybody outside to be able to track my movements through the house. I got back up to lock the bedroom door, wishing I had a chair to jam under the knob, but not wanting to go back downstairs to get one from my library.

The previous night I'd gotten halfway through a mystery novel, but last night it didn't tempt me a bit. That's all I'd need, a suspenseful plot full of things I hadn't yet thought to be scared of. It was too dark to read, anyway. I wasn't going to turn on any lights with that big bow window right there.

I was stiff, I guess from the stress of the day, so I kicked off my shoes and did twice my usual number of stretches, and then I crawled into bed fully dressed and tried to relax. Lying there staring up at the night shadows on the ceiling I pushed away the memory of Angus's hug and thought about what I'd told Jerry about having heard about a job that might suit him.

I've got to come up with something.

I hit a sale on plain white tab-top curtains and load up the car with those and a bunch of tension rods. Some of the other rods were nicer, but I don't want to have to put nails or screws in my pretty window frames.

At home, I go around and put them up in my most-used rooms first, lugging the ladder with me.

"I could've done that for you." Angus fills the dining room doorway, watching as I slide the last set of drapes onto the final rod. His eyes glow in the newly muted light, his spiky black lashes a dramatic frame for the bright blue-green.

I ignore the little leap of my heart. Two nice days after a

couple of weeks of silence and grumpiness, and now I'm having to fight a crush? Stupid heart. I'm too old for this shit. "No need, but thanks. Does this look straight?"

At his nod, I climb down and fold the ladder to carry it back out to the garage.

"Let me take that for you, at least." He lifts it from my hands, his calloused fingers brushing warm against mine.

My heart gives another one of those annoying little skips.

He pauses in the hall. "Listen, I put up some motion detector lights in the back and side yards. Rabbits and squirrels shouldn't trigger them, but taller stuff will. Thought that might make you feel safer."

I'm speechless. Who is this big thoughtful man, and what did he do with the cranky hermit who used to work here? That guy seemed a lot safer.

CHAPTER 8

Rose

THE DAY AFTER ANGUS FINISHES the laundry room, my brand-new washer and dryer are delivered. I'm so excited I strip the bed and throw my sheets and towels in for a celebratory first load, even though I just washed them a couple of days ago. It seems like such a big deal that, before I know it, I'm down grabbing two beers from the fridge and tugging Angus away from his lunch, dragging him upstairs.

He looks at me a little sideways as I pull him into my bedroom and on through to the laundry. "What's up?" His voice is a hesitant croak.

I hand him a beer, push the button to restart the wash cycle, and clink my bottle to his. "Ta-da! Little celebration. First time in my life I have ever done a load of laundry without having to feed in quarters." *Or, when things were* really *tight, swirling clothes around in the bathtub.* I toast the cheerfully chugging washer, admiring its churning suds.

He raises his brows. "No kiddin'. Hm." He clinks bottles

with me again and takes a drink. He waves a finger at the house around us. "This whole thing is really a treat for you, isn't it?"

I nod, dead serious now. "You know what, just about every single second of it. I don't want to take anything for granted. My mom never had anything like this, and neither have I, until now."

We drink our beer in silence for another couple of minutes until it's clear the washer is performing as it should, and then we go back downstairs to our respective work.

I've figured out how to help Jerry and Lydia. I just need to find the best bookstore and get up the nerve to talk to Mr. Ahmed at the market again. Then I can set my plan in motion.

I've also got swimming pool installers coming next week. I'm ahead on class work, so I'm going to make a landscape plan for the backyard for after the pool's in.

After school Friday, I check out every gardening and landscape book the library has. Do I know a damn thing about plants? Nope. Never even had a potted one. I'll have to read nonstop between now and planting weather to have a chance of this ending well.

I stash the books in my car and head across the square to meet Sabina for an early lunch at July's. July joins us for a few minutes, sliding in beside Sabina, looking like her much bigger, stronger, exuberant daughter. Both have bright eyes—July's gray, Sabina's blue—but where Sabina is calm and serene, July is restless, always moving.

Before the rush starts, we catch up on each other's news. They make the mistake of asking for a progress report, so I pull out my phone to show pictures. “I’ve got a downstairs powder room now! So that’s wonderful. And I can do laundry in my own house! We had a little ceremony about that…” I flip to the next picture (my sheets in suds, Angus’s big fingers around a beer bottle at one corner) before noticing how quiet they’ve grown.

Sabina’s brows are up near her hairline.

“You and Angus had a laundry ceremony?” July is completely deadpan.

“Yeahhh… He didn’t really know what I was dragging him up there for. Probably thought I was crazy.” I shrug. “We just had a beer toast and then went back to what we were doing.”

July nods. “You had a beer toast. With Angus Drummond. Over a washing machine.”

Sabina, the jerk, is holding in a giggle. She’s supposed to be the mature one of this group.

I frown. “Well, way to make it weird.”

They burst out laughing.

“Honey, that ship sailed long before Sabina and I got to the dock,” July informs me. “So I guess I don’t need to ask if you’re still scared of him? What with you dragging him through the house for impromptu laundry festivities and whatnot?”

“What?” This is a surprise. “I was never *scared* of him. I just wasn’t sure if I wanted to work with somebody who hated my guts. We’re getting along okay now. He’s been nicer lately. He laughs more.” Mostly *at* me, but.

July eyes me as she stands to go back to the kitchen. “Yeah… pretty sure no one has seen him crack a smile in years. Maybe decades.”

Angus isn’t there when I get home. The day is so nice and warm that I take a few library books out to the front porch. I’ve got no furniture there yet, but the floorboards and the wall behind me are warm with sunshine. This will be a great place for a couple of rockers, maybe a little table to hold an icy glass of lemonade.

I'm skimming the table of contents of a southern gardening book when I hear a child's babble from somewhere up the street. Well, a baby, really. It's not saying distinguishable words. Maybe the daycare crew is out and about.

I wait until it sounds like they're past the professor's house, and then I look up, ready to wave.

There's nobody there. Huh. Wait, there *is* somebody... But only one very small person, toddling its way along the fence, talking to itself. It's wearing tiny tennis shoes and jeans and a wee turtleneck under a sweatshirt with a duck applique. No sign of an adult.

I push myself up off the porch and move down the steps to my front walk. Surely this is a prank. This baby's not really on its own, out for a noontime stroll, right? I squint, looking for hidden cameras, but there's nothing and nobody on either side of the street for as far as I can see.

The Lone Baby trundles closer, looking like it might overbalance at any second if not for its hand on the fence. It's almost to my gate. Still alone. Still tiny and defenseless.

What the fuck? This is *so* not okay.

Angus

When she grabbed those beers and dragged me up to her room yesterday, for a minute I thought—I hoped—I was afraid that—well, clearly I was way off base.

Maybe I'm getting too used to this place. That's always a danger on longer-term jobs...that I'll get too comfortable with somebody else's property. This is a good house. Shaping up real nice. Satisfying.

The Wednesday morning therapy group caught me whistling the other day. Al, the mouthiest of the bunch, said it shook 'em up real bad—said I had to "cut that shit out." Dennis hopped right on the bandwagon. "We need to know there are things we can count on here at home, Angus. You know, like humidity. Good food. You being a grouch."

Jackasses.

But Rose seems so damn excited over every bit of progress on the house, it's fun to see. I can't even remember why I was so set against her. She's fair. Generous. Practical. Smart. There's just nothing not to like.

She pays whatever I ask right away. Hasn't mentioned needing to trim her wish list. 'Course, her living room and dining room and spare bedroom are completely empty, so maybe she's choosing renovations over furniture.

How am I supposed to make a dent in my debt to the universe if the person I'm supposed to be helping gives me more than I give her?

But today is a *gorgeous* day, so I'm not going to worry about that. I walk down to the Chinese restaurant off the square to pick up lunch. Enough to share in case Rose wants some.

She's in the front yard when I get back.

I let myself in the gate. "Hungry? I got plenty." I hold up the white takeout cartons.

Her eyes are glued to something at the fence.

There's a child there, squatting, examining a patch of bare

dirt near the corner of the yard. "Oh. Rose. You've got a baby." I sound ridiculous.

"Seems that way." She's using her rare not-pleased voice.

I look back and forth from her to the child. She doesn't explain. Just stands there silent and grim. Maybe I can lighten things up. "You turning that other bedroom into a nursery?"

"Let me tell you, my friend, we are all in trouble if it has come to that."

I've got no clue what's happening here. "Oh?"

"I've never had to deal with a small child. Well, every now and then when I was waitressing, I'd touch one of their grubby little paws by accident, bringing them crackers. But that's it. If anyone is depending on me to care for a child, we are all in deep shit." She claps her hand over her mouth. "Oops—shit! Oops! *See*? I'd be a *terrible* role model for a young person."

"Rose"—I make my voice as soft as I can—"why is this child in your yard?"

"I let it in."

"You...*let*...it in?"

"Yeah. I opened the gate, and once it was inside, I trapped it."

"You *trapped* it?" I admit, my calm is slipping.

"Yes. It was wandering down the street, all by itself... What the fuck are people think—? Oops! Shit! Oops! Angus, stop me before I cuss again! And I couldn't let it just keep going. It would have come to a street, or a driveway, or some evil person's house..." Rose gazes up at me, misery clear in her eyes. "I had to let it in. But now," she waves her arm, "here it is."

Okay. This is unusual, but not an emergency.

The child pokes at a piece of red paper stuck in the fence.

I nod. "I see. Okay then." We stand in silence for a minute, listening to the baby chant something at the paper. "So, police?"

"Already called 'em." She holds up her hand, phone still in it.

Together we watch the baby, who is pretty much oblivious to us, until a squad car pulls up. Same officers who responded to the burglary call last week.

"Welcome back to the house of weird things," Rose greets them, pointing to the baby. "Wait, that sounds mean. As far as I know, that baby is not weird. Not that I would know. I don't know that baby. What I mean is..."

One of the officers, nephew of a guy I went to school with, crooks a brow and leads Rose up to sit on the porch steps to answer some questions. The other one stays down near the baby and talks to me.

Rose shoots me an evil eye, probably because she can hear me laughing as I tell the officer my part of the story.

Eventually, just as the police radios crackle with a report about a missing toddler, a woman comes trotting up the street toward us, three other babies in a stroller and an infant strapped to her chest. Apparently, the wandering baby had crawled out an unsecured doggy door and gone adventuring. The woman scoops up the child and holds it tight, tears streaming down her face. She looks almost as relieved as Rose does.

A little while later, mystery solved, daycare woman and child reunited, everyone else leaves and Rose and I head inside. She mutters, "Thanks for mocking my pain, you big jerk."

I can't help it. I burst out laughing. "I wasn't mocking your pain, Rose."

She scoops a pile of books from the porch and yanks open

the front door. "I saw you when that officer led me away to grill me like I was some kind of baby collector sociopath."

I've got tears blinding me, I'm laughing so hard. "Okay, I might've been a little amused. But you gotta admit, Rosie, that was really, really funny." I wipe my eyes with the back of one hand, pinch the bridge of my nose, trying to get hold of myself. "I'm beginning to think I should pay you to let me hang around here."

"Fork it over," she snarls, jerking one of the carryout containers from my other hand and stalking away to the kitchen, her cute round butt twitching with each stomp.

I follow, still laughing, forcing away the sudden impulse to scoop her up and kiss her until she's laughing too.

CHAPTER 9

Rose

YOU'VE GOTTA ADMIT, ROSIE...

Nobody's ever called me Rosie before. Never had a *nice* nickname. In no universe could "Udderly Alice" or "Dairy Barns" have been considered nice. Or fond.

"Rosie" sounds fond the way Angus says it. I like it.

I am beyond pathetic.

The pool installation crew comes and I spend too much time watching them work, imagining how it will be when everything's done: a big, graceful, kidney-shaped pool edged with broad flagstones and gorgeous landscaping. Warm water the color of Angus's eyes. I'll get a floppy straw hat and a floaty chair with a cup holder for fruity umbrella drinks, and I'll work on my first adult tan. I'll know the names of every shrub and flower and tree, and just how to take care of them all.

My private paradise where nobody can ogle or heckle or

kill my joy in any way. I'll swim laps every morning. I *love* to swim.

But it's been sixteen years since I last swam and I need a bathing suit, so I head downtown to see if Naomi at the lingerie shop can fix me up.

On the way, I stop by the indie bookstore on the square. When I'd checked out a used bookstore yesterday with my plan for Jerry and Lydia in mind, I was sorely disappointed. They had plenty of books, but their only furniture was an occasional tiny rickety chair crammed between overflowing shelves. I gathered a big armful of children's books I wanted to make a selection from and went to the little counter up front. "Hello. Do you have any place sturdy I could sit to look at these?" I'd asked the clerk, who I suspect was the owner but who in no way resembled my friend Mr. Brown.

He looked me up and down, his face sour, and said, "No room." No "I'm sorry, we don't," or any suggestion of anything that might help me be comfortable while choosing which of his books to buy. Just "No room."

I'd gazed back at him for a long minute, imagining how awful it would be to have to deal with such a hard-eyed man regularly. Then I quietly put the whole big stack of books on the counter and walked out, ignoring his outraged sputters behind me.

Today the indie store gives me a totally different experience from the moment I walk in the door. This is the place I'd visited on my first full day in Galway. It's bright and well lit, with room for me to move comfortably between shelves. Sturdy chairs and tables where I can sit if I wish. A clerk calls out a greeting and says to let her know if I need help finding anything. I browse through their children's section, and when I'm satisfied, I find the clerk to talk to her about my plan.

Angus is working on the kitchen now, framing the refrigerator, filling in missing cabinetry, and refinishing the wood. I'm probably driving him crazy, bouncing from window to window at the back of the house, reporting on every fascinating thing the pool installers do. Which, to me, is pretty much everything.

But he seems interested in the process too. The first evening after the crew leaves, he and I go out and poke around to see their work up close. Wednesday afternoon late, the day he usually doesn't get here until after lunch, he sticks his head into the library where I've got graph paper and landscape designs scattered across the table. "Hey, I'm starving. Missed lunch and I've got a couple more hours of work to do. If I order a pizza, would you eat some?"

I sit back and study him. "Is this where I follow your example and insist on paying half? Or where I set a better example by graciously agreeing to let you pay and then thanking you for your kindness?"

He doesn't crack a smile, but his eyes crinkle at the corners. "You just won't let me get away with a thing, will you?"

"Nope." I wave at the counter. "We could pay for it out of the Cuss Jar."

He's been putting quarters in too lately when he curses.

"Nah, let this be my treat. As thanks for you letting me stay late to catch up."

We both go back to what we were doing. When the delivery person comes, he gives them a hefty tip and we settle at the table with cold drinks, the pizza box between us.

"Plates. Glasses. Napkins. Classy." He's every bit as much of a smart-ass as I am.

"I *even* have forks. If you know how to use utensils."

He grunts. "Blasphemer. Nobody eats pizza with a fork."

Talk about the pool progress leads to talk about swimming, and how and where we learned. Galway Lake for Angus. That's at the edge of town. I've driven along part of the shore a time or two, and it's lovely even in cold weather. It must have seemed really great to a young boy during long steamy North Carolina summers. I can almost see him, a sunbaked little guy with wild curls shining as he takes a running leap into the blessed cool of the water.

"Public pool for me. City pool passes and swim lessons were cheaper than daycare. The lifeguards were basically my babysitters."

"You're probably a better swimmer than me. I never had an actual lesson." He steals a drippy glob of cheese off the end of the slice I'm lifting onto my plate. "How about college? What made you want to go back now?"

Must tread carefully. "Would you say 'go back' if I never started college in the first place? I always wanted to but I… had some things happen and ended up dropping out of high school." I bite off the skinny point of my slice and chew, remembering that hellish time. "It looks like a bad decision, now, but at the time it seemed…necessary. For survival. Anyway, I went to work. Got a GED. Then my mom got sick and I didn't end up ever starting college. I guess this finally feels like the right time." Maybe he won't notice I didn't really answer his question.

He nods and chews for a minute. He's got more he wants to ask, I can tell.

I head him off at the pass. "How about you? Did you go to college?"

"Yeah. After the army." He eyes the remaining pizza. "I liked college, mostly. Had some problems when I was first discharged, but going to school helped, in some ways."

"What'd you study?"

"Psychology. You declare a major yet?"

"Nah. Too early to decide. There's a lot I want to learn about."

"I saw your list on the fridge." He points with his Coke can.

A big silly smile spreads across my face. "Oh, that's not school-related; it's just life things I want to do before too long."

He nods. "Making a good start, Rosie."

His approval, if that's what it is, is a warm surprise. Not that I'm doing those things for anyone's approval. It's just lovely that he cared enough to notice and mention it.

Angus

When she's not spying on the pool crew, Rosie's at her library table with a big pad of graph paper, sketching landscape designs. Elbows propping open two different books, an index finger marking her place in a third, pencil between her teeth as she types things into the search box on her browser. Her sketches get more elaborate as the week goes on.

Thursday I bring my lunch over from the fridge and settle at the one seat not covered in paper or books. "You've done this before?" The design next to me is pretty damn impressive.

She looks up from her screen and takes the pencil from her mouth. "Ha! No. I don't have a clue. I've never even had a cactus. Never had anything it was my job to care for. Well, except for Mom."

I'd like to hear more about that, but her mind's not on the conversation. She frowns at her drawing and starts pestering me about how many hours of sunlight different parts of the backyard get each day, and which sections of the yard get the most shade, and would I consider her property to be well drained.

That afternoon, I get the worst kind of crisis call. Kind of client I'm not sure I can help.

She's an army vet with PTSD. That much I know like the back of my hand. Suicidal risk assessment? I've got tools to help with that. Problem is, she won't talk to me.

I shake her hand, wave her to the best chair in my office, and sit across from her, like I do with everybody. "I'm glad you're here. I'll do my best to help."

She flicks her eyes at me, knee jiggling. "Yeah, not sure that's possible."

"Tell me a little about what brought you in today."

She squints at the framed stuff on the wall behind me. My discharge papers. Diplomas. Photos of me in uniform, with buddies, with family. Without. One shot Lenny took of me after I got home, my eyes haunted and unfocused, my new beard scraggly around the angry red scar on my jaw.

He didn't give me the photo until a couple of years ago. "I was afraid we were going to lose you," was all he said when he put it in my hands.

It's only on my wall now because I see that same haunted

look in the eyes of every vet I work with, at least at first. It's all over this woman's face now.

"You're not going to shock me or say anything I haven't heard," I tell her. "Wasn't all that long ago *I* was in that chair."

She snorts, weary bitterness in every movement as she shifts in her seat. "Man, you've never been where I'm sitting."

I change direction, ask softball questions about how long she was in, where she trained, what made her join up. She bites out two-word answers. Doesn't loosen a bit. Keeps darting glances at my hands where they rest on my knees.

"This isn't gonna work." Her voice is so low I can hardly hear her.

"Some kinda hope brought you in. What'd be the best-case scenario to come from this?"

"I just—" She rubs her eyes one at a time as if she's afraid to stop watching me. "I don't know. I just wanna be able to sleep. Feel normal again."

I nod and wait.

And wait. And wait.

She shifts in her seat again but can't seem to speak.

"Some things are hard to talk about. That's okay. Normal. You're not sleeping well… How you eating?" I lead her through questions about her symptoms. Try to gauge the severity, the risk level. Give her some suggestions for handling panic attacks, relaxing enough to rest. She agrees to call if she hits a crisis point.

She calls at ten thirty the next morning, voice jagged. "Those exercises don't work. I couldn't sleep at all again. I can't take this."

I meet her at the office. She's even jitterier than the day before, up and down from her seat, never turning her back on me, keeping herself between me and the door. I'm beginning to have suspicions about what happened to her.

"It's a nice day." I nod toward the window. "Wanna sit outside?"

She agrees but still seems ready to bolt at any minute.

I keep my movements and my voice slow and easy. Give her the yard chair closest to the gate.

Five minutes of silence while she stares at my hands like they're giant spiders about to spring.

"This is what I'm thinking," I say finally. "I'm wondering if you might rather work with a woman. Would that feel safer? I could introduce you to a friend of mine; she's really good."

Her eyes dart from my hands to my face. Back to my hands. "She a vet?"

"No. But she works with women who've survived assault. Helps them get their lives back."

She's shaking her head. "If she's not a vet, she won't understand." She doesn't deny the assault part. Crosses her legs, bouncing her foot at top speed. Glances away, then back at me. "Know anybody who's both? A woman and a vet?"

My turn to shake my head no. "Wish I did. There's nobody for a few counties around us." I let that sit for a beat. "But you're not the first person to want that. Couple of times, my friend and I have worked together to help somebody. Wanna try that?" It's not common, and it's not easy, but it's better than our other alternatives.

She frowns. "I can barely afford one therapist."

"We're both sliding scale. We can work something out." Need be, I'll donate my time. I'm so fucking sick of young vets not getting enough support, in service or out. Robin feels the same way about assault survivors.

My client nods finally. “Let me think about it.”

When she leaves, I call Robin. Give her a heads up, make sure she’s on board. Then I drive back to Rosie’s, hoping to god she does something wacky today to distract me from this frustration and helplessness that makes me want to break shit.

CHAPTER 10

Rose

ANGUS IS CHATTY. I DON'T know where he went when he left here earlier, or what happened there, but having him come back chatty is unnerving.

I'm eating a sandwich and marking up my three best landscape designs, x-ing out parts I don't think I want, circling the parts I do.

He goes to the refrigerator for his lunch and then joins me at the table, picking up one of my drawings and studying it. "I can't believe you didn't have any training for this."

"Learning as I go." With one thick pencil stroke I eliminate a bed of coral bells and hosta.

"What'd you do when you dropped out?"

"Pardon?" I fumble the pencil. *What the fuck?* It wasn't my fault. *I* didn't *do any*thing. And high school is off limits for casual lunch conversation. Timmy Johnson and those other assholes don't deserve one more second of my life.

"You said you dropped out and went to work. What kind of work?"

"Oh." Whew. Misread *that*. "Picked up more shifts at the restaurant where my mom worked. It was a block and a half from home, and I was already washing dishes there a couple times a week. When…I left school, they were needing somebody full-time, so…good timing."

He's silent for a minute, frowning and chewing his PB and J, then cuts those eyes over at me. "That nice, working with your mom?"

I snort before I can catch myself. "No. She was pissed for two whole years. I would rather have worked somewhere else, but she refused to drive me and wouldn't let me use the car. Said I should be in school, should've stuck to the plan. College." I need to lighten this conversation. "So she'd be really happy I'm finally doing it."

"She probably thought you were wasting that brain of yours."

"Those words might've crossed her lips, yeah."

His eyes laser in on me. "And you love learning stuff."

I nod. No point denying that.

"Must've taken something pretty serious to make you want to leave school." His jaw tightens, his expression grim, but he doesn't seem angry with *me*, exactly.

Eat your sandwich, Big Man. We're not going there.

"How about you? What other kinds of work have you done?" I wave my arm to indicate the whole house and yard, because this situation calls for a big distraction. "How'd you learn all this?"

He lets me get away with it. "My grandpa. Learned more in the army. Still had to get certifications when I came out, but I already had most of the knowledge." His turn to look away. He stows his trash in his lunch bag. "I do some…other work with veterans now. That's what I use my schooling for."

That explains his occasional unexpected exits and those phone calls he gets. He always takes them in another room, his voice low and calm and serious. "Are you some kind of counselor?"

"Yeah." He doesn't say any more and I don't pry. No wonder he has X-ray vision.

I take my plate to the sink and change the subject to the beautiful kitchen he finished last night. "You know what this means." I point at the cabinets and counters and island.

"No, what?"

"Time for me to learn to cook." I run my hand over the silky blue countertop. Somehow he's made concrete look like lapis lazuli.

His mouth quirks up. "Should I be scared?"

"Probably. I sure as hell am."

He packs away his lunch gear and stands. "Aw, come on, how bad could you be?"

"I can read directions on frozen pizza and I can operate a microwave, sometimes without causing an explosion."

"Oh shit." He wisely retreats to the living room to begin refinishing the floor, his quarter clinking in the Cuss Jar as he passes.

The kitchen's ready. I just need groceries. And the courage to brave the lion in his den. Before I can talk myself out of it, I grab my purse and the recipe I've chosen to start with and I head for Ahmed's Market. I need his help for the Jerry and Lydia plan.

"You," he says when he sees me, his dark eyes sweeping over me and my cart. Even the raw chicken quivers.

I straighten my spine to my full five-foot-one-inch height. "Mr. Ahmed, could I talk with you for a minute?"

He doesn't answer, just waits, so I plunge on. "Would it be

possible for me to set up an account for someone else to use? I mean, could I give you four or five hundred a month and tell you who will be coming in to shop with it?"

His eyes haven't moved off of me. "Why?"

"It's for a literacy program. Snacks and sandwiches and stories for kids."

"And you would be paying for it every month?" His words are bullets.

"Yes. Ahead of time. Well, not me, really… The money's from—"

He cuts me off with a nod. "Your grandfather. I know. Why do I feel like you are not telling me the truth?"

Because I am a lying, lie-ee, liar-pants. "Mr. Ahmed, I promise, there is nothing bad or illegal or in any way hurtful to anyone about this project. I swear."

That, at least, he seems to believe. He sighs and gestures me to follow. "Come. Let's get you set up."

I wake up optimistic. This week I'll talk to Jerry and Lydia, and also I'm thinking it'll be warm enough soon to use my new pool. I dig through my beach clothes for loose cotton capris and a T-shirt and then head for class, only to learn that not only is it a gray day but also cold and windy.

Okay, so, soup weather. After class I buy the ingredients and do prep work for pasta e fagioli.

Angus is at the table eating when I come over to look at my most recent landscape drawing.

"I think this might be the one." I tilt the notepad in his direction.

"Yeah?" He leans over to look, his broad shoulder brushing my hip, his warmth delicious.

I heroically ignore that and tap the page with one finger. "This path's in a slightly different place than we originally talked about. Will that work?"

"I'm done eating. Let's go look." He clears away his mess and follows me outside.

Puffy gray skies sprinkle on us as we pace off widths for planting beds and a path, but rain's been half-heartedly threatening all day, so we pay it no mind. But just as Angus asks whether I want a matching path on the right side of the yard, the sky splits open with a massive crash of thunder and in seconds we're drenched.

I race for the back patio, Angus right behind me, his hand warm on my elbow. The shaky latticework overhang provides just enough shelter that I stop, not wanting to soak my wooden floors. But fuck, that rain was freezing. "Holy moly, it's cold!" My teeth chatter as I try to wring water out of my shirt.

Angus doesn't answer, unless you count a tiny choking sound. But he seems okay, turning away when I look at him, peeling off his own shirt and twisting the fabric to squeeze water out.

I can't help it. I gape. I've never been so close to anybody so big and strong and manly and half-naked. *Don't think about naked.* He's all massive muscle and warm sturdy flesh and curly dark hair that cushions his chest and trails down his midsection. I catch his scent of soap and laundry detergent and something that's just him, and my knees go shaky.

It's possible I'm going to pass out.

Breathe.

Breathing, yes. I suck in air like I've just come up from a deep dive, and start to feel better, but then I notice his jeans. Apparently, wet jeans can really highlight a man's powerful thighs and calves and... Good lord, is that—? Aren't men supposed to shrink up in cold water?

Jesus Christ. I should probably sit down. Maybe find smelling salts. What are smelling salts, exactly? Ammonia? Like cat pee? Yeah, that sounds awful enough to snap me out of this nonsense reaction. I'm thirty-two, for god's sake.

I cannot let Angus catch me staring, no matter how... overwhelming he is.

"I'll grab us some towels." I yank open the door and dash in. Thank heavens for my convenient new powder room with its solid wooden door.

Angus

Thank god. Relief leaves me dizzy when Rose goes inside. Holy moly is right.

I've been doing a good job of not looking at her body. A *damn* good job, ever since she caught me ogling her chest like a horny kid at the restaurant. Usually her clothes disguise her enough that it's easy. Bulky, baggy sweats hide a lot.

Thin wet cotton doesn't.

Rosie's got the most amazing breasts I've ever seen. And now, thanks to an icy rain shower, I know their exact size and shape and perky nipple placement, and all I can think about is what kinds of sounds she might make if I scrape my tongue across them.

I don't need that particular addition to my dreams. And that nice round ass of hers, as she spun around to go inside? Didn't need to know so much about that, either.

She almost caught me staring. *That* would've sucked. I'm hoping she didn't notice my—Well, I held my shirt in front of me to hide it. Because that's *not* an appropriate reaction to someone I'm working for.

She's back in a second, tossing me a thick hand towel and then retreating into the house. I rub my arms and torso till they sting. Floors. Today I'm working on floors. That's where my mind should be.

She opens the door again, towel in front of her as she dries her face. "Here, toss me your shirt and towel and I'll go up and throw them in the dryer."

I watch her go, imagining her progress up the stairs, through her room to her new shower, dropping wet clothes in her wake, her warm, rounded body gleaming in the watery light from her windows.

Shit. Not okay. That's not just a body I'm fixating on. It's Rosie. My employer. My...friend.

This relationship just got a lot more complicated.

I head back out into the rain to my van. Grab my gym bag and take it to the powder room to change. Wipe up the rain we've tracked in. Try to unsee what I saw.

She's back downstairs in fifteen minutes, pink-cheeked and soft-looking in extra-big, extra-fluffy sweats, her hair in damp spirals around her sweet face. She hands me my newly dried shirt without looking at me. She leaves then and stays gone the rest of the afternoon.

I sand the dining room floor, glad for the mask that covers

most of my face and the plastic sheeting that separates my work space from the rest of the house, making it easier to forget where I am and what just happened.

But I drive home later with these new images of Rosie still seared in my brain.

Robin and I start meeting together with our new shared client. As I'd hoped, Robin and Nikki hit it off. Nikki looks at her when she's talking about the assault itself and at me when she's describing the bureaucratic nightmares of navigating sexual assault in the military.

At Rosie's, I finish the floors and paint the living and dining rooms. Takes Rosie and me a few days to get back to our usual ease with each other, but eventually we do.

She spends part of each day on cooking experiments. Couple of them qualify as disasters, but most of her stuff turns out great. Far as I can tell, the woman is across-the-boards competent at everything she does. She writes everything down in a notebook she's labeled *Kitchen Adventures*. Always has some kind of idea how to make each recipe better next time.

She asks me again, this morning before she goes to school, what sounds good.

I know she'll offer to share, and after spending all day surrounded by delicious smells from her kitchen, I have a hell of a time saying no. I sigh and pull out my wallet. "How about some kind of Mexican recipe tonight?"

She pushes the wallet away, her hand warm on mine. "Dang it, Angus, keep your damn money. I can buy my own groceries."

I ignore her, the way I always do, and pull out a ten. Lay it on the counter. "Dang it, woman, it's ridiculous, you thinking you can do all the work on it, feed me, *and* pay for the groceries. In what universe would that be fair?" My scoreboard would be screaming.

And later, I'll wash the dishes. She can maybe dry, if she insists. Which she will.

She's never said anything about having money problems, but there's still that uncrossed-off *figure out $* line on her refrigerator list. And recently, books lying around with titles like *Money Management* and *Financial Responsibility*. Unlike landscaping or sociology, she never talks about the money books.

Probably embarrassed. I try to give her openings to tell me she needs to whittle down the remodeling list but she's silent. Stubborn woman.

So I watch for ways to save money without cutting quality. She's put so much into it, it'd be great if she could actually afford furniture. Woman doesn't even have a TV. Or a sofa to watch it from.

One night, over amazing lamb kebobs, I ask if she's an only child. I know her mom died, but maybe she's got other family she can turn to in a pinch.

"No, it was just me and my mom. How about you?" She takes a bite of rice and pepper with her meat.

"I'm an only child too. My grandparents raised me."

She nods. "I don't even know if I've got any relatives still alive. Never met my dad or his family." She spears a piece of onion and pops it into her mouth. Shrugs. "I'm used to being alone."

God damn. So, no family to help her out.

"How come you're not married?" None of my business, dammit.

She frowns and picks at her kebob. "I've never gotten close enough to anybody to want that. Have you? Ever been married?"

She always turns questions back on me.

"Yeah. For a few years. Didn't last long once I got out of the army."

Her brows quirk up. Must've been expecting the hairy giant to say no. "Oh. I'm sorry. Do you miss being married?"

Fair question. Clearly I'm lonely enough to bum dinner off my employer most nights. Jesus. A sigh escapes me. "Sometimes. When things are good, it's great. But when things go bad, and you can't fix it... Nothing worse. Living with somebody, feeling like you don't have a damn thing to offer? Not good."

"No, I guess not." She pushes rice around her plate with her fork. "Do you have kids?"

"Nah." Another way I let my wife down. At least she's got some now, with her new husband. "How about you, didn't you ever want kids?"

She gives me a half smile. "No. Kids are like aliens to me, Angus. I'm never around them for more than a few seconds at a time. Just never got interested in them."

I have to laugh. "Totally explains your attitude toward the Scary Wandering Baby That Might or Might Not Have Been Weird."

Her frown is severe. "There you go again with the mockery."

CHAPTER 11

Angus

I'M ON SCHEDULE WITH THE inside renovations by the time I start painting Rose's room. Not a color I would have chosen—purplish-blue?—but it'll be good for sleeping. Peaceful. Not depressing, not too dark, with white woodwork and all the natural light.

Best part of the room's that bow window. Comfy chair or two, good book, relaxing before bedtime...I can definitely see Rose enjoying this space.

I try not to picture myself up here with her, but images flash through my brain anyway. I keep my eyes off the bed.

Finished the ceiling yesterday. Now I move the furniture to the middle of the room, put down drop cloths, and start applying painter's tape.

Ceiling fan's making a ticking noise. Probably needs balancing. I move the ladder over and climb up to fiddle with it. Problem's easily corrected—just a loose screw—but when I go to step down, I miss the bottom rung.

I land hard and off balance, staggering, slamming into the back of the dresser. Only keep from falling by grabbing the headboard. Unfortunately, my collision with the dresser rocks it forward. Top two drawers shoot out, crash to the floor, spill bright silky clothes everywhere.

Cussing myself for my clumsiness, I scoop up the top drawer—miraculously undamaged—and a handful of things that have fallen from it. Bras and panties. Rosie's bras and panties. Beautiful, sheer, expensive-looking, and very pleasing to the touch. I freeze, holding them. These are not at *all* what I'd expect a no-nonsense solitary woman like Rose to wear. I glance at the stuff on the floor. Maybe there's some plain sturdy white cotton everyday underwear there? Maybe some chain mail?

Nope. Only these soft sexy scraps of fabric and lace. Who'd have thought…?

Focus, dude. Gotta clean this up quick.

Too late. Rose appears in the doorway. "Are you all right? I heard disaster noises…"

I look from her face to my hand, horrified to see that I'm stroking her sexy underwear between my thumb and fingers. Like it's precious. Treasure.

"Oh." I clear my throat. I've got nothing for this situation. "Well. *This* looks bad."

After an eon of silence, I drop the undies into the drawer I'm holding and shove it back into the dresser.

She's spooky when she's this quiet.

I pick up the second drawer and its contents.

Nighties. Verrry nice, very silky, very flimsy nighties. Almost transparent. *Shit!* It takes a heroic effort to stop imagining her curves gleaming through the delicate fabric. I set the drawer on the bed and try to fold the slippery siren garments.

She looks on straight-faced, making no attempt to help. Sadistic woman. But she did just catch me feeling up her panties, so. Should I explain, or would that make it worse?

She's smart, though. Her eyes go from the ladder to the fan to the crooked dresser and then back to my face.

I duck my head, hoping I'm not blushing or some such middle-school bullshit. Hold one of the silky things against me to fold it in half, and then in half again.

"Probably not gonna be the most flattering fit," she drawls. "The aqua one goes better with your eyes." Then she turns and heads back downstairs, leaving me with a fistful of sexy negligee.

Which I'm also caressing. "Shit!"

And then "Shit!" again later, when I'm back on the ladder, painting the top of one wall, and realize I'm wondering what her underwear today looks like. And whether she might someday show me.

As the weather warms and Rose's classes end, I start on the roof.

Rose goes out each day and buys plants for her landscaping design. I think she's also swimming when I'm away. Lot of the time there's water around the pool ladder when I get back. And her skin is taking on a glow. Reminds me of fresh, warm peaches.

I spend way too much time wondering if her swimsuit is as nice as her underwear.

None of my business, dammit. Not the swimsuit, and for sure not the underwear.

But today I come back from a session with Robin and Nikki, and find Rose still in the pool, asleep in a floating chair, a straw hat shading her face and a soggy paperback floating a few feet away.

Suit's pure white. Looks like something a 1950s movie star might wear. Niiice.

Who'm I kidding? I'm not admiring the suit. I'm admiring her curves. Her breasts would fill even my big hands. Thick round hips, a bottom made for gripping... *Aw, dammit.* I can't let her see me in this condition but I need to wake her up so she won't burn.

I force my eyes away, reach for the skimmer pole. Focus on scooping up the ruined paperback. Takes me a minute to get things under control. "Rose, wake up! You're gonna burn."

"Mm?" She turns her head away, knocking her straw hat crooked.

I hold out the skimmer pole and let some water dribble on her shin. That wakes her up.

"Hey. You fell asleep. You're gonna burn if you don't get out. Plus, you ruined this really great book, uh..." I squint at the soggy cover and read off the title: *An Affair to Surrender.* "What the hell's that even mean?"

She does a half-assed paddle toward the pool ladder. "Bad book. Threw it," she mumbles. "Deserved to die."

I try not to laugh. "Yeah? What's so terrible?"

She reaches the edge. Maneuvers the chair so she can step directly onto the ladder. "'She smiled moistly.'" She makes air quotes with her fingers, her pretty lip curled in disgust.

"Aw, Jesus." I toss the book back in the pool. "I don't think it's all the way dead yet. Best just leave it."

I reach down, take her hand, and haul her out. She stumbles against me and I put my arm around her to steady her. Very curvy. Very, very curvy. Lots of soft sun-warmed silky curves pressed up against me.

I'm rock hard again, and if I don't move, I'll do something one or both of us will regret. I step back, supporting her from an arm's length away. "You okay there? I'd better get back to work." I'm across the yard and up the ladder to the roof without waiting for an answer. Spend the rest of the day with my eyes firmly fixed on the shingles.

Rose

When Angus spilled my underwear, I wanted to curl into a ball, maybe hide under the library table. To have my most personal things on display… I hope he couldn't tell how mortified I was.

At least my drawers aren't full of old cheap faded undies with holes and tattered elastic anymore. The thought of him seeing *those* makes me want to puke.

And thank god he hadn't knocked open the nightstand drawer. He'd have found my stash. My romance novels.

I've been devouring them. I picked one up in the library last week for the first time in my life. The New Arrivals section had books displayed covers out, and on one of them was a dark-eyed guy who otherwise looked like Angus. Tall, brawny, powerful shoulders, broad chest, massive arms… I couldn't not get it.

I'd tucked it between the money management materials in my stack. Brought it home, read it that night, and was hooked. I can't stop. I keep going back to the library and checking out more, which I keep in my bedside drawers and devour when he isn't around.

Maybe I should get locks for my nightstand drawers. *Sure, Angus, feel free to root through my underwear. Just not my books.*

Oh my god, the look on his face when I walked in and caught him holding my panties, though...priceless. *Oh. Well.* This *looks bad.*

As I'd fled the room with as much dignity as possible, I'd gotten a mental flash of him caressing my undies with me still wearing them. I could almost feel his big hands gentle on me. Because he would be gentle. He'd—

The fantasy made me miss the last step. I had to grab hold of the banister to catch myself. Pretty sure my whole body was blushing. I left as fast as I could, glad I had something important to do to take my mind off...things.

I went to the address Angus had given me for Jerry and Lydia.

Their little cul-de-sac is several blocks past Ahmed's Market. The houses and lots are small. Some need sprucing up, but Jerry and Lydia's looked well loved, with bright shutters and window boxes and a whimsical submarine-shaped birdhouse hanging from the tiny porch roof. Jerry was out near the curb, hammering in a sign that read *Custom birdhouses and flower boxes* with a phone number and website. He didn't look happy to see me.

I turned off Lillian and tried to put his fears to rest quick. "Hey, Jerry. You still looking for work? I know of something that might be perfect for you and your wife."

Without getting out of the car, I gave him the basics: a literacy program called "Stories and Snacks" for kids. Jerry and Lydia would make sandwiches and take them and children's books to parks and playgrounds in the less wealthy parts of town. Jerry'd get Lydia set up so she could sit and read a few stories to the little kids and then part of a chapter book to older kids, while Jerry passed around snacks and juice boxes. Then Lydia would do a book giveaway while Jerry'd pack everything back up, and they'd go to the next place. "When she starts to get tired, then just head home for the day."

His obvious worry and skepticism faded as he listened. When I told him the amount they'd earn weekly, his posture relaxed so much I feared he might fall over.

"Do you think you might be interested? Is Lydia home—? Could we talk?"

We went inside. Again, the house was small but well kept. Lydia was pale and looked like a stiff wind could blow her away...if she were wide enough to offer any wind resistance. But her smile was warm and sweet. She set aside her fuzzy throw, got up from the couch, and led the way into the kitchen, where Jerry poured us all tea from a pitcher in the fridge.

I ran through the whole plan with her as we sat around their table. "The funding is from an older gentleman—a friend of mine who ran a bookstore and cares a lot about literacy." I prayed for forgiveness for making them think my friend is still alive. "He especially wants to reach kids who don't have as much access to books at home, and he wants to make sure that hunger isn't a distraction for them. So...you all would plan your route each week, put up flyers and pick up the snack stuff from Ahmed's Market using the account we set up. There's another account set up for you at Corey's Books, and Lydia, with your teaching experience, you should be the one to choose the books each week. Be sure to get extras for giveaways at each stop. You'll have to figure out the fairest way to handle the giveaways."

Lydia's eyes glowed as she listened. Jerry's eyes glowed as he watched her.

Another idea struck me. "Jerry, are you the one making those adorable birdhouses and window boxes?"

Lydia beamed at him and then at me. "He is. He's really talented."

"I'm wondering if you could build some of those cute little free-library boxes they have in a lot of neighborhoods. If you all are interested in this project, we could add that on. I could set up an account for supplies for that, and we could use the Corey's account to stock them with books. It'd be extra work for you, of course, so we'd figure out what the pay for that should be. Hey, you could build a practice box first for your own yard. And one for mine."

They hold one of those wordless conversations I've seen really lucky couples have, and then Lydia nodded and Jerry turned to me. "When do we start?"

I laughed out loud, I was so happy. "As soon as you all can get set up. Plan your route. I'm authorized to pay you today for the prep work."

Lydia actually hugged me as I left—this is one hugging town, and I don't mind it a bit—and Jerry took my order for two birdhouses, one for my front porch, one for out back. I drove home whistling. Or, well, trying. Ineffectually blowing air out my lips, till I learn how.

And the next day Angus started on the roof, damn him. I took a break from studying for final exams to go outside with my landscape plan to try to picture how everything would look when the plants reach maturity.

I stepped into the backyard and glanced up at the roof where he was working, earbuds in, whistling something that sounded like "Born to Run." I only recognized it because Mom was a Springsteen fan. Also because Angus is a pretty good whistler, damn him.

He was facing away from me, and as I watched he raised the hem of his T-shirt to wipe his face. Then he reached over his shoulder, grabbed the back of it, and pulled it off entirely.

Daaamn.

It must not have been the first time he'd worked shirtless, because he was all golden-brown skin stretched over broad, solid muscle. He had a rhythm to his work, steady and graceful and quick. Every movement caused things to flex in a way that was mesmerizing.

I hope my mouth wasn't hanging open.

I half wanted him to come down off the roof so I could touch him. I just wanted to know how he'd feel under my hands. I didn't have any other intentions except that I am a pathetic creeper.

I managed to shake myself out of his spell just before he turned and saw me.

He waved and pulled out an earbud. "Need me?"

Um.

"Naw, just..." I waved the landscape drawing vaguely and turned to face the backyard.

Over the next couple of days, I found lots of reasons to go outside.

Now finals are over and suddenly I've got a lot more time for ogling and cooking and stuff. I'm getting more ambitious, figuring out how to fix whole meals and make everything be ready at the same time. Angus stays for dinner most nights.

I enjoy time with him more than I should. I don't harbor

any romantic fantasies—no way could *that* turn out well—but I'm a little worried about how much I'll miss seeing him and talking to him when he finishes up here and moves on to his next job.

Normally, aloneness is my default. My comfort zone. Something to seek rather than avoid. But Angus has been in my life as long as this place has. The house feels like home partly because of his work on it and partly because of his presence in it.

I don't want this crush to grow stronger. I don't want to embarrass myself. I don't want to depend on him. I don't know what to do about all that.

On a more positive note, now that I've taken care of the Jerry issue, I've got an idea of what to do with the money: keep enough to pay for school and house stuff, and then maybe set up some kind of charitable organization, get somebody to help me run it. I can make a career out of philanthropy. I'm not sure yet how to go about that, but I can learn. I'm working my way through all the books in the Money and Wealth Management section of the library. Once I have a better handle on financial stuff, I'll look for someone local to advise me and walk me through the steps.

Somebody local who can keep a secret.

That's what I was thinking about a while ago when I nodded off after giving up on that ridiculous impulse-purchase book. I cast it a dirty look where it floats at the opposite end of the pool.

Is there no end to my embarrassment around Angus Drummond? I sigh and paddle my chair over to the edge.

After all my care to keep him from seeing me in a swimsuit so as not to subject myself to the usual harsh judgments about my body, it seems I needn't have bothered. He reaches down, wraps one big warm hand around my wrist, pulls me out of the pool, up against all his deliciousness, and then leaps away like I'm contagious.

I watch him scale the ladder double-time and then I go inside to get dressed.

Men and their fear of fat women. No point trying to hide my pool time anymore. The hell with it. From now on I'll swim whenever I want, whether there's anybody around to see me or not. This is *my* damn house and yard and pool, and I'm going to enjoy it.

CHAPTER 12

Rose

WHEN I FINALLY FIGURE OUT how to access my grades online. I stare for a second and then shoot straight up out of my chair, fists raised in triumph, squealing like a boiling teakettle.

Shit. Angus is *right there*, eating his lunch. I sit my ass back down.

Still chewing, he raises a dark brow.

I'm not sure what's proper in this situation. I've never had anybody to brag to.

I nudge the corner of the laptop, turning it so he can see the screen.

"*I* am a straight-A student. In *college*." Insufferably smug, I know. Blame the grade report: *Algebra I: A. Sociology: A+*.

He swallows his food. "Looks to me like there's a plus on there too. You are an A-*plus* student. In college. Didn't know they even gave pluses in college."

"Probably started the practice just for me." I wriggle in my chair, afraid I'm about to emit another god-awful *eeeeee* sound.

He stares at me, a twinkle in those eyes. "You need a victory lap, don't you?"

After a beat, I nod. No use denying it. I explode out of my chair, waving my hands in the air, and circle the room twice, singsong-ing, "I got all A-ee-ays, I got all A-ee-ays!"

He leans back, grinning. "Way to go, Rosie. That's great. What are you going to do to celebrate?"

That stops me in my tracks. "I should! I *should* celebrate." I drop back into my seat. "Maybe I'll...have a little dinner party. My first party! Will you come if I invite Sabina and July one night?"

He tips his head in a nod. "I'd be honored."

July's closes early on Sundays, and the weekend crowd usually clears out of the B and B by mid-afternoon, so we decide to hold the celebration on Sunday evening.

Sabina brings wine, July brings fancy chocolates, and Angus shows up with a big bouquet of roses. Lavender, peach, and cream, delicate and gorgeous together.

No one's ever given me flowers before. I hide my face in the fragrant blossoms, lump in my throat, moved beyond all reason. I'm ridiculous. This crush is going to be the death of me. "These are beautiful. Thank you, Angus. You didn't have to do this."

He bends and actually kisses my cheek, his lips warm, his beard and mustache soft against my skin, treating me to the scent of freshly showered man. "Special occasion, Rosie. You worked hard, you did well, you deserve flowers." His voice is gruffer than usual.

My vision blurs. I don't look at anyone as I head to the kitchen to find something to use as a vase. I need to get a grip.

This is just him paying for his meal in a prettier way than usual. God forbid he accept free food.

"The house looks so nice!" Sabina takes everything in with bright eyes, kindly refraining from commenting on my lack of living room and dining room furniture.

I probably should've bought some before having people over. But I'm a newbie at entertaining—and friends—so sue me. It's a dinner party. We've got the library table to eat from.

"Something smells wonderful." July inhales deeply. "What are you feeding us?"

"Chicken Kiev." I'm nervous about this whole idea now. Sure, my cooking experiments have been mostly successful. And when it's just Angus and me, we can joke about the occasional failure. But Sabina's a marvelous baker and July can make anything perfectly. What was I thinking? I still struggle to get everything done at the right moment.

They follow me into the kitchen and ask what they can do to help. I ask Angus to toss the salad and take it to the table. Sabina plates the rolls, hot from the oven, and carries them in. July puts the new potatoes into another bowl while I fill two plates, one with chicken, one with asparagus.

At least I remembered to buy a white tablecloth and some candles. My dishes are plain, but everything looks good by candlelight, even though we have to drink Sabina's wine out of water glasses.

We pass the platters and serve ourselves. I always loved it when families did that on TV. My heart's a little swollen in my chest from finally having somebody to share with.

Everybody digs in and for a minute there are only soft sounds of appreciation.

"Rose, this is delicious."

"Mm, mmm."

"You've outdone yourself, Rosie."

Halle-freakin'-lujah.

The food disappears and the volume ramps up. July and Angus tell a funny story about their friend Lenny from high school.

"You met Lenny, Rosie, that day you waited on us at July's."

I remember him. Reddish hair, glasses. Seemed sweet.

"Wait, wait," July gestures between us, "So you all met *before* you started working on the house?"

"Twice."

"But we didn't know it."

Angus and I tell the story, interrupting each other and laughing, and by the time the big jerk finishes exaggerating how hard I hit him with that candy bar, Sabina and July are howling.

"So," Sabina pauses to wipe a tear from the corner of her eye, "you hated each other at first? That's hard to imagine."

Which is July's cue to tell how we both called her with doubts about working together. And then Angus tells about the Wandering Baby.

Really, we haven't had enough wine to be laughing this much. My face and my sides hurt. All these stories seem to be at my expense, but with Sabina squeezing one of my hands and Angus nudging my knee with his under the table, all I can feel is warm. It's...lovely.

"What's next, Rose?" Sabina nibbles one of July's chocolates and sips her after-dinner coffee. "More classes?"

"Yep. Haven't picked my next quarter's schedule yet, and I don't have a major. But I'm really enjoying it."

They tell me about great and terrible courses they've taken and teachers they've loved or hated. Angus had an Abnormal Psych professor whose class periods flew by because she told fascinating stories from her decades in practice.

Sabina tells us about her English professor decades ago who used the phrase, "That is to say," so often it's all Sabina could remember from the class. "Forty-six times in an hour and fifteen minutes. That was her record. I kept a tally. As a good student does."

July imitates a chef in her culinary school, a French guy who liked to hover menacingly over students, crooning, "Are you nair-voos?" and then shouting, "Imbecile!" when they screwed up.

I'm going to be sore tomorrow from laughing. This has been the best night of my life.

They insist on helping me clean up. There aren't any leftovers to speak of—Angus pops the last half of the last new potato into his mouth—so soon everything is tidy.

Angus leaves first.

I walk him to the door, thanking him once more for the roses. For a second he tilts like he might kiss my cheek again, but then he squeezes my elbow, smiles, and ducks out.

Sabina and July come down the hall as I close the door behind him.

"I saw a whole new side of Angus tonight, Rose." July slides an arm into her sweater sleeve.

"He lights up around you." Sabina pulls a key ring from her pocket. "I've never seen him laugh like that."

"Maybe he didn't at first, but he likes you fine now, babe." July gives me a one-armed hug.

Sabina gives me a longer one. They congratulate me on my successful first college term, compliment the food again, thank me, and then they're gone, leaving behind a silence that echoes with the laughter and warmth of friends. And the scent of roses, and the memory of a way-too-important-to-me kiss.

Best. Night. Ever.

"Rosie, you like blues music?"

"Guess so. Haven't listened to it much." I'm poking around in the fridge for raspberry jam. "Want some toast?"

"Naw, thanks, I ate already."

We've perfected a morning kitchen ballet in which he puts his lunch away while I'm getting my breakfast out. We rarely crash, darn it, but I can usually catch the clean scent and heat of him. If I lean in far enough.

"Some friends of mine—remember Lenny?—have a band and they're playing downtown this weekend. I don't get to see them very often because they travel a lot. They're really good. Wanna go hear them Saturday?" He's swirling his coffee in his cup, not looking at me.

I could never afford to go out in Indy, and I never had anyone to go with anyway. It's never occurred to me to go to a bar here.

I'm just beginning to understand how limited my range of experience has been.

Is Angus asking me as a friend or a date? Friend, almost certainly. Definitely.

Either way, I'm in. "Sure." Saturday is five days away. Sometime between now and then, he's bound to drop a hint that will let me know how to think about the outing.

But by that night I still have no clue whether it's a date or a friends-hanging-out thing. I study the clothes in my closet, not sure what to wear. I Google the bar, Lindon's, to see if it seems like a fancy place. It does not.

Eventually I decide on an outfit I haven't worn yet, mainly because it's not baggy: stretchy jeans, a soft fuzzy black V-neck sweater, flats, and some dangly green glass earrings.

Angus shows up just before nine, as promised. "Well, you look very nice."

"Thanks. You look very nice yourself."

Understatement of the year. He's in a long-sleeved dark Henley and jeans that show the power of his big body. Again I get that urge to touch him, to see how he feels under my hands. Instead I turn to lock the door behind me.

"Your shoes comfortable? Want to walk?" He peers at my feet. "It's about five blocks. I can drive if you'd rather."

"It's a nice night. Let's walk." I swing my purse strap over my head so my hands are free.

Angus holds the gate open for me and then ambles alongside, his hands in his pockets. He must be matching his pace to mine—he's at least a foot taller than me—but somehow he doesn't seem awkward or clumsy. He makes no attempt to touch me.

Okay, no hand-holding. One point for not-a-date.

We talk about next week's tasks when we'll be working together out back, him hardscaping and me planting.

"You gonna try to do everything yourself and not let me help?" He reaches around me to open the door to Lindon's.

"You gonna try to pay me and pout if I won't take your money?" I stick my nose in the air—the better to sniff him with—and sail past him into the bar.

His hand is at the small of my back as we weave through the little tables in front of the stage and settle at one next to the wall.

Even through my sweater, my skin tingles from his touch.

Angus

What in the hell was I thinking, asking Rosie to come with me tonight?

This is *not* a date. I don't date customers, for Christ's sake.

But she's so pretty it's hard not to touch her. She just kind of...glows. Her hair looks all soft and shiny, waving and curling. Makes me want to wrap it around my fingers. Doesn't help that those little earrings catch the light like they're flirting.

Her clothes aren't tight, but they show a lot more of her curves than her usual baggy stuff, and it's distracting as hell. I should've never put my hand on her waist. Now all I can think about is resting it there again. Maybe rubbing her back. Sliding my arm around her.

Getting damn hard to be just friends.

But even if she weren't my customer, I'm not sure this'd be a date. Her interest seems platonic. For all I know, she prefers women. Or some different type of man. I need to get a grip. Remember our circumstances and chill the fuck out.

She tries to pay for our drinks. Then argues when I won't let her. Cute little pain in my ass. I finally have to put down my foot. "*No*. My invitation, my friends' band, my tab."

She frowns like she's going to take that snotty tone she uses when she wants me to think she's pissed off, but she just gives me the evil eye and turns her attention to the band taking the stage.

I hide my grin.

Lenny sees me, then nudges James and Rashad. Their eyes move from me to Rosie and back. All three of them quirk their brows at once. Jackasses. I rub my nose with my middle finger. They snicker and turn back to their instruments.

Rosie misses all of this. I'd expect her to be watching David—everybody attracted to men always does—but she's looking at Chris. "I think it would be so much fun to play drums, don't you? If you had a bad day, you could beat on them until your frustration actually sounded good."

Hard to imagine her doing that, but okay. I'm sure she could pick it up fast like everything else. "That going to be your next project?"

"Naw, Spanish is next." She's serious. "Tell me how you know these guys again?"

"Lenny and James and Rashad and I were in school together. Played football in high school." I point each of them out to her.

"Wow. Lenny and James and you, I could see. But Rashad? He looks like a history professor."

I laugh. I'll have to tell 'Shad that one.

She's not wrong, though. The rest of us are big. Tall and broad. Lenny's red hair is almost as wild and kinky as James's afro. Rashad is medium height, lean and elegant. Close-cut hair, round wire-rimmed glasses. He could wear tweed and look right at home in front of a college classroom.

"He was the fastest wide receiver in western North Carolina in high school. Great hands. Too small for the pros, but he prefers music anyway. You'll see when he plays that guitar."

The guys confer on stage. David and Chris glance out at us, and Chris grins. No good can come of this. They take their places and Lenny leans into the mic at his keyboards.

"How y'all doing this evening?"

The bar filled while we were talking. The Blue Shoes aren't just good, they're hometown favorites who only play Galway a few times a year. When Lenny asks his question, the crowd roars in approval.

His fingers ripple over the keys like water. "We'd planned to start off a little different, but I see our buddy Angus is here tonight. This one's for him..." Points straight at me and waves. Gives me a big cheesy grin.

Aw, hell. Sure enough, they go straight into that old Southside Johnny song about having the fever for a girl, Lenny raunching it up for all he's worth on vocals, James strutting through the bass line, singing the deep echo, Rashad and David side by side, their guitars and shoulders swaying in perfect sync.

I'm afraid to look over at Rose. The lights are focused on the band, but I'm sure I'm redder than Lenny's hair. It's not just the band; most of the people in the bar are shooting us looks and grins. At least three of 'em wink. Assholes.

Rosie's eyes are enormous. A million expressions cross her face before she finally leans over and tugs my sleeve. Shit. She's going to throw up. No, she's going to punch somebody. No. She's going to ask to leave, and I'll have to come back later and murder my best friends. I bend to hear her.

"You *sure* these guys made it through middle school?" she hollers, as in the background Lenny wails about having the fever for her and the whole band chimes in with *oo-oo-oo-oo-oo*s.

I can't help it. I laugh. My girl is the master of this situation too. I wrap one arm around her and hug her tight for a long perfect moment.

What the hell. Not my girl. I turn her loose, but even that slipup can't stop me from feeling good down to my bones.

Next time Lenny looks our way, she points and shoots him an evil eye much like the ones she gives me. He grins and winks without missing a note.

By the third song, she's totally under their spell, leaning forward in her chair, a tiny smile on her pretty lips. Watches each guy in turn. Probably teaching herself to play all the different instruments just by observation.

Finally her eyes land on David. Can't believe it took her so long. Dude's prettier than most of the women in the bar. He's not tall but he's got dark and handsome down pat. The guys are always giving him a hard time about all the phone numbers people shove at him.

She tugs me down so she can speak in my ear. "Is that his girlfriend?" She nods at a woman in a white dress at a nearby table.

"Don't think so. He's been single as long as I've known him." But he *is* looking at the woman in white almost nonstop. "She's not sitting with James and Rashad's wives. They just came in the door. See?" I wave at Tisha and Shay.

Shay's eyes go wide when she sees us. The curiosity is going to eat her alive. There's no room at our tiny table, so they have to find their own seats.

"Ooh, interesting! Let me watch for a bit. I'll have the story for you by the end of the night." Rose settles back in her chair, poking at the lime in her rum and Coke, her gaze moving between David and the woman in white.

I smile down into my beer and fight the urge to put my arm around her again.

We stay till almost one o'clock. I introduce her to the guys and wives when the band goes on break. Tisha and Shay give me semi-subtle thumbs up. James and Rashad clap me on the shoulder. *They* all think it's a date. And they approve.

Lenny spends too much time leaning in close to talk to Rosie, but the guys head back up on stage just as I'm considering kicking his ass.

When we finally fight our way through the crowd and step out into the cool night, it's all I can do not to reach for her hand. I can't remember the last time I wanted to hold somebody's hand. My marriage? High school? Either way, it's been years.

Rosie bumps my elbow. "They just met today."

"What? Who?"

"That pretty David guy and the woman in the white dress."

I turn to look down at her as we walk. "How'd you figure that out?"

She grins up at me. "Lenny told me." She interlocks her fingers and stretches them out in front of her, cracking her knuckles, as she gives me a cute, smug little look. "He said David laid eyes on her and was 'poleaxed.' Lenny's word." She frowns. "That actually sounds a little sketchy. David's not a creepy stalker type, is he?"

The thought makes me laugh. "No. He's one of the nicest people you'll ever meet."

"I wonder, then…" Her voice trails off.

"What?"

"Do you believe in love at first sight? Could it just happen like that, do you think?"

I'm considering my answer when I see her shiver. "You okay? You cold?"

"A little chilly. It's okay. We don't have far to go." But she doesn't object when I wrap one arm around her and pull her in against my side.

I get a faint whiff of her orange scent. She feels just as soft and nice as she did that day by the pool. After a minute she puts her arm around my waist. That doesn't feel too bad either.

"I don't *not* believe in it," I tell her.

"Pardon?"

"Love at first sight. I don't *not* believe in it. Maybe it works like that for some people. I haven't experienced it, but…who's to say?" I rub my hand up and down her arm as we walk. Just to keep her warm. "What about you—you believe in it?"

"I don't know, Angus. I don't know what I believe about a lot of things."

I wouldn't mind walking another couple of miles with her tucked in warm at my side. We reach her house all too soon. I hold the gate for her. Force myself to stop there. "Thanks for going with me tonight, Rosie. I had fun."

She blinks up at me, her eyes shining dark in the night, a half smile on her pretty lips. "Thank you for asking me. I had fun too."

I watch her let herself in. Wave and leave, closing the gate softly. Wish I was done with the work on her house, up on that porch with her after a real date, kissing her good night. Or maybe, if I was really lucky, she'd take me up to her pretty room with that wide comfortable-looking bed, so I could make sure she stays warm all night.

CHAPTER 13

Rose

SO, NOT A REAL DATE, then.

I was unclear on that point up until the very last second at the gate there where, if it had been a real date, there would have been the good night kiss issue.

Angus didn't show the slightest hesitation in saying goodbye or leaving, so…not a date.

Don't know how I could've thought otherwise.

I lean against the wall in my dark front hall, watching his loose stride to the van. Watching him drive away. My side feels cool, even inside the house, without him here beside me.

What would it be like to have him wrap his big strong arms around me, look at me with his ocean eyes, and give me a long slow kiss?

I shiver from something that isn't cold. Something that's part nerves and part…eagerness?

It seems like forever ago that Galway was an unfamiliar place and Angus just a cranky stranger. He may never return my other feelings, and he's still a little cranky, but he truly is a friend now.

Despite my not-a-date disappointment, I feel every bit as rich as you'd expect someone with a bunch of millions to feel.

Sunday I visit the library, collecting a weathered paperback here, a new arrival there. It's past the worst of the brunch rush when I finally get to July's. Miz Ames is nowhere in sight. Probably at church. Probably hanging from the belfry.

Sonya's on break and waves me over to join her. "Sit and talk with me. I need to think about non-restaurant stuff."

"Bad day? You all need help?" I look around but everything seems calm and clean and normal in the dining room.

"No, we got it covered. It's Bonita's day for the kids, but she's got some kind of stomach bug and so do a couple of the kids, so Kip stayed home to keep the sickies separate from the well ones."

"I didn't know Bonita and Kip lived together." I shove the menu aside. I want quiche and fruit.

"You didn't? Bonita, Kip, Donna, Tina, and me. And our kids."

I blink. "Wow! That must be a really big house!"

"It's a four-plex. July bought it when she found out how bad rents are. She's letting us rent-to-own." Sonya finishes her sandwich as another server brings me water and takes my order.

When she's gone, I turn back to Sonya. "That sounds like a good arrangement."

She nods, gathering her dishes. "Yup. Works out great all around. We have a decent place to live, we all share childcare, and July gets ride-or-die employees."

As I watch Sonya disappear into the kitchen, I remember Sabina saying, the day I met July, “July knows everyone.” I’ve seen the photos all along the hallway to the restrooms: Little League teams she’s sponsored, Girl Scout troops, group shots with well-dressed adults I assume are town bigwigs... July might be able to help me with my money situation, if I can find the right way to ask questions.

She’s a lovely friend, but my guts clench when I think of confessing my money secret. Can’t do that just yet. Got to be subtle.

July herself brings out my food on a tray with her own lunch. “Mind if I join you?”

“Please.” The fates are kind to deliver her straight into my unprepared clutches.

We unload the tray and she tucks it away on the bench beside her. She asks about the house and I show her my most recent photos.

“Next we tackle the back landscaping.” I’ve been envisioning it for days.

“Nice!” She pushes the breadbasket closer to my plate. “You’ll have to throw a pool party after that. Break it in right.”

“Ooh, yeah, good idea.” I close my eyes, savoring the quiche of the day. Roasted red pepper and caramelized onion. “Geez, July, this is fantastic.”

She grins. “I’ll tell Donna you said so. That was her creation.”

We talk food for a few minutes before I figure out how to word what I want to ask her.

“Hey, remember when Sabina introduced us, she told me you know everyone and everything about Galway? I’m hoping you can help me with something.”

She doesn't hesitate. "Sure. What's up?"

"I've been wondering what kinds of volunteer opportunities Galway has, or what kinds of needs there are. Can you tell me about the different places around town that help people?"

She pokes at her salad, spears half a grape tomato with her fork. "Hm. Well, I guess we have the same problems and needs as other places. Homelessness, poverty, domestic violence, lack of access to affordable medical care. I mean, we have a free clinic, but it's only open once a week, on Mondays. What if somebody gets hurt or wakes up sick on a Tuesday?"

I nod and nibble a slice of orange, willing her to keep talking.

"So we could definitely stand to have a clinic that's open more, if not every day." She chews her tomato and swallows. "Affordable housing's a problem for almost everybody. I wish we could pull together and do better on that." She chases a piece of arugula around her plate. "Childcare...never enough good safe childcare. Wages are too low in most jobs. Like everywhere."

She eats the arugula with a sliver of boiled egg. "But you're wanting to know about volunteer work. Hm. The women's shelter can always use volunteers. They do a big training every year for that. Um, the free clinic needs people to provide meals and cleanup, host fund drives, stuff like that. The school district and the Youth Home are always recruiting tutors and mentors. Need to pass background checks for them. The Food Pantry and the Community Closet always need donors and people to help organize donations."

She's a gold mine of information. I eat and nod and listen and try to memorize every word she says.

Angus

It's a warm week for working on the backyard. Rose amends the soil and then plants and mulches one bed at a time, while I lay flagstones around the pool and put in brick walkways. It's hard physical work. Monday she asks if I've got my gym bag in the van. When I say yes, she says, "Let's jump in the pool." So instead of sitting inside for lunch, we wolf down our sandwiches and then take cold drinks outside and float around for a half hour before we get back to work. That sets our lunch pattern for the week.

She brings a little speaker outside and we take turns choosing music. By Wednesday I'm pretty sure she's trying to pick a fight, especially when she cranks up *West Side Story* for the fourth time.

"Show tunes *again*, Rosie? I swear, if you weren't my boss, I'd pick you up and throw you in that pool right now."

She bobbles her head, snark oozing out her pores. "Angus, Nirvana is good. Blues are fine too. But if I have to listen to any more of that godforsaken improvisational jazz shit—"

I stop shoveling the sand base for the path and cup a hand over my ear. "What's that? I can't hear you over Maria feeling pretty..."

She stomps back over to where she's been putting in those weird-looking elephant ear plants near the bamboo. "I *said* if I wanted to hear a bunch of people warming up on twelve random songs all at the same time, I'm sure I could drop by any preschool class."

But when I glance at her a minute later, she's laughing to herself.

She's not cooking this week. I bring my little charcoal

grill from home and we have meat and foil-wrapped potatoes, or takeout.

By Thursday night we've got the backyard mostly done according to plan. Our steaks taste extra good and between us we finish off three potatoes.

Afterward, Rosie sprawls on her back at the edge of the pool, hands cupping her belly. "Is it weird that I'm enjoying working so hard I can barely move at the end of the day? Waking up and having to stretch my sore muscles before I even get out of bed?"

I settle a couple of feet away on the warm flagstones and clink my cold bottle to hers. "I think everybody likes to work hard and then see what they accomplished. Yard looks great, Rosie."

She stares up at the sky turning lavender-blue above us. "You feel like that about your counseling work?"

I look away across the pool. "Sometimes. Progress is slower. Less obvious. Still feels good to see it. Great, when the client can see it too."

Like the client Robin and I share. I still give Nikki plenty of space and a clear path to the door, but she's stopped staring at me like I'm going to jump her. And yesterday after her EMDR session, she smiled back at me and Robin and said, "I slept six solid hours last night before I woke up." There was hope in her voice.

Rosie raises herself up enough to drink from her bottle, then lays her head back again. "Is that where you are on Wednesdays when you're not here till after lunch?"

I nod. "A therapy group and some individual clients, yeah." Saturdays too, but Rosie and I don't share our weekends, so I don't mention that.

She swirls her feet in the pool, seeming to sense that I can't talk about clients. She doesn't ask any more questions.

Rosie's got this place looking great. She's been slowly furnishing the empty rooms—I guess money's trickling in from somewhere, or she's taking on more debt...but I don't like thinking about that—with pieces that make you want to stay awhile. Big comfortable couch and chairs in the living room, all different colors, somehow looking good against her cool green walls. Flat-screen TV above the living room fireplace, a funky bright piece of fabric art on a rod that swings right over the top of the screen to hide it. I don't get how she can look at some of this bright stuff and know it'll be good together, but she can. And it does.

Problem is, I feel like I'm coming home whenever I let myself in her gate. Like I'm somewhere cold and impersonal when I go back to my place.

I am way too comfortable here.

Way too comfortable with Rosie.

Mornings when I side-step her to get my lunch in the fridge, it's all I can do not to put my arm around her. Pull her in for a kiss. And when she comes out of the pool, water sliding over her, her big brown eyes and smile bright, I want to take hold of her and do a lot more than kiss.

She should cross *suntan* off that goddamn refrigerator list. She's a really pretty shade of tan now. Sun's bringing out red in her hair. I'm sure she didn't do that chemically. Wouldn't be like her.

Then again, I'd thought she was a white cotton granny panties kinda woman, so what do I know? And why the hell am I still thinking about her damn silky underwear?

Should be focusing on prepping the exterior of the house for paint. Rose wants light cocoa with spring green shutters and trim in cream, green, and burnt orange. Gonna make the place even more welcoming. Dammit.

It *cannot* be healthy for a man to walk around with a hard-on all day. Heard warnings about that on TV. If I have to see her in another one of those clingy, old-fashioned, sexy swimsuits, my dick's going to explode. Why'd she stop waiting till I'm not around to swim? Is she *try*ing to make me nuts?

Thing is, I'm pretty sure she's got no idea how she affects me. Pisses me off. If I'm a giant knot of lust, seems fair she should be uncomfortable too. But no, she's cool as can be. Doesn't bat an eye when I work without a shirt. Other places I've done jobs, I've had to be careful to keep a shirt on, no matter how hot it got, if I didn't want comments—sometimes touches and invitations—from people already in relationships. Here I could strip naked and strut around in nothing but my tool belt, and Rosie would never raise her nose out of whatever she's reading. Goddammit.

I wipe sweat off my forehead with the back of my hand and go back to scraping peeling paint. Mr. Invisible, that's me.

CHAPTER 14

Rose

I AM FREAKING *TORMENTED* BY the sight of him every day. Jesus Christ, how can a man be so big and rugged-looking and have so damn much muscle under that smooth tanned skin?

Maybe next quarter I'll take an anatomy class. Maybe he'll let me take a Sharpie and label all his various yummy bits. As a totally innocent study aid for an A-*plus* student.

My obsession with his body is really pissing me off. Some days it feels like I might need to tie my arms to my sides to keep from smoothing my hands over him. But even if I did touch him and he didn't slap my hands away in horror, I'd be scared about what might happen after that.

Why, as hot as it is, isn't his hair ever flat or greasy? Why does even his sweat smell good to me? And how bright can one man's smile be against his tanned face? He's not supposed to even *be* smiling. I was told that's not something Angus Drummond does.

Not that I've seen any smiles lately. That's another irritating thing. He's been really grumpy this week. Not yelling or snapping—although I suspect he wants to—but just grunting his answers or turning away with a word or two instead of talking to me like he used to. He hasn't stayed for dinner the past couple of days. We're friends, aren't we? So what changed?

I rack my brain trying to think of how I might've upset him, but I've got nothing. He must have something else going on in his life.

He should either talk about it with me, like friends do, or stop taking it out on me.

Day Three of Angus's Terrible No Good Very Bad Mood, I find him on the front porch scraping the sills and frame of the bow window. "Hey." I try not to look at his big lovely bare chest. Difficult, since his freakish height puts it right at my face level. "I'm going shopping for a dining table and chairs. Need anything while I'm out?"

He doesn't even glance my way. "Huh-uh."

I wait but he doesn't add anything. Apparently I no longer even rate real words. I wait some more.

He *knows* I'm right here, but he won't look up from his work.

Okay, that's enough. "Dammit, Angus, what the hell is wrong? Are you mad at me?"

He stops scraping and stands for a long moment staring at the peeling window trim. Eventually he seems to reach some decision, because he draws in a deep breath and lets it out in a long sigh. He tucks the scraper in his pocket and turns to look at me for the first time in days, his aqua eyes, as always, sending a shock right through me. "I think we need to talk. Let's go out back."

Oh god, this does not sound good.

He leads me through the house and out the back door, across the yard to the gate, digging his key ring out of his pocket as we go. Once we reach the alley, he comes to a stop in front of his van and looks down, fiddling with the keys. When his gaze comes back up, there's an emotion I've never seen on his face. Worry? Dread?

Now I'm really concerned. "What's wrong, Angus? Are you okay?"

He presses something hard into my hand. His copies of my gate and house keys.

My heart jerks. "What's this?"

He can't just leave me! I haven't done a single one of the inappropriate things I fantasized about. I've been really, really well mannered. I can't imagine anybody else showing such self-restraint. This isn't fair!

My voice comes out as a croak. "Angus, are you…quitting?"

"Not unless you want me to, after I say what I need to say." His voice scrapes my heart.

Oh god, what? What in the world have I done? I grit my teeth, squeezing the keys until the metal bites my fingers. "Tell me."

"Rosie, I have feelings for you."

What? I freeze, my panic suspended in midair.

When I don't speak, he takes another breath. "I didn't mean to. Totally inappropriate, I know. Was gonna ignore it until I finish up my work here. Told myself I'd wait a couple of weeks after that, then maybe call and ask you out." He huffs a little laugh. "But clearly I'm not handling things well if I'm being a dick. You deserve to know why. Sorry. I know it's uncomfortable."

Feelings. I must've stayed in the pool too long. Water in my ears. I'm not hearing him right. I tug my earlobes, tilting my head to one side and then the other to see if anything comes out. I've heard hopping on one foot helps. I try that.

Nothing, unless you count the peculiar expression that crosses Angus's face.

I've been taught my place in the world, and it's not beside a big beautiful well-liked man like him. I'm the little fat girl with the big boobs. The world hates fat girls, big boobs or not. The world thinks guys like Angus should be paired with somebody equally attractive, according to the world's definition of attractive. Doesn't matter what I think.

I'm the one people ignore until there's an opportunity to torture me. Or punish me for forgetting my place.

I'm the one nobody wants until I get eighty million dollars.

Oh, fuuuck.

Could Angus have found out about the money?

Icicles form and splinter in my gut, stabbing me.

"Rosie?" Angus reaches out, cups my forearm where it's hugging my waist. "You all right?"

I don't know what to do. If he *doesn't* know about the money, I sure as hell don't want to tip him off. But also if he doesn't know, I need to get to the bottom of this unfathomable confession of his. Is it possible…? Could he really…?

I take a step closer. Peer up into his eyes. "Angus, not to go all middle school on you, but did you just tell me you *like* me like me?"

"Yeah." His mouth quirks up on one side, but I can tell he's dead serious. In his face I see bewilderment and worry, but no guilt. No evasion. No glancing to the side like people do when they lie. He keeps those amazing eyes on me.

God help me, I believe him.

Stranger things have happened, but I'm not sure I've experienced any of them.

Angus

She's quiet so long I don't know what to do.

"You okay? Should I leave for a while, let you think?" I go to rub her arm, comfort her, but it seems presumptuous. I drop my hand.

She glances up fast, like she'd forgotten I'm here. Man, *that's* flattering.

"I'm sorry. I don't have any experience with this kind of thing. This is...a real surprise." She searches my face. A prelude for the it's-not-you-it's-me talk? Shit.

I nod. "Listen, if this makes you uncomfortable, I can find somebody else to finish the work for you. Not gonna pressure you, Rosie." I shrug. "It is what it is. I can go home and make some calls." And definitely not cry like a big sad baby.

She tips her head back and scowls at me. "Angus, you don't *honestly* think I don't like you?"

All right, now I'm confused. "Well...*like* me, like me?"

"What if I did? What if I do?" Her gaze bores into me. "What would happen next?"

Is she—? Does she mean—? My words come out slow. Thick, pushing through my fear I'll screw this up. "Well, if you *did*... If you *do*... Whatever you want, Rosie."

"What—?" Her voice cracks and she clears her throat. "What would you normally do in such a situation?" She shifts a fraction of an inch closer.

"In such a situation I might...ask if I could kiss you." I'm almost whispering, I'm trying so hard to get it right.

She presses her lips together, her eyes moving to my mouth. "And...are you a gentle kisser?"

Woman, I'll kiss you any way you want. "I can be. Unless you want something different." My turn to shift closer, but I don't touch her. She's got to be sure.

She's so close I can see her pupils dilate. Her gaze shifts from my mouth to my eyes and back again.

"Maybe you should ask me." Her voice is tiny. Shaky.

Hallelujah. Something loosens in me, almost buckling my knees. I touch her jaw with my knuckle. "Rosie, may I kiss you?"

She nods.

She doesn't even come to my shoulder. I lean back against the van and take her hands, tugging her to stand between my knees.

Her cheek is just as smooth as I'd imagined. My fingertips glide to her jaw, into her silky curls. Her faint orange scent wraps around my brain as our lips meet. Her mouth is the softest, sweetest thing I've ever known. I kiss her upper lip, suck the edge of her lower lip into my mouth for a second. She opens a little on a gasp and I taste her. Softest. Sweetest. Ever.

Ah, god, I could do this all day. I settle against the van and push my other hand into her hair too.

Her fingers trace my ribs, trailing fire.

I pull her tight against me to feel her softness all up and down me. And that's when I realize that, although her kisses are sweet and willing, she's shaking. Her arms, her back, all her muscles are so tense she's quaking under my hands.

"Rosie." I lean back so I can see her eyes. "You okay?"

She nods, a quick jerk of her chin, and tries to smile. There's some kind of war going on in her.

I don't have any experience with this kind of thing.

I...had some things happen and ended up dropping out.

At the time it seemed...necessary. For survival. Never got close enough to anybody to want that.

All the pieces click together. Maybe Rosie's a virgin. Nervous. But maybe somebody assaulted her. Rage rears up in me, rage like I haven't felt in years. The urge to tear apart anybody who would hurt her.

I stroke her hair and press a kiss to her forehead so she doesn't have to look me in the eye if she doesn't want to. "Rosie, are you a virgin?"

"No!" The denial comes quick and sure. Then she snorts, but it's not her usual amused sound. "I kiss that bad, huh?"

I shake my head and hug her close, but only for a second. I let her go before she can tighten back up. Slide my hands down her arms and weave my fingers with hers. "No, you're a lovely kisser. You said you don't have much experience. Your muscles were tense." I stroke her knuckles with my thumbs. "You don't have to worry, Rosie. I won't push."

For a minute I think she's going to deny that there's a problem, but she just pulls in a slow breath. "Thanks." Honest to the core, that's my girl.

I study her face. She believes me, I think, but she's still unsure. Seeing Rosie scared opens a little fissure in my heart.

I squeeze her hands. "You be in charge. You want a hug or a kiss, you let me know. I'll only do what you want. I promise."

Her eyes fly to mine. "That doesn't sound very fun for you." But there's a thread of hope in her voice.

I shrug. Try to hide my desire to kill whoever made her think what she wanted wasn't important. "Wouldn't be fun to do anything you weren't wanting." I nuzzle her temple. "But having you tell me what you'd like? Boss me around? That's got possibilities."

"But—" She catches herself, stops. "Okay. But if you decide I'm too boring, I'll understand. Just let me know."

That world-class nonsense makes me laugh out loud. "Rosie, you're the least boring person I've ever met." I tuck a loose curl behind her ear. Let my fingertip linger on the baby-fine skin there. Watch her give a little shiver that matches my own.

Her face softens and she stretches a hand toward my cheek, then stops when she sees she's still holding the keys. "Why did you give me these?"

I shrug. "In case what I told you made you so uncomfortable you didn't want me to have access to your place anymore. Wanted you to feel safe."

I swear, her eyes flood with tears, but I only see for a second, because she looks down, takes my hand, and presses the keys into it, folding my fingers around them.

She lifts my knuckles to her soft lips, then turns and goes back inside, leaving the gate and the back door wide open behind her.

I can feel the big goofy grin on my face a few minutes later when I come to my senses and follow her inside, her keys securely back on my key ring. She and her car are gone, but that's okay. She didn't fire me. She kissed me back.

She *likes* me likes me.

CHAPTER 15

Rose

I'M SURPRISED I CAN DRIVE with this storm inside me.

Angus has feelings for me. *Angus* has *feelings* for *me*? I'm 99.5 percent sure he was telling the truth about that, and that he doesn't know about the money.

What the hell do I do with this? Besides, obviously, kiss him every chance I get.

What a difference the man can make. At a stoplight, I glance in the mirror. My lips are tingling but not bleeding. *Nothing* is bruised or bleeding. Timmy Johnson had kissed like he was attacking my face, grinding my lips into my teeth, shoving his tongue down my throat while he climbed on top of me.

I shake that out of my head fast so it doesn't taint my experience with Angus.

Kissing Angus was...a lovely way of getting to know my sweet friend better. How can a man who could break me in half with his hands be so incredibly gentle?

He tasted like...security and spice. And he held me like I was treasure.

Wanted you to feel safe. Lordy.

At the furniture store, I come out of my daze enough to choose a round dark wood dining table and sturdy straight chairs that are the perfect size for my dining room. To my surprise, I also buy two—not one—recliners that don't look like recliners for the bow window area of my bedroom. Two. But I'm not ready to think about that yet.

I end up at July's with no memory of driving there. None of the staff is on break, so I head for an empty table, and then I see her. My pearl-wearing, perpetually sour-faced, geriatric nemesis. Oh hell no. *Not today, Satan.*

I walk straight to her booth and slide in across from her.

Her eyes go wide. Swear to god, she literally clutches those pearls. "What—what do you think you're doing?"

She's outraged, yeah, but her voice is a little quavery. I'm probably the only adult in here who's not got several inches on her, but I'm at least forty years younger and almost certainly faster, stronger, and less breakable. I guess a person can be unpleasant and still get scared.

So I speak quietly. "Miz Ames, my name is Rose Barnes. We haven't been properly introduced, but it seems to me that every time I'm in here you glare at me. If I'm wrong, please tell me and I won't take any more of your time. But if I'm right, I'd like to know why, because the looks you give me are enough to spoil my enjoyment of July's good food."

Apparently deciding I'm not a threat after all, she purses her lips, sweeps me with an up-and-down look, and mutters, "You could stand to skip a few meals." Then she sits back and folds her tiny veiny hands on the table in front of her, her face smug.

I sit back against my seat. “Jesus. I bet you were a real bitch in high school. I thought Southern ladies were supposed to have manners.” As the words leave my lips, I see Sonya bringing me a menu and a glass of water.

“Hey, Rose. How you doin’?” She looks nervous, her eyes zinging between Pearl and me. “Everything okay over here?”

“Hey, Sonya. Yeah, I’m just going to keep Miz Ames company today.” What the fuck, mouth? Worst idea ever. Right up there with getting in a car with Timmy Johnson. But at least I get to see Pearl’s smirk evaporate. “Quiche of the day for me, please. With fruit.”

“Okey-doke.” Sonya hurries away.

I refocus on my sourpuss companion. “So, are you saying you stare at me because you disapprove of my body?” I watch her around my water glass as I take a drink.

She sniffs and glances away. “Everyone disapproves of bodies like that.” She rakes me with another look meant to wound.

And normally it would wound me, but suddenly in my mind, I’m back in that alley with Angus, his arms cradling me, his mouth warm on mine, his fingers in my hair, his gruff voice telling me he’s got feelings for me, and I know she’s wrong. I smile. “You’d be surprised.”

She frowns. “You know, you shouldn’t be ordering quiche. All that cream. There are many healthier things on the menu here.” She nods to her empty salad bowl, a dry crust of roll and the untouched pat of butter on a small plate beside it.

“I wanted quiche today. And besides, you glare at me on the days I get salad too.”

She raises her brows and purses her lips, deepening the furrows on her face. "It's not healthy for a person of your size to just eat whatever she wants."

"Oh, thank heavens, this is about my health! I was worried you didn't like me." I am so over this bullshit. "Maybe you could give me some advice. What should I have eaten differently for dinner last night? And breakfast this morning?"

She answers promptly, despite not having witnessed me eating either of those meals. "Cut out all the fats and starches. And while you're at it, get some exercise."

I think of last night's baked chicken, some of which (Angus's uneaten portion, from when he was still, in his words, "being a dick,") I'd eaten cold for breakfast this morning. Of the stretches I do morning and night, and the laps I swim each day till my legs ache. Of walking my neighborhood, meeting people, including the care provider of the Wandering Baby, with whom I'd had a nice long conversation. Of walking up here to the square and, often, beyond it to the B and B to visit Sabina.

I could list all these things out loud. Argue to this judgmental old woman that at least some of the time I'm a "good fatty," not like whatever stereotypes she has in her head, but that wouldn't make her believe me. And it certainly wouldn't change her personality. "Have you always followed your own advice, then?"

"I certainly have. I had the smallest waist in town when I was a young girl. They had to take my wedding gown in three times, and I'd gotten the smallest in the store. My husband said he hardly noticed carrying me over the threshold when we got married. He said that's just how a woman should be."

She looks smug again but, Jesus, I can't for the life of me imagine why. Angus would never say anything like that. He'd probably be griping at me, something about "Of course I'll carry you in—I'm not a monster," his ocean eyes smiling down at me, his massive arms supporting me, his laughter gusting out of him when I tease back.

I leap away from that fantasy. Fantasies have only brought me trouble in the past.

Miz Ames is looking at me oddly. I clear the hearts out of my eyes and look right back. "And did he appreciate other things about you too?"

Sonya brings my food before Pearl can answer. She's silent, watching me eat, and then we pay for our food and go our separate ways, me to get more twenties from the ATM—I always give away small bills because of the way shop owners look at shabbily dressed people with big bills—and her to, I don't know, haunt an abandoned building.

The next morning Angus actually knocks on the back door before coming in. He hasn't done that since his first week here.

I'm sitting on the kitchen island. My hand barely trembles as I set my toast on the plate beside me.

He stops just inside the door and looks across the space that separates us. Nods. "Rosie."

This is so weird. Normally he'd already be setting his coffee down in preparation for wrestling me for a position at the fridge.

"Angus." I take a slow deep breath for courage. "Can we talk about what happened yesterday?"

A muscle twitches in his cheek and his big shoulders stiffen like he's bracing himself. He sets his tool belt and coffee and lunch on the counter beside him before turning back to me. "You mean what I said. What I did."

He's taking all the responsibility for the kiss? That doesn't seem fair. "What *we* did."

He waits, expressionless, his aqua eyes wary. No sign of the cranky man I first met or the laughing man who is my friend. Or the achingly gentle man who kissed me yesterday.

Well, this is fun.

"Angus, why'd you say it wasn't appropriate for you to let me know how you felt before you'd finished your work here?" I lace my still-trembling fingers together in my lap. I don't hop down from the island. I need these extra inches of height.

He moves slowly into the room to lean against the counter across from me. Sighs. "I didn't have any clue how you'd feel if I told you. What if you weren't interested? I might've freaked you out. You might've started to feel like I was invading your privacy." He drops his head and scratches the back of his neck. Huffs out a laugh. "It's not like you didn't already catch me with a handful of your underwear."

I snort. "Fair. But now don't we have another problem?"

He meets my gaze square on. "You don't have to worry about me trying to cut corners or take advantage of you, Rosie. I'd never do that."

"Jeez, Angus, I know *that*! I mean me. What if I accidentally take advantage of you?"

He frowns. "I'm not sure how that could happen."

God, this is embarrassing. "What if…I get used to kissing you and hugging you, and I expect you to do it whenever I ask, but you start to lose interest in me and don't know how to tell me no? What if you feel pressure to kiss me when you don't want to, out of fear of losing the job?"

His shoulders and his shields drop. My friend is back. He

steps forward, braces himself on the counter, his hands on either side of my knees. “Two things, Rosie. One: I’ve already offered to turn the work over to somebody else if it will make you more comfortable. I wouldn’t do anything against my will just to keep a job. Two: Unless some part of me is literally on fire or being torn to pieces by wild animals, I’m not going to pass up any chances to kiss you.”

My suddenly unlaced fingers spread across his broad shoulders. “Yeah?” Omigod, I think I just flirted. “Promise. Promise you’ll just tell me if you lose interest. It would be horrible to find out later that you’d been, like, kissing me out of pity. Tell me right away.”

His big hand comes up to cup the side of my head. “I promise.” He leans in, his eyes holding mine. “Still interested, Rosie.”

He touches his lips to mine. “Still interested.” He settles his mouth over mine. I taste toothpaste and coffee and Angus. His beard and mustache are a soft tickle on my face, his skin so warm, his touch so tender. It’s a long heavenly moment before he pulls back enough to whisper, “Still interested. How about you, you still interested?”

“Oh, yeahhh.”

He laughs at that. I can’t blame him. I’ve probably got cartoon heart eyes again.

He tilts his head and I discover how lovely it is to be kissed by a big smiling man who smells of fresh laundry, a man with a wide sturdy chest and arms as strong and sheltering as oak.

Finally he leans back and I retrieve my hands from where they’d locked around his neck. I tuck them between my knees as he runs his fingers through my hair, massaging my scalp.

“Still interested.” His voice is husky. He turns away to

scoop up his lunch and stick it in the refrigerator, his T-shirt stretching mesmerizingly over his back and shoulders. "There is something else we should talk about, though." He comes back and cups my elbows with his big hands.

"What's that?"

"Two things. I've gotta be careful not to get so distracted that I'm not getting the work done on schedule. And we've gotta make sure you still feel okay telling me if you're not happy with my work."

I reach out a finger and trace it over his biceps, up and down, up and down. "I admire your ethics, Angus."

He grins. As he leans in to drop another quick kiss on my lips, his forearms flex in a magical way.

"I'll try not to interrupt you for gratuitous kissing. I can always go out for a while if it seems like I'm distracting you." Up, down. How can his skin be so smooth and the muscle underneath be so hard?

"Rosie."

"Hmm?"

He waits until I look up. He doesn't quite manage to wipe his smirk away before I see it. Insufferable man. Insufferable, giant, mesmerizing man.

"Focus, Rosie! I think you should practice telling me I've messed something up and you want me to fix it."

Well, that's no fun.

I sigh. "All right." I corral my imagination and channel my inner critic. "Okay. Angus, I don't know who told you that Pepto-Bismol pink was a good color for hallways, but it's completely unacceptable and, frankly, nauseating. Please fix it. And take your shirt off while you do it, as penance for your many wrongs."

He ducks his head. I swear he's blushing, even as he grins. "Clearly I was wrong to think you couldn't handle the situation." He glances around, reaches for his tool belt. "I should get to work."

"Wait! One more thing."

He stills.

"I want you to practice telling me that you're not interested. Just so I won't embarrass myself by asking for kisses you don't want to give."

"Rosie, I don't think that's gonna—" He shakes his head and stops himself. Comes back to me, nudges my knees apart, and stands between them. "Okay. Just practice. Fiction." He draws a deep breath. "Rosie, I don't want to do this anymore. I've stopped finding that smart-ass little dimple you get right here"—he reaches out one gentle finger and touches my left cheek lightly—"irresistible. I don't notice anymore the way your eyes go bright when you talk about something you care about. I don't listen for your laugh, or your cussing, or your wacky stories. I've become immune to the way you look in those swimming suits of yours, and I haven't thought about your fancy underwear in days." He's lost his smile. He looks miserable.

"Aw, Angus, that's really sweet." I pull him in, feathering kisses all over his face until he grips my waist and takes them deeper, tasting me, daring my tongue to play with his.

Cue a little throat-sigh sound I'm sure I've never made before.

"Okay! Okay." He shoves back, breathing hard, and rubs a hand down his face. "I gotta get to work, devil woman. Go cast your spells somewhere else."

CHAPTER 16

Angus

DON'T KNOW WHAT TO CALL this new stage of our relationship. Boyfriend would be ridiculous. I'm thirty-six. But it all seems too new for me to assume I'm her man. I mean, I am, no doubt about that on my end. But we haven't discussed it. I wouldn't presume to call her my girlfriend, but I sure would like her to consider herself my woman.

Over the next week, I finish scraping the outside of the house, replace damaged wood, and start on the painting, in between lots of kissing with Rosie. Good thing that's so much fun, because the damn woman sure does give me a hard time about every other damn thing in the world. But we kiss when I get there, when I leave, when we pass in the hall, when we sit down to lunch. In the yard, in the pool. In doorways and the middle of rooms, Rosie pressed up against me so soft and warm it makes me ache.

We must have a similar sense of what's too much. Every time I start feeling like I'm not getting enough work done, she takes herself off somewhere. Sometimes she leaves the house, but other times she hunkers down with her laptop. She's tackling Spanish, using a free online program. She bought some beginner's Spanish books too. I see them lying around with her other books. Some days when I come inside, she's listening to one of the local Spanish-speaking radio stations or watching telenovelas.

She winces and blushes and grins the afternoon I walk in on her rolling her Rs like a big seductive cat as she's kneading bread dough. "Stop laughing. I need to get used to making that sound."

I want to propose other uses for that tongue, but...not till she's ready.

I have no doubt she'll master Spanish just like everything else I've seen her try. Rosie's strong. Creative. Hardworking. And the best part? She's exactly what she seems. Up front about everything. No pretense, no show, just honest what-you-see-is-what-you-get.

And I really like what I see.

I'm there for dinner almost every night. Now that the house is actually furnished, it's even harder to leave her to go back to my supposed home. Most nights we watch TV in the living room or just hang out, swimming or rocking on the front porch.

I make her let me clean up the kitchen when she cooks. Sometimes she actually cooperates. Unless I grill the meat, and then our arguments lift the roof a few inches, until one of us grabs the other and starts the kissing.

Hardest thing for me is leaving her at the end of the day. Seems the most natural thing in the world to hold her and kiss her whenever she's in reach. What doesn't feel right is having to let go. To keep myself in check when all I want is to wrap myself around her. Have her bare skin against mine. Touch her in all the ways I think will give her pleasure. Be inside her. I want to go with her up to her room and say "good night" instead of "goodbye" every night.

Sometimes, saying goodbye, it's like I'm tearing off layers of my skin and leaving them with her. The woman's killing me, I want so badly to make love to her, but that move has to come from her, or she'll never feel safe. As much as she likes me and enjoys my kisses, she hasn't said she's ready for more. I know something bad happened in her past; I'm just not sure what. Got to earn her trust so she'll tell me and then we'll have no more secrets. Nothing between us.

She showed me her finished bedroom with the new chairs, but since my work upstairs is done and I don't want to rush her, I pretend there's not even a second floor anymore. Every night I make it a point to leave before she has to ask me to go. And every night as I step out that door, I hope she'll ask me to stay.

Probably just as well she hasn't. I can't even imagine how hard it would be to tear myself away from her warm sweet body in the mornings to hit the gym. And there's always clients waiting for me there. My very first client, Gary, owns the place and opens early for us three days a week. We walk or roll or limp in to work out as a group. It's not official therapy—it's a lot sweatier, and free—but it builds community, and that's as important as anything I do.

It's not just my life Rosie's affected. One morning I get to her house early and find Jerry Hawes waiting for me outside the fence with the world's most decrepit lawnmower. "Jesus, Jerry, what's holding that thing together?"

"Gum and a prayer," he says, pushing himself away from the fence. "Think it'd be okay if I cut her grass? I didn't want to go in till you got here, but I sure would like to do something to thank her for hooking me up with that job."

I got no idea what job he's talking about, but I open the gate and wave him in.

Then the very next day a new client shows up at my office. Frank. About my age, but with lines on his face and the hollow eyes of a man looking into hell. I start by asking what brought him in to see me.

His answer, when it comes, is slow and dripping with shame. "My wife. Says she can't do everything by herself anymore. Said I need to get my hopeless, lazy ass off the couch or she's gonna kick me out." He raises red-rimmed eyes to me. "I was halfway through yelling that if she wanted me to leave, I'd leave, but then I heard myself. Shut my stupid mouth, sat right back down."

He spreads his hands helplessly. "She's right. This isn't who I am. Not how I want to be. And I don't want to let her down too."

That one little three-letter word at the end there tells me much of what I need to know.

"Soon as I stopped yelling, my wife sat down beside me. Two kids hanging on to her shirt, baby in her arms, and she sat down and told me about you."

"Me?" It's rare for me to hear something that surprises me in this room.

"Wife runs a daycare from the house. One of the toddlers got out one day, wandered down the street. A neighbor lady took him into her yard and kept him safe until my wife could come get him. I guess now they talk whenever they see each other out for a walk. My wife said something about me getting back from Afghanistan not too long ago. Neighbor lady said she had a wonderful friend who works with vets who need help adjusting to being back home. My wife looked you up after that."

I'll be damned. Rosie's spread her magic all the way to the house of the Wandering Baby.

Saturdays I'm busy with counseling work, but Sunday I pick her up and take her on a surprise trip to Asheville with Lenny to wander around, eat some good food, and listen to live music at a venue he wants to check out. We almost lose her to Malaprop's Bookstore, but we lure her out by promising to bring her back one day when we've got more time.

Lenny cements it by hooking his arm through hers and pulling her up the street toward Tupelo Honey, saying, "C'mon, Rosie, I'm starving. Let's go eat and I'll show you old pictures of beanpole Angus."

Aw, hell. Old photos. But Rosie throws such a dubious look back at my chest that I can't help but be flattered.

They seat us in the sidewalk café area and after we order, Lenny whips out his phone. "This was scrawny little freshman Angus." He hands the phone to Rosie and she looks back and forth from it to me in disbelief. It's gotta be the one where my eyes take up half my hairless face.

"Angus, you're so cute!"

Lenny makes a disgusted noise, shaking his head. "Rose, you're missing the point. Angus was five eleven here and weighed thirty-eight pounds soaking wet."

I roll my eyes. "I weighed at least seventy. Dry."

Lenny ignores me and swipes to the next picture. "Then by sophomore year, he'd grown another couple of inches and started figuring out how to eat enough to gain some muscle."

I know which picture he's showing her. Me and Lenny on the porch of somebody's cabin in the mountains, him with his perpetual sunburn and me squinting into the sun, our long skinny arms on each other's shoulders, beer cans in our underage hands.

Rosie's gazing at it with a sweet, misty look on her face, Lenny peering over her shoulder.

He frowns. "Hey, I think that was the Goodbye Earl party."

Ah, lord. "Lenny—"

But there's no stopping him when he's in storyteller mode. "No, no, this is a good one. Really lets you see what kind of guy Angus is, Rosie."

I'd rather not be stuck at the table during the telling of this, but I can't leave Rosie alone with it. I settle back and wave a waitress down for more sweet tea.

"So it's spring break and a bunch of us are up at Gary Waycomb's family's summer cabin. Most of us are out front, but then over the music, we hear James's girlfriend Tisha—they're married now, you met her, remember?—yelling, 'You get your filthy hands off of her!' One minute Angus is beside me in the yard, and the next second the screen door's slapping shut behind him and he's up in the cabin. Next thing I know, he's back out on the porch, holding this junior kid over his head like a piece of driftwood. The kid's screaming and Angus rears back and throws him halfway across the yard like he weighs nothing. The kid bounces and rolls and jumps up looking like he doesn't know what hit him, and Angus bellows, 'Get the *fuck* outta here! And don't you *ever*... If I *ever* hear of you doing something like that again, I'll hunt you down and kick your ass, and then I'll haul you to the police station myself!' See, one of the girls had had too much to drink and was passed out in the back room, and Tisha went to check on her and found the junior kid with his hands up her shirt."

Lenny's on a roll. "Kid jumps up and whines, 'But I need a ride...' and Angus roars, '*Walk*! You don't *deserve* a ride!' The kid hesitates and Angus starts toward him yelling, 'I'll throw you off the mountain myself,' and the kid screams a little and takes off running down the dirt road. And up on the porch, Tisha and James start dancing and singing that 'Goodbye Earl' song about some abusive asshole nobody missed when he disappeared."

Lenny stops talking as the waitress arrives with our food. We watch her unload the tray.

Rosie's eyes are enormous, shifting from me to Lenny and back again. When the waitress leaves, Rose takes a deep breath. "Well, that was some powerful peer pressure." She stares down at her fried green tomato omelet for a long minute, and then she sets her fork on the table, reaches up to wrap her hand around my neck, and pulls me down to her level. She presses a sweet kiss to my mouth, right in front of Lenny, and says, her voice all soft and husky, "Thank you, on behalf of girls and women everywhere."

I'm sure I'm fire engine red. Rosie picks up her fork and takes a bite of omelet, and when I shoot a look at Lenny, he gives me a self-satisfied smirk and digs into his cheese grits.

CHAPTER 17

Rose

BEFORE MR. BROWN DIED, I considered myself basically contented. Life wasn't exciting or stress-free, but it had familiar not-too-scary rhythms. Walk to work as the sun was rising, drag myself home later smelling of every food the diner had served that day. Shower, eat something cheap and easy for dinner, curl up with a book. On days off, I loaded up my bag with return items and headed to the nearest library. Sometimes I'd take a bus and check out other branches, especially ones near interesting parks. Usually I couldn't afford to eat lunch out, so I'd take a peanut butter sandwich.

I didn't have any real friends until Mr. Brown. The other servers were either younger and caught up in party plans or had families and too many responsibilities to juggle.

Maybe it's stretching it to call Mr. Brown a friend, but I sure talked to him more than anybody else. I knew bits and pieces about his wife who had died and his kids who had moved away, not wanting to take over the running of his used bookstore. He knew I loved to read but hadn't gone to college. I tried to time my breaks so I could sit and eat with him when he came in, and he brought me books he thought I'd like.

Home was a shabby studio apartment in the old building where Mom and I had lived as far back as I can remember. No matter how much I scrubbed or swept, it never seemed clean. The carpet was thin and stained, the paint scratched and dingy, and the only working window had no screen. The hallways were narrow and dark and full of the sounds of my neighbors' arguments or crying children or TV laugh tracks. Walking from the stairs to my door, I could identify what everyone had cooked that day by the smells. I knew better than to call the landlord about leaks or drips until the problems got too serious to ignore. My strategy for keeping bugs to a minimum was to scrub everything with bleach and wipe up every drip, every spill, every dirty dish immediately. But still they came, looking for food they were never gonna get from me. Hope must spring eternal in the insect thorax.

But I thought I was doing okay. I could usually meet my bills on time if I picked up extra shifts here and there. I was basically healthy. I had some privacy in my locked apartment, and as much safety as most women.

So now when I come in my sturdy Galway front door and shut out the sounds and smells and people of the world, it feels as cool and clean and peaceful as a chapel. And when I step into my backyard, it's like being transported to one of those vacation spots I've only ever seen on TV. When I spend time with Sabina, or when I go to July's and someone waves and calls me by name, it's like slipping under a warm shower after a long cold journey home.

And when Angus sees me and lights up, it's...god, it's indescribable. I never imagined how different life could be with someone by my side. He wraps me in those big arms and cuddles me and teases me and asks me questions about silly little things, just because he wants to know. What was my favorite book as a kid? What's my favorite movie? My biggest childhood fear? How do I feel about this or that issue?

He listens, and he tells me his own answers, and then lord, how he kisses me, his mouth warm and gentle, his hands on my face or in my hair or moving up and down my back like he's making sure I'm still there, still okay.

And every cell of my body and heart sings.

One of these days I'm going to get up the nerve to take our physical relationship to the next level. I want to, that's for damn sure. If anybody could make sex good, Angus could. But I'm afraid of hurting him if I ask for more and then hate it. It would be awful to have to tell him I don't want to do...whatever... anymore. And I so don't want to ever hurt him.

So I don't ask.

He talks with me about everything but his therapy clients. I just know anonymous bits and pieces about his work with them. They're all veterans, mostly struggling with PTSD or having trouble adjusting to civilian life.

One evening when we're sharing a beer on the front porch steps, I ask him about something I read. "Is it true a lot of vets are homeless or really hurting for basic stuff?"

A muscle twitches in his jaw. He raises the bottle to take a drink, then passes it to me. "Yeah."

"Does that mean people who need therapy aren't getting it?"

He sighs. "Yeah, in a lot of cases. I've got a fee sliding scale for that reason. One guy used to pay me in fresh eggs. Not gonna turn anybody away if I can help it."

"I thought vets got medical benefits for free. Doesn't that include counseling?"

He shakes his head and I hand the beer back to him. "It's complicated. We *should* provide benefits to all the vets, but they don't all qualify under the rules. Some who do qualify don't want to use VA services, or they think it's a sign of weakness to need mental health care. And even for people who qualify and want the services, there's a lot of red tape and long wait lines. When somebody's in crisis, they can't wait."

I scoot closer and lean in, my head against his shoulder. We wave at the Lightspeed Family—my name for them—as they pull up next door and race each other into their house.

Angus takes my hand. "There's a problem that's been coming up more and more often. I'm not sure what to do about it." He offers me the bottle, and when I shake my head, he sets it on the porch behind us.

"A counseling problem?"

"Yeah." He looks down at our twined fingers. "Have you heard anything about sexual assault in the military?"

I nod, his T-shirt sleeve soft against my cheek. "Yeah. I've read a couple of articles, and there was a documentary a while back that really got to me."

He nods too. "Huge problem. We're not handling it well. Not doing enough to stop it, not prosecuting enough, not providing enough support to soldiers who've been assaulted. Not all the victims are women, but there are more women in the military now, and we're seeing more and more cases. When people who've been sexually assaulted leave the service, they've got all kinds of other trauma heaped on top of the 'regular' PTSD. And we aren't even providing enough services to vets with the 'regular' kind."

Another neighbor couple strolls by on the sidewalk and we wave greetings.

I watch them move on down the street before I speak. "And this is affecting the work you're doing?"

He sighs again. "Yes and no. I'm willing to provide the counseling, I'm qualified, and I think I could help, but...not if they can't trust me. I can't, you know, force trust, and women vets don't always feel comfortable or safe coming to a man. Especially a big one."

I squeeze his hand. "They would if they knew you."

He squeezes back. "I got a friend I went to school with. Robin. She's not military, but she works with survivors of sexual violence. So a couple of times we've teamed up to help somebody, and it's worked pretty well. But doubling up cuts the number of people we're able to serve, and the need is growing."

He stares off in the direction the neighbors took. "We're working on writing a grant to bring somebody to Galway. Preferably a woman with both military experience and training in sexual assault trauma counseling."

His voice drops lower. "Those vets are at really high risk for hurting themselves. One study not too long ago found a hundred percent of them—a hundred percent!—had suicidal thoughts. I'm afraid if we don't get help soon, we're going to lose somebody here."

I sandwich his hand between both of mine and hold on. We lean on each other in silence.

How can I help my big sweetie without letting on about the money?

I haven't seriously considered telling him about it. I just can't picture any way that could turn out well. It changed every single relationship I had in Indiana, once people found out. Well, except for Mom and Mr. Brown, because they were dead. But everybody else I'd ever known acted differently after that.

I'd been okay with casual surface relationships and lots of alone time. At least people's disinterest was honest. But the damn money brought an avalanche of attention, smothering, demanding, scary, and often fake, if my instincts were accurate.

The thought of my romance with Angus becoming twisted like that makes me want to cry and throw up at the same time. I just can't risk it. When he looks at me, there's warmth in his eyes. Tenderness in his smile. Affection in his teasing. I can't stand the idea of looking at him and having to wonder what he *really* wants from me.

I can't tell him. Especially not with everything between us so new.

Maybe someday, if we become lovers and are still going strong. Later, after I figure out a way to crawl out from under the money, to turn it into a charitable institution, maybe I can tell him. I can describe it as a past-tense thing, a done deal, nothing that could affect our present or our future. The money won't be mine anymore, so it won't be able to wreck anything.

I have regular Wednesday phone conversations with my money people in Indiana, just to keep on top of what's going on. I've learned a lot about money management and wealth, enough that I can actually formulate questions about potential issues, but god, it's deadly boring and slow going.

The money people seem perfectly competent and honest. I'd checked their reputations before I hired them, to make sure they were the best. But still sometimes, particularly when I don't understand something or I catch them off guard with a question they didn't expect, they're a little defensive and mansplainy. They try to hold their patience in check, I'm sure because I'm one of their wealthiest clients, but I sense condescension there under the surface. It irritates me and makes me hate dealing with the money even more.

Thank god Angus isn't around on Wednesday mornings for those calls. He'd sense my frustration and get all protective and nosy, and then what would I say?

Angus

Wednesday I let myself in the back door in time to hear Rosie say, "No, I'm not worried. I just want to be careful. You know I'm not experienced with money. I'm just trying to understand. Trying to handle everything right."

She glances up at me, big-eyed, says goodbye to whoever she's talking to, and ends her call.

I've brought sandwiches for us to share. I put them on the library table and grab drinks from the fridge. "Was I interrupting anything? Need me to leave?" I kiss the top of her head and settle into my seat.

"No, I'm good. You're fine." She doesn't reach for me for another kiss. That's a first.

I pretend I don't notice. Line the sandwiches up between us, point to each one. "Cheesesteak. Turkey and swiss. Reuben." I unwrap them all and pick up half of the cheesesteak for myself.

She's quiet, examining the sandwiches.

I can't just let it go. "Rosie, you'd tell me if you were having some kind of money problem, right?"

She takes her time choosing half the Reuben. "I don't know." She lifts a corner of the bread, redistributes the meat more evenly. "But I'm fine, Angus. No trouble."

I wait, finishing my half sandwich and starting on half the turkey, but she doesn't say anything else. I try again. "It's just, I noticed all the money books lying around. Wondered if maybe you need me to hold off on some of the renovations. Maybe scale back?" I can donate my time. Make my scoreboard *and* me happy to help her out.

She flashes me a quick, sweet smile. "No, we're good." But she shifts in her seat like she's uncomfortable.

"And I'm not, like, eating you out of house and home? 'Cause I can start buying the groceries. Helping out..."

She rounds her eyes at me. "Angus! I'm fine! No money worries, I promise." She sets her sandwich down, only a single bite missing, and comes over to my side of the table to kiss me on the forehead, nose, and lips. "But you are very sweet to offer." She heads for the stairs. "I've got a couple of errands to run. Need anything while I'm out?"

"No. Thanks."

She clatters back down the stairs with her purse, waves and blows me a kiss before closing the front door behind her.

Well, that was weird.

I eye her abandoned sandwich as I finish eating. She's never hopped up and run off in the middle of a meal before. And it's not like her to just leave food lying around. Usually she fights me for cleanup duties.

I think back to the conversation I'd overheard. What she'd said was troubling, but her tone wasn't worried exactly. Not sure what it was. Not happy, but not scared. Irritated? Impatient? Who was she talking to? A bank? A creditor? I've got no clue.

When I asked my questions, she didn't seem concerned about money. But there was something... She was hiding something.

That bothers me. Not because I think we should know everything about each other already; it's early days. It's just, it's not like I have a whole lot to bring to a relationship. If she needs something I can provide, I want to help.

Maybe she has trouble accepting help.

But she could *talk* to me about it, at least.

My sigh shivers the sandwich wrappers. I clean up the lunch mess and get back to work. Need to be patient. Eventually she'll trust me.

Until then I'll just...put more in my savings. Be ready to help when the time comes.

Couple days later, I come back from errands to find Rose in the backyard, standing by the pool in my favorite of her swimsuits—red, strapless, one-piece. Makes my mouth water.

She's got a hose trained on her landscaping.

I stroke her smooth shoulder as I pass, fiddling with my phone to end a call from Lenny. No sooner do I get by her than I hear "Oops!" and a chilly blast of water hits me right between the shoulder blades. I toss the phone onto a lounge chair and spin around, already knowing what I'm going to find.

Her brown eyes are shining and I catch her mid-laugh. She sprays me in the chest, but before she can say, "Oops," again, I'm on her.

I scoop her up in a half tackle, half carry, and we go flying into the pool.

She comes up spluttering and shrieking with laughter and heads for the ladder, but I catch her fast, reaching out one arm to wrap around her, tightening to pull her back to me. But as my arm angles across her rib cage, she bobs in the water and my hand closes over her full, perfect breast.

"Oh shit!" I leap back. This is so not how I wanted this to happen. "I didn't mean to do that, Rosie. I'm sorry."

She takes hold of the ladder with one hand and looks over her shoulder at me. "Sorry about which part? The football move? The near drowning? Or feeling me up?"

She's trying for nonchalance, I'm pretty sure, but with that last bit, a tiny wince suggests she's shocked at her own words.

I tread water, studying her face, a little less worried than a minute ago. "Which one upset you the most? Pretty sure that's the one I'm sorry for."

She presses one finger to her mouth and scrunches her face up in thought. "Well, the airborne tackle was kind of exciting. Kind of fun, since it didn't actually, you know, kill me or break any of my bones. The near drowning wasn't as much fun, but that was my own fault. I know better than to laugh when I should be holding my breath." She pauses. "As for feeling me up," she shrugs one pretty shoulder, "that didn't last long enough for me to know. I can't judge without more evidence."

I swim a little closer. Make sure I heard her right. "More evidence?"

"Yeah." Her voice is shaking but determined. "To help me decide: terrible or nice." She turns away as if to climb the ladder.

I come up behind her and set my hands on her waist. I think I know an invitation when I hear one, but—gotta be sure. "I don't want there to be any confusion. Maybe we could go ahead and gather that evidence? And then you can let me know what you decide?"

"Okay." She sounds breathless now. She doesn't look back at me.

I move closer, ease my chest up against her bare back and shoulders. Run a finger up her arm and watch goose bumps form in its wake. I wrap both my arms around her waist and lower my mouth to her neck, tasting chlorinated water and sunshine and Rosie.

She sighs and drops her head back onto my shoulder.

Her nipples draw tight under the thin material of her suit, and I want to take her right there. Her throat is cool and firm against my lips, her body warm and soft as I smooth my hands up over her ribs to palm her perfect breasts. They're just as I imagined them, generous and firm and soft.

She gasps and I cup her, gentle as I can be, plucking her between my thumbs and fingers. She gives a soft moan, her back arching, pressing her sweet round bottom against me just where I'm hardest.

I have to kiss her mouth *right now.* I turn her to me. Her arms come up around my neck and I watch her face as I lean in, holding her against the side of the pool with my body.

Her lips are already parting for me. Her eyes are wide and dark, her pupils huge. There's no fear there.

I kiss her deep and her arms tighten around me as she kisses me back just as fiercely. My hands find her breasts again, tug down the top of her stretchy suit. Bare her to the water and my eyes. I don't know which of us makes the hungry sound as I take her in my hands again. Maybe both of us.

Her skin is incredibly soft, her nipples tempting little raspberries against untanned curves.

I cup her bottom and raise her out of the water just enough that I can take one nipple in my mouth. She gasps as I suck her in. Locks her legs around my waist. God help me.

"Angus!" Her eyes are wide and wild. "No, don't stop, please! That's lovely!"

I turn my attention to her other nipple.

She clasps my head and murmurs my name, hands in my hair.

I don't think she knows she's rubbing herself against me under the water. I've never wanted anything as much as I want to tug that suit aside and plunge into her, right here in the pool, in broad daylight in the middle of her backyard. The thought of that sets me on fire and brings me to my senses at the same time.

I raise my mouth to hers, trying to control my breathing and the drum of my heart, caressing her as I pull her suit back up to cover breasts I'm going to be dreaming about for the rest of my life.

"But—" Her voice is a sad little wail.

I stroke her cheek with my knuckles. "I've gotta stop, Rosie. Or else I'll be giving you more than you want. Without any protection. And your neighbors will look out and see us, and we'll both end up in jail. Or on YouTube."

She stiffens, clutches my shoulders. "And then your reputation will be ruined." She frowns up at me. "Or maybe enhanced? Do you have women trying to seduce you all the time?"

More than a few. But I rarely give in, and never until after the work is done. And I'm not going to tell Rosie any of this. So I deflect. "That's all I need, Rosie…calls for 'emergency plumbing jobs' at all hours."

She snorts and bites my chin and slides her arms back up around my neck. "Either way, I'd rather not get my own reputation as a watery tart, seducing men in swimming pools."

CHAPTER 18

Angus

NEXT JOB'S THE BACK PATIO. The old one spans the width of the house, but it's narrow, paved with stones that have popped up in some places and sunk in others, so the surface is unsafe. Rosie wants me to tear out all the old stones, give them away—stubborn woman won't let me sell them for her—and replace them with flagstone all the way out to the pool.

After that she says she'll go buy outdoor furniture so we can cook and eat out back more. Table and chair set. Couple of those outdoor gliding chairs. Side tables. A double-wide chaise lounge. She says she'll have me help her pick out a grill so I don't need to cart mine back and forth. A big one fit for entertaining.

I can picture, as she describes it, how great it'll be, but damn, that's a lot of shopping.

I know, she started from scratch with an empty house, so of course she's had to buy lots of things. But why so much so soon? The guest room could have stood empty for a while. She never has anybody stay over. Dammit.

Not that I'd want to be in the guest room anyway. I ache for her. My brain and all my senses stay full of her...the little sounds she makes when I kiss or touch her just right. The taste of her, the feel of her in my hands, in my mouth. The light, sweet scent of her, all of her pressed up against me, firm and round and soft.

But that's not the point.

She never uses the dining room. That could have stayed empty until she gets on firmer footing. She doesn't have to buy so much patio stuff all at once. Even the landscaping could have been done gradually, in phases, as she could afford it.

I should butt out. This is none of my business. She's told me she doesn't have money problems. I should just leave it at that until she tells me different. But I'm seeing more and more books on money lying around, including at least one on loans, and I'm afraid for her.

I can't shake the worry. She makes it clear she doesn't want to talk about money so I try to find other ways to help. Last Sunday I came over with a bunch of groceries, thinking I could at least make sure she's not paying to feed my giant self. Instead of seeming relieved or happy, she yelled at me.

"You big sweetie! What are you doing? We're not going to be able to eat all this before it goes bad. Look!" She threw open the door to the definitely-already-full refrigerator.

We ended up shoving as much as possible into the freezer and spending the day cooking, hosting Lenny and Chris and Sabina for dinner to help use it up. That was fun, I admit. Seeing Lenny's eyes light up at the feast spread out on the counters, hearing his big laugh roll out as he filled his plate all three times, while Chris, who's usually the King of Quiet, jostled him for position in line, his own plate heaped to overflowing. Sabina just beamed at everyone like a proud, fond mother.

And we'd had fun cooking it all before the guests showed up, even if Rosie does have a weird fixation on how I chop vegetables. Kept bossing me around, telling me to push up my sleeves to the elbow, then watching me like a hawk, then interrupting my work to make out with me... Woman's gonna kill me if she doesn't take me to bed soon.

Rosie loaded the guys up with leftovers. Before they left, she showed them around the backyard, skirting my patio construction mess. "Next summer I'm going to try growing my own vegetables. See all these annuals here in these sunny spots? Those places will be perfect." She rattled off the veggies she wants to put in. I listened, wondering if it's a cost-saving, budget-tightening strategy. All the beautiful fresh produce she's been feeding me has to be really expensive.

The next Sunday, thunderstorms wash out my plan to take Rosie to Boone for the day. Too nasty to window shop and wander up and down random streets the way she loves to do.

I'm stiff and sore from hauling flagstone anyway. We decide not to go anywhere. Just have a lazy day with carryout and movies.

"Wanna come over here? My house isn't as nice as yours, but I never got rid of my DVD collection. Got just about anything you might want to see, up until the last few years."

Kind of touching, how excited she sounds at the prospect of seeing my place. I give her directions and then race around making sure everything's tidy and the bathroom's clean.

My little house was built in the 1940s. One main room, two small bedrooms, and a bath. Spare bedroom's my office. Just enough space for a desk and file cabinet against the inside wall, and a love seat and two comfortable chairs in front of the windows to the backyard. I keep the place neat, but it's borderline shabby. My clients seem more at ease in barely noticeable surroundings.

Rosie parks Lillian in the driveway and dashes through the rain to the side door. "This is cute!" She looks around, her eyes bright, as I give her the tour. "You do your counseling work here too, right?"

"Yep."

She nods. "I can see people feeling comfortable here. It's really laid-back."

I pull her to me for an overdue hello kiss. "You are very perceptive. Thanks."

She slides her arms up around my neck, and we're just getting serious when my cell rings.

Robin. Damn.

"I'm sorry. I need to take this. Pick something? Anything." I wave her toward the video shelves along one living room wall and head to my room to take the call.

Rose

This week has been unsettling. The knowledge that I practically had sex in full view of anyone upstairs at my neighbors' houses, that someone could've put video of us online, for anybody—including Indianapolis people—to see, makes me want to vomit.

The realization brought all my high school shame and

humiliation flooding back. Even after Angus covered me up, I felt unbearably exposed, bracing for whatever terrible thing would surely follow.

But Angus didn't say or do anything to hurt me. His eyes crinkled, warm with something like delight. "Watery tart? You're a Monty Python fan? Rosie, you're the perfect woman."

I'd lost hold of the ladder and my feet weren't touching the bottom. Angus was holding me up, his strong arms cradling me, his heart thudding against mine, his lips soft on my neck, my throat, my jaw. He kissed me again and touched my cheek, looking down into my eyes for a long minute before rumbling, "Aw, Rosie. Everything about you is such a lovely surprise."

I slipped my arms around his waist and we just held each other, my heart rate slowing as I listened to his, the lump in my throat receding, calm creeping back in the comfort of his embrace.

Ever since then, my mind's been on a constant loop, replaying everything we did and said, everything I felt. It was overwhelming, physically and emotionally. Did Angus think so too? Probably not. Probably just me with my unfortunate history. My issues.

I always figured people were exaggerating about sex.

Have I ever experienced physical pleasure with another person?

Mom must've hugged me at some point when I was growing up. Probably when I fell down and scraped a knee. But we weren't a touchy pair.

I've never met my dad. He went home to the wife he'd forgotten to mention before my mom even knew she was pregnant. Mom wasn't even sure he'd told her his real name. I've got no siblings (at least none that I know of—I'm afraid to take a DNA test), no grandparents, no contact with any aunts or uncles or cousins. So no hugs or kisses there.

No dates or lovers, because after Timmy Johnson, I expected every guy to be a user. A braggart. A bully.

But if my first experience had been with someone like Angus...his sweetness, his kisses, his big hard body pressed to mine, his little growl against my breast before he kissed it...

The thing is, even though I'm not a virgin and haven't been for half my life, I've never had anyone touch me with a desire to bring me pleasure. I've never even had anyone kiss me softly just to be kissing me. Never had anyone hold me just because. In the last couple of weeks Angus has given me more pleasure and affection than everyone else in my entire life put together.

Something fierce and tender rises in me for this gentle, generous man. This immensely lovable man.

The most unbearable thing, I decided long ago, is romantic hope, because it brings heartbreak and loneliness and shame. But Angus makes me feel hope.

And now I'm in his house. His tidy little home.

The man must be a movie addict. One whole wall of floor-to-ceiling DVD cases.

He's pulled his door partway closed but I can still hear him. I'm trying not to eavesdrop but there aren't any other sounds in the house to block his voice.

I hum in my special no-musical-ability-whatsoever monotone and focus on the titles—everything from action films to chick flicks to sci-fi and drama. Makes me smile. I could've predicted that he'd have eclectic tastes and a soft side.

There's the *Die Hard* movie with Justin Long in it. I identify with young hackers to a ridiculous degree. I think if I could do high school all over again now, I'd be a white hat hacker. Bring justice to the bullied and doom to the bullies. Hell yeah. I pull down the case with that disc.

Maybe I should choose a second one to balance out the nonstop action. Maybe something with Meryl Streep or Whoopi Goldberg.

"No, *no*!" Angus's voice booms out, full of anger and something else. Frustration? Despair?

I fumble the case, drop it, and bend to pick it up.

"Fucking hell!" he roars in the other room.

Oh shit. He doesn't cuss nearly as much as I do. I've never heard him really mad.

This is bad. I straighten, no longer trying not to overhear.

"God*dam*mit." There's a quiet spell—he must be listening to the caller—and then he says in a lower, sadder voice, "She leave any family?" Then after another couple of minutes, "I don't know. We'll have to figure out a plan B." Pause. "No, no idea. Let me think about it. I'll call you this week. You okay? Okay. Yeah, thanks. Bye." There's a thump, as if something has been thrown hard into something soft, and then the squeak of bedsprings, and then…nothing.

I wait, trying to choose another DVD, but the silence is unnerving.

After a few minutes, he still hasn't reappeared. Would it make things worse if I go check on him? Would he be upset to learn that I overheard his end of the conversation? Would I be intruding? Or would it be a comfort? Which mistake would cause more harm: to offer him comfort that's unwelcome, or not to offer it when it's needed?

If there's even a small chance he needs me, I've gotta go in there.

I set the disc on the couch and move as quietly as I can to the bedroom door.

CHAPTER 19

Rose

HE'S ON HIS BACK ON the bed, up near the pillows, bare feet on the floor, his phone facedown beside him, the heels of his hands pressed to his eyes.

I ease in and sit at the foot of the bed, not looking at him in case he's crying and doesn't want me to see. "You okay?"

"Yeah. No. Shit, I don't know." He sighs. "Yeah, I'm okay. Somebody else isn't, though. Two pieces of terrible news."

I nod, tracing the stitching on his bedspread with my finger. "Wanna talk about it?"

He sighs again, sounding as old as the world. "That was my friend Robin. The one I told you was working on the grant with me? She just found out we don't qualify for the one we were going for. So as she was getting ready to call to let me know that, she got another call. A young vet from Brevard—somebody we haven't seen yet but who needed the services we could have provided with that grant—died last night. Self-inflicted gunshot wound."

Instant tears blur my vision. "Shit." Poor Angus. Poor Robin. And that young vet and her family. I swing around and reach for his hand.

He pulls me to his side, cradles my head on his chest, and we lie like that for a while in silence.

I remember something I read about veterans and suicide. "That happens a lot, doesn't it?"

"*Way* too often." He breathes out a sigh. "It's a fucking disgrace. We put young people in harm's way and then we don't take good enough care of them, in service or out. Rosie, sometimes I get so frustrated I don't know what to do."

I wrap my arm around his waist and squeeze.

Maybe talking will help. I ask another question, then another, hoping he'll open up and let some of his feelings out.

And he answers. He trusts me, and he answers.

He's so much better at that than I am.

Then again, he's got those diplomas on the wall in his office. Bachelor's in psychology, master's in therapy. He *should* be good at it. Whereas I…but today's not about me.

We lie on his bed talking the rest of the morning, until my stomach growls like a bear. Jesus. I cup my hand over my belly, as if that could subdue the beast. "Sorry."

"We need to rustle you up some lunch, don't we?" I hear a smile in his voice.

"No hurry. Don't reward it for bad behavior." I reach for him again without looking. My hand lands on his stomach, on bare hot skin just above his waistband, where his T-shirt has hiked up. Immediately my own midsection starts a backflip routine.

Totally inappropriate, Rose! Calm the fuck down. But I'm

frozen, staring at my hand. Would it be less awkward to leave it in this too-personal place, or to move it? As I'm trying to decide, I see movement just beyond my fingers. It takes me a second to realize what it is.

Angus hasn't shifted or made any sound, but...I'm pretty sure he's growing hard. Pushing up against the fabric of his shorts.

Shit! Now I really don't know what to do. Ignore it? Joke about it? Reach for it? *Shitshitshit.* Does he know I know? How would he feel about that? The last thing I want is to cause him discomfort or embarrassment on an already hard day. No pun intended. *Shit, Rose, stop!*

How could a simple accidental touch do that to him? And how can thinking about it cause *my* body to do this ridiculous melty, achy thing?

My fingers want to explore this uncharted part of him.

What would it be like to be naked with him? To have sex with him? Would it hurt? Would it even be physically possible for him to fit inside me? I eye his shorts. I'm dubious. He looks enormous.

But the indecision and the suspense and my usual damn curiosity are killing me. Finally I can't stand it. "Angus." My voice comes out a whisper.

"Yeah, Rosie?" He sounds perfectly normal. Nothing to see here, folks. Move along.

"Please forgive my wildly inappropriate timing. I've gotta ask. Do you think you might be ready for us to take another step in our physical relationship?"

He actually chuckles. Squeezes me. "Pretty sure I'm ready any time you're ready, Rosie. What'd you have in mind?"

"Well, I—I'm not sure I'm ready to have sex yet, but I've never..." I break off with a sigh. "Angus, I'd really like to see you naked. I love your body and I'd like to see it." There. I said it.

He's silent for a moment. "You want me to take off my clothes so you can look at me?"

"Yes."

"And you would leave your clothes on?"

"I'm not sure. Probably. At least some of them."

"Is there something you're scared about, Rosie?"

So many things. "I—well—I've just...never seen a man naked in real life."

"You haven't?" He pauses, then asks very gently, "Rosie, are you sure you're not a virgin?"

"*No.* I mean, yes, I'm sure. But I don't have much experience. And...he didn't undress. And I'm a little nervous about your size."

"You worried sex might hurt?"

"Well. Not in general. I don't have much experience, as I said, but you seem...um, really well endowed."

"Rosie, I'm six four. It would be embarrassing if I weren't, uh, proportional." Is that a grin in his voice?

I'm turning the color of a tomato here and he's grinning? Men and their damn penises.

My gaze is locked on his shorts. "Really? That's just... proportional? Because I've been lying here wondering if you've ever put anybody in the hospital with that thing."

He bursts out laughing. "Christ, Rosie, I can't believe you said that."

"No, seriously, haven't your partners been...like, sore afterward? Or during? Hasn't anyone ever had to ask you to stop?"

"No..." he drawls. "Mostly they have asked me *not* to stop." He's still laughing, but I'm pretty sure he's not joking.

"Really?" I've gotta get to the bottom of this. "What kinds of things have your lovers said about your...size?"

He seems to consider this. "Hell, I don't remember, Rosie. It's been a while. The last one—I can't be sure she was talking about my size."

"What'd she say?"

"Three words: 'Oh my god.' I remember 'em clearly because she said 'em over and over. The last few times she was pretty loud." Still laughing, the big jerk.

I don't see how anyone could ever have thought him a humorless, silent giant. He's a real comedian today.

"You are not the humble, modest man I thought you were, Angus." I make my tone as severe as possible.

Still he laughs. "Rosie, I would never tell anybody else this stuff. This is the weirdest conversation I've ever had."

I'm regretting starting it, that's for sure. Clearly any other topic would have been better. I blow out a sigh. "Okay, Mr. Smarty Pants. I have never taken a physics class, but I am aware that there are laws about these things, and I just am not confident that *that*—"I point at his crotch"—will fit in me."

That sobers him. "It will, Rosie." He puts his other arm around me too. "When you're ready. But if you're not ready, we just won't do it, okay?" He presses a kiss to the top of my head.

"Okay." I tilt my head and pull his face to mine. "But can I see you naked today?"

His tender kiss makes me sigh. "Sure, if you want." He gets up, tugs me to a sitting position, and yanks his T-shirt over his head. He's barefoot, so all that's left is for him to pull off his shorts and boxer briefs. Mm, he wears boxer briefs. Wears them well. He steps away from the bed to take them off, I guess so he won't be right in my face, and stands patiently, letting me look.

And I stare, taking him in from the top of his wild curly head to the graceful curving arches of his feet. "I am beginning to understand the 'Oh my god!' reaction," I admit finally. "Angus, there's no part of you that isn't beautiful."

I think maybe his penis flexes a little at this, might have grown even larger—*holy mother of god*—but I'm on sensory overload and can't be certain. I'm not even sure penises do that.

Truly, the man is magnificent. His hips are narrower than his acre-wide shoulders, his legs long and powerful, beautifully shaped, like he's used to supporting the weight of the world. He's all smooth skin stretched over thick, solid muscle and flesh, a smattering of hair thrown in for believability.

Jesus.

In a daze, I stand and circle around behind him. Beneath the broad back I've admired so many times is a perfect butt. Untanned and perfect, rounded, with indentations conveniently located for my fingers to grip. I swallow. Magnificent.

Against the paler skin, a raised white mark catches my eye. Just above his left buttock is a scar about an inch and a half long. There's a matching scar on his left hip in front.

"Angus, may I touch you?" I'm whispering again.

"Yeah." His voice is serious now. Hoarse.

I reach out with both hands and touch the two scars. "What did this to you?"

He hesitates, as if there are multiple correct answers. “Shrapnel,” is the single word he finally chooses.

I meet his wary eyes. Hold his gaze. I kiss my fingertips and press them to each scar. His muscles visibly relax.

I move behind him, reach around, and run my hands up his body from his thighs to his chest. He leans back against me, his breath hitching. I explore him, touching my lips to his triceps, his biceps, the sides of his chest, his breastbone, his shoulder blades, the dip in the center of his back. Caressing his sturdy abdomen, his taut butt.

When I finally touch his penis, I’m surprised by its heat and hardness. Its silky skin. He gasps as my fingers stroke him. He keeps his arms at his sides, but he’s shaking.

I’m operating on pure instinct. My hands move to my blouse buttons, making quick work of them, dropping my shirt to the floor beside his clothing. Dazed, feeling like I’m possessed by some other woman with more knowledge, I go to stand in front of him again so he can see me.

I would swear the sound he makes at the sight of my flower petal bra is involuntary. There’s a tiny hidden button that allows me to lower the petals one by one, but if I try that with my fingers trembling this badly, I might tear it off.

“Will you undo my bra?” I turn my back to him. His fingers unfasten it in a second, his knuckles brushing warm against my skin. I face him again, holding the sheer cups to my breasts, the straps sliding off my shoulders.

His “Mm” seems purposeful this time, a deep exhale accompanying it.

It is impossible not to feel sexy when this man makes that sound at me.

I move behind him again, letting the bra drop to the floor, pressing my breasts to his back, and reach around to stroke up his thighs and across his hips.

His big body quakes in my arms. "Christ, Rosie." He grinds the words out.

I step back a little, so that just the tips of my breasts are brushing him. Trail my fingertips over his butt as I press tiny nibbling kisses to his back.

He groans like he's in actual pain, but he doesn't move. "Rosie, I have to hold you. Can we lie on the bed?"

If I say no, he'll honor my wishes, even if it kills him. The knowledge fills me with a sense of power but, more importantly, with trust. I take his hand and pull him onto the bed with me. His arms come around me and his lips find mine.

These kisses are different. Always before, they've been lingering, a source of pleasure on their own. These are questioning, searching, saying more, demanding more.

Now it's me saying, "Mm..." into his hungry mouth.

I'm caught up in his taste, his scent, the feel of his powerful body holding me, wrapping around me as he murmurs my name.

His big, calloused hands roam my back, tracing down my spine and back up over my shoulder blades, raising shivers and goose bumps, cupping my shoulders, holding me in place as he drags his mouth over my collarbones, my throat, and then lingers on my breasts.

My back arches without permission, pressing me tighter to him, and my own hands fly over him, exploring, squeezing, gripping him.

This feeling, this desperate, frenzied feeling, must be what those novels are talking about.

CHAPTER 20

Angus

I'M A STARVING MAN AT a feast. Rosie's kicked off her sandals and she's in my bed, barefoot and topless, almost everything I've dreamed about. There are fifty different things I want to do with her, ways I want to give her pleasure, and for the life of me I don't know where to start.

Because above all, I don't want to scare her.

And I'm twice her size, so I should probably start by not smashing her. I roll to my back and tug her on top of me.

Damn. Excellent view.

She traces my nose, my cheekbones, my brows, and then captures me in another drugging kiss. I don't think she's even aware she's making tiny, sweet sounds, sighs, murmurs, bits of my name. I *know* she's not aware she's moving on me, rocking her soft hot center against me just where she'll make me the craziest.

I fill my hands with her breasts and she whimpers, rocking harder. Woman's going to be the death of me, but damn it's a good way to die.

"Angus!" She tears her mouth from mine, her face flushed, her big brown eyes a little wild. She slides to one side, levers up on her knees, and touches me, stroking with one finger, her eyes widening as my cock jumps. "Now what?" Her voice is smaller than before.

Her cheek is velvet soft under my hand. "Whatever you want, Rosie." I've got a brand-new box of condoms in the bedside drawer, and I deserve a goddamn medal for how normal my voice sounds right now. But I am not—*will not*—push her.

She sits back on her heels, her mouth clamped shut, her eyes tinged with panic. "I don't know what I want."

"What if...?" I hook my index finger in the waistband of her shorts and stroke her soft belly with my knuckle. "What if you take these off and then lie back down, and we do what we were doing a minute ago? You liked that, right? We could try it with no clothes between us."

That way she'll be on top, with control. I won't be trapping her against the mattress.

She nods. Crawls off the bed and tugs down her shorts. I get a flash of sheer green, the same color as that impossibly sexy bra, and then that's gone too and she's climbing back up, straddling me, not looking at me. Shy.

My heart squeezes a little. Despite my screaming dick, I want to gather her in and cuddle her into feeling better.

"Rosie." I tip her chin up and kiss her. Wait for her to raise her pretty eyes to mine. "One of these days we're going to go through your drawer, and you're going to introduce me formally to every one of your bras. Every single pair of panties."

Her eyes crinkle and my Rosie's back with me. "Oh, like you haven't taken liberties with them all already."

"Yeah, but this time I'm going to name them all. 'Sweet Jesus.' 'Gift from heaven.' 'Wowser.'"

Our smiles meet and open, and we're kissing again. Her hair curls around my fingers and her hands stroke my neck, my earlobes, my shoulders. Long, slow, soft kisses deepen to kisses that feel like communication. I care about her and she cares about me. I like her and she likes me. I want her...and she wants me.

She's moving on me again, and my hands glide over her body. My sterile little bedroom becomes something different, something special, filling with her scent and her warmth and the sounds of our pleasure. My life becomes something different. Something special.

"Oh! Oh, Angus." She's straddling me, killing me with pleasure, sliding back and forth over me, grinding into me, her eyes holding mine like a lifeline as she comes in for another kiss.

Too overcome to speak, I take her fine ass in both hands, squeezing, pressing her to me at an angle that makes her gasp and has me seeing stars.

"Angus, this feels...amazing." Her breaths come out as little pants, in time with the little circles her hips are making on me.

Amazing is right. I don't remember sex ever being so... intoxicating? Even the first few times in high school. And I'm not even inside her.

She's got her concentrated, learning-something-new face on now, and she's beginning to move more. And lord help me, the woman can move.

She may be new to this, but I'm not, so why do I feel like I'm learning something profound right along with her?

Then we're rocking together, and I'm meeting every

breathless "Oh, Angus!" with my own surprised-sounding "Rosie!"

And then she stills, pressing hard against me, shaking as I hold her tight, her eyes sliding closed, a tiny "Oh, oh, ohhh" escaping her lips.

Her expression turns from wonder to pure contentment, melting me, bringing tears to my eyes. A few swift strokes and I'm right there with her, falling back from the heights, surprised and awed and completely at peace.

She tucks her head under my chin and cuddles close. I wrap both arms around her to keep her there. I want to savor this perfect, special, tender moment.

"Son of a bitch, Angus," she says. "Now I totally fucking get why people like getting naked."

My laughter shakes her until she levers up to give me a dirty look.

I kiss her nose. "There she is. There's my Rosie."

"Sometimes regular words won't do." She lowers her head again and strokes my chest. "If we're going to keep doing stuff like this, I'm going to need a bigger Cuss Jar. A Cuss Vat."

I let her words settle. "You wanna keep doing stuff like this with me, Rosie?"

"*Hell* yeah."

I might never get this smile off my face.

We lie there holding each other and kissing, squabbling half-heartedly over who's going to get a washcloth from the bathroom—"I'll go," "No, I'll go. I've gotta pee anyway," "No, you are *not* going to take care of my sticky mess!" "I think it's *our* sticky mess, dude"—until her stomach growls again. Then I dig the phone out from its refuge under the bed and call for pizza as I head to the shower. I wish my tub weren't too small to bring Rosie in with me…but we can do that some other time, at her house. In the shower stall I built while trying not to imagine us using it together.

"Shirts in the drawer here if you want one." I toss her a washcloth, grab clean clothes, and give her some privacy.

She wanders out into the living room a few minutes later, tugging at her dripping hair with the comb I rarely use. My UNC Asheville shirt hangs nearly to her knees.

I can see every movement of her breasts under the soft fabric, and I'm hard again before she makes it to the couch. "Can I do that?" I hold out my hand for the comb and turn sideways on the sofa so she can settle between my legs. Damn, how can my own soap and shampoo smell so much better on her?

"I found a new toothbrush in your cabinet and used it. I'll get you a replacement tomorrow."

"No need. I keep a bunch." I sweep her wet hair away from one side of her neck. Taste her there.

She shivers and clutches at my knee. "For clients?"

"Yeah." We're quiet as I work the comb through the snarls we've made in her hair. Then I raise the issue that occurred to me while she was in the shower. "Rosie, that step we just took… You didn't do that today just to comfort me, did you?"

"Did it comfort you?"

I pause with my detangling. "Yeah. But being with you means a whole lot more than comfort to me."

She turns to look me in the eye. "It means a whole lot more to me too. If it comforted you, that's a nice side benefit."

"The timing of it… You didn't rush ahead of what you wanted, just to help me through a rough time?"

She twists the hem of the T-shirt in her hands, giving me a flash of her warm, soft thighs. "I figured stuff would happen sooner or later. I don't have a specific timeline in mind. I just… want everything to feel right."

"And today it did?"

"Oh, yeah."

I bring the comb up and go back to work on her hair. "So, you worry about physical pain with sex?"

She keeps her face turned away. "Some. I—have some other fears and insecurities that go way back. But I think being around you has helped."

Easy, now. Don't push. "Wanna talk about it?"

"Not today."

"Okay." I let it go, focusing on her curls.

Just as I finish, the doorbell rings. I have to battle her to pay, of course. Pretty sure I only win because she's naked under that T-shirt. She darts into the bedroom—a pleasure to watch, though only briefly, because she's much speedier than I expected—while I answer the door.

We settle on the couch, pizza box on the coffee table, and put in the *Live Free or Die Hard* disc. The woman is fucking *perfect* for me.

"I love this one," she says around a mouthful of sausage and mushroom, gesturing at the screen as the opening credits roll, "even during the more preposterous moments."

I hook an arm around her neck and pull her in so I can lick a little speck of tomato sauce from the corner of her mouth. "I love you, Rosie, even during your more preposterous moments."

Holy shit, I said that out loud.

CHAPTER 21

Rose

I'M DOING A DAMN GOOD job of impersonating a person who does these things. Goes to the home of a sweet, beautiful man. Gets naked with him. Has an *orgasm*, for god's sake.

Takes a shower in his bathroom and helps herself to his stuff. Lounges casually, barely dressed, around the living room with him afterward, because of course he wants to hang out and eat with an awesome person like me.

Into whose fairy tale have I fallen? And how do I keep anyone from questioning whether I belong?

I want to snuggle close and study his face and think about all this for a while, let it seep slowly into my bones and my heart, but I know that in a strange land you have to act like the people who live there. So I take a bite of pizza and tell him I love this sometimes-preposterous movie.

And he totally blows my mind. Puts his arm around me, pulls me over where I want to be, gives me a little licking kiss and says, "I love you, Rosie, even during your more preposterous moments."

Just like that, my pretense shatters. I'm clearly not yet fluent in the language of this land. "I'm sorry, what?"

His aqua eyes are a bit rounder than usual. Not panicked, exactly, but not calm. "I—didn't know I was going to say that. But you heard me, Rosie."

I grope for the remote and pause the movie. I'm totally off script, with zero idea how to handle this situation. This... amazing, unbelievable gift.

"How does it feel? How do you know? What does it mean?" Well, hell. My visit to this place was nice while it lasted.

He takes my hand. Stares down at my fingers. "Real answers?" There's a flash of humor in his quick glance up. Humor and an Angus-sized warmth that curls my toes.

I nod and snuggle closer.

"Well, it's not as much of a surprise to me as it seems to be to you. Hadn't planned to mention it yet, but I've been feeling it for a while." He traces my little finger with one of his. "It feels really nice, Rosie. I've got something to look forward to every day. Somebody I want to be with."

I mull that over. Yeah. I nod. "Me too. But also like I've got an ally. Somebody who'd have my back if I needed it."

He slides his fingers through mine, locking our hands together. "You do, Rosie. I've got you. Whatever you need, I've got you."

I meet his eyes. "I've got you too." But my voice is tiny. Terrified. Now what? "I don't have any experience with this, Angus."

One side of his mouth quirks up. "I don't have all that much experience with it myself."

"But you've been married."

Angus

I sigh and nod. "Yeah. Seems like somebody else's life, it feels so long ago. Like I'm a different person. And our relationship was nothing like yours and mine."

Her turn to examine my hands. "What was that relationship like?"

I've thought about it a lot. Not hard to explain. "Met her when I was twenty. Home on leave. Married her six months later. We were so young...so young. Did okay for a couple of years, but then I had a really tough deployment. I was a mess when I got out. Pissed off all the time, hair-trigger temper, nightmares, drinking too much."

Sandy deserved so much better. "I wasn't fit to be a husband. Couldn't even take care of myself, much less be a decent partner. She stuck it out almost two more years, but one night I tripped over some little footstool thing. Got mad, broke it to pieces, and threw it out into the rain. Hadn't even noticed she'd spent weeks doing some kind of fancy needlework on it." That memory still twists my gut. "She didn't cry, didn't yell. Just sank down on the couch and told me the person she'd loved and married was gone, and she'd given up hoping he was coming back."

Rosie slides her hand over mine and holds on.

"She asked me to leave. She was right." I shrug, helpless all over again. "I was broken. Can't imagine how she lasted so long, or why anybody would've wanted to be with me. I had nothing to offer. She's married to somebody else now. Has a couple of kids. Seems happy. I'm glad. She's a good person."

Rosie wraps her arms around me. Lays her head on my chest, rubs her soft cheek over the hair there. "You're a good person too."

Her hair's still damp when I kiss it. "What about you? How come you never got close to getting married?"

She tenses under my hand and doesn't answer right away. Then she sighs. "There was this guy in high school. We didn't really date. But...he was awful. That squashed any dreams I had of romance. And after I dropped out, the only men I met were restaurant customers. I didn't look at them, they didn't look at me. I didn't really do anything outside work, so I never met anybody new. Not until I moved here."

I pull her up onto my lap. Slide my fingers over her jaw to tuck her hair behind her ears. "I'm glad you didn't stick with somebody awful, Rosie."

She presses her lips together and nods, one hand smoothing across my shoulder to tickle the nape of my neck. "I'm so sorry about your marriage, Angus. And I'm so glad you were single when I met you."

I wrap both arms around her and hold her tight. "Me too, Rosie. Me too."

Then she's kissing my neck, my shoulder, my jaw, her lips as soft as summer nights, and I forget the pain of a marriage gone wrong, because this feels so, so right.

And when I ease her down on the couch and ask if I can kiss her a few other places, she squeaks. Her eyes go huge as she watches me slide down her body, watches me press her knees apart, watches me lower my mouth to her. She nods once, twice, three times as my lips find her petals and my tongue her core, and then her head drops back and she fists her hands in my hair and I show her how happy I am to be sharing something new with her.

And afterwards, before her breathing even slows to normal, she's reaching for me, sliding her hand down the front of my gray sweats, taking hold of me, putting her sweet mouth on me. Turns out she's a fast learner with every goddamn miraculous thing she does. And I am a lucky, lucky man.

We do eventually restart the movie after reheating our pizza. We watch from the couch, her back to my front, my leg hooked over hers, and my arm holding her secure.

Afterwards, when I ask her to stay, she says yes. She cuddles up to me like a kitten in my bed, one hand on my chest. I fall asleep holding her. When I wake in the middle of the night, I get up and take the kitchen trash out, just so I can come back in to her.

CHAPTER 22

Rose

I'VE NEVER FELT SO SAFE in my life. It should have been weird to sleep in a man's bed, next to his big furnace of a body for the first time, but when Angus wrapped his arms around me and tucked my head under his chin, my bones and my worries dissolved, and I slid into a happy place. With anybody else, I'd be tense all night and extremely self-conscious the next morning, but when I wake up, Angus gives me a sweet sleepy smile and such tender kisses I can't doubt his pleasure at having me there. He makes love to me again with his mouth, so slowly and with such care that even if he hadn't said those unexpected three words the day before, I'd know it from his touch.

Afterwards as we're getting ready to caravan to my house, I tell him not to go through the Dunkin' drive-through. "Come make your own pot at my place."

He looks like he wants to argue, but then his face softens at something he sees in mine, and he grumbles, "Okay, but from now on, I buy the beans."

With the patio finished, he starts building shelving for my library room. In no time at all, we're back to squabbling over music, although in his defense, he doesn't complain when I want to listen to a Spanish language station. "I guess I could stand to learn too," is all he says.

Keeping our hands off each other is a challenge. We fool around in just about every room of the house and sleep in my bed every night. I haven't yet shown him the condoms I bought, but that time is approaching. He makes everything so safe and so lovely that it's hard to remember there's anything to be scared of.

Happiness is affecting my life in peculiar ways. One day, after pulling the "Ma'am, you dropped this" routine at the market with a harried-looking woman with a crying baby and a hole in her shoe, I go to July's and sail straight across the room to Miz Ames' booth.

She does not look happy to see me.

Especially when I wave over Naomi from the lingerie shop who comes in a minute later. Naomi's my dealer now. My enabler. We have a codependent relationship in which she texts me whenever she gets in a new shipment and I race over and we spend half an hour oohing and ahhing before I leave with a bag of new fancy stuff.

"Join us!" I say to her now.

"Are...you sure?" She looks dubiously from sourpuss Pearl Necklace to me.

I flap my hand and scoot over to make room. "Oh, sure. Miz Ames loves when I sit with her. Gives her a chance to count my carbs and think up forms of exercise that will both punish me and make large portions of me disappear."

"Um...fun?" But Naomi slides in beside me and nods to Miz Ames, who spends the next several minutes telling me what I should order from the menu if I "ever want that handsome Angus Drummond to fall for" me.

Naomi leans back and surveys me. "I don't know, Miz Ames... Looks like she's got quite a glow. I bet he notices her plenty." Sonya, beside her with an order pad, nods.

I nearly snort my water, wondering whether I should tell Pearl just how many times Angus "noticed" me yesterday. And this morning. And in the shower an hour before I got here. "Yeah, he seems to like me just fine," I say and give my order for pasta salad.

Naomi and Sonya squeal and high-five me. Pearl's frown takes on a thoughtful quality.

The next day, Sabina and July nearly catch Angus and me in the act. They show up unexpectedly to see the progress on the house. Angus and I are out back on the double chaise lounge on the surprisingly private back patio when the doorbell rings.

I know I'm flushed and rumpled when I answer the door. "I'm so glad you're here! Let me show you around!" I'm trying to act normal, but my voice is high and breathless.

Good friends that they are, they ooh and ahh over the house and patio, not teasing Angus for being as disheveled as I am. They even pretend not to notice when, out back, I nudge my favorite bra under the chaise with my toe.

The only indication that they know what was going on comes when we're saying goodbye. Sabina gives me a big hug and whispers, "You go get him, tiger."

And I do, as soon as I close the front door behind them.

There is one small thing I feel a little guilty about. I tell

Angus a tiny fib. "What's your colleague Robin's last name? I think maybe I've heard July or Sabina mention her." Totally not true.

But once I have the name, I find her contact information and sneak off to call my money man and lawyer in Indiana. My instructions are specific: "Wait a few days and then contact these two therapists. Tell them you represent a funding source for people and agencies providing services to returning veterans. Don't tell them how you learned about them. If they ask, let them think you found out from somebody they've worked with before. Tell them your client is interested in seeing proposals and ask them to submit one. Then we'll look it over and I'll fund it. But nobody—and I mean *no*body—can know I'm involved."

I hate fibbing to Angus, even over something tiny, but they need that money, and I'm not ready to tell him about mine yet. He wouldn't want to take money from me anyway, and that would piss me off, and I don't want to fight when things are so lovely between us. This way, I can save him some agonizing, help people who need it, and still keep my secret.

Angus

One morning, Rosie runs downstairs for my coffee and her Coke while I shower. There's an unwelcome development afterward when I'm brushing my teeth.

I look down. "Oh, *come on*, Junior, really? It's been, like, twenty minutes. You think I don't have other things I need to do today?"

I hear Rosie on the stairs and debate wrapping a towel

around myself, but a towel's not going to hide...that. "Jesus Christ. This isn't junior high, buddy."

"Who you talking to?" She steps in with my mug, just in time to catch me frowning down at my dick.

Rose and I look at each other over Junior's head.

"Guess I shouldn't ask what's up, huh?" she drawls, coming over to lean on the sink next to me, extending her hand. Stroking me.

Junior jumps with joy.

"Mm." Not sure who says it.

I pull her against me, grumbling. "I just opened the cabinet for toothpaste. That's all I did. But your lotion was in there and I could smell your scent, and suddenly all the blood in my body rushed to my dick. I have no control over myself anymore. It's embarrassing."

She sets our drinks on the edge of the sink. Reaches behind me to clasp my butt, rubbing her belly against me in the process. We both groan.

"Come back to bed. I'll have a little talk with him." Her voice has that catch I can't resist.

"Rosie, it hasn't even been half an hour! I think I should tough it out and get to work." It's a half-hearted protest. I lean over to clasp her round bottom through her flimsy nighty, squeezing her to me.

She eases one hand between us to cup my balls and I'm lost. Thirty seconds later we're back in bed, our kisses and hands ravenous.

Afterwards we lie damp, limp, arms around each other, waiting for our heartbeats and breathing to slow back down.

"You've bewitched me, woman. I can't think about anything

else. How do you do that?" I tickle her arm and her breasts with one lazy fingertip. Memorize her pretty flushed face.

"Angus, I don't do anything. I don't know anything. Oh!" She gasps as I capture her nipple with my lips. "I…was only ever with somebody one time…oh! And it was awful. This bewitching thing is all you."

I stop what I'm doing. I've gotta ask. I press my forehead to her shoulder and wrap both arms around her waist. "There's more to the story, isn't there?" It takes effort, but I keep my tone quiet and even. "Something bad happened. Had to do with you dropping out of school, didn't it? Will you tell me?"

She goes completely still.

I'm pretty sure I'm going to be sorry I asked.

CHAPTER 23

Rose

I TRY NOT TO BE obvious about sucking the air back into my lungs. How do I answer?

He's a good man. He loves me. If I tell him, he'll make up his own mind. His feelings for me won't be changed by what a bunch of hateful high school kids did half my life ago.

Still, shame has been my companion for so long it's nearly impossible to hold at bay. I never imagined sharing this story. Never imagined anybody caring enough to ask. But I feel how he's holding me, and I think of his clients, and Lenny's Goodbye Earl story, and… I'm going to tell him.

"Angus, I've never talked about this. If I tell you"—I have to stop to clear my throat—"remember I'm not that person anymore. Okay? She was a 16-year-old kid. Ignorant—no, let me be fair to myself. Innocent. Defenseless. I'm not her anymore, okay?" I comb my fingers through his hair, his soft beard tickling me as he nods against my neck. "So if you feel sorry for her after this, just remember I'm *not* still her anymore." I swallow around the dryness in my throat. "I'm a grownup, and I'm fine."

"Okay," Angus rumbles. His hands are warm, anchoring me.

I draw in a long shaky breath. "In high school I was invisible. Mom and I didn't have anything. She worked all the time to make ends meet. I was working part-time too, to help. We planned for me to get a scholarship to a local college, live at home, and go to school. I always loved to read and learn stuff, and Mom said it would be my way out. She said I had to depend on myself, not make her mistake of assuming I could depend on some guy. My sperm donor of a father had apparently forgotten his marriage just long enough for an out-of-town fling with my mom, and then disappeared back to his wife. So my life was all about school, study, work. Helping out at home. Not so far as learning to cook, obviously."

Angus snorts and presses a kiss to my collarbone.

"But, you know, I was sixteen! I still had hope I could have more than what Mom had—some guy who'd gotten her pregnant and abandoned her. I'd started developing pretty young, and this one day I wore a sweater that was a little too tight—I'd outgrown it the year before, but it was my favorite and I couldn't afford to replace it and didn't want to get rid of it—and this cute boy in one of my classes complimented me. He asked me out. Invisible me."

Angus stays quiet. Doesn't rush me.

"There was this romantic in me who thought, *This is it! My love story! My fairy tale*. He took me for a ride in his car. We went through a drive-through and got soft drinks. He poured out part of both of them and added some kind of smelly whisky. Then he said we were going to go find the moon. That's what he said, 'Find the moon.' Romantic, right? He drove us up some hill in the middle of nowhere. Parked the car, drank his drink. I didn't like the taste, but I didn't want to hurt his feelings or make him think I was wasting it. Mom and I were always careful not to waste stuff. So I took a sip every now and then. And he drank and talked. Not about anything important or interesting, but I thought he was just nervous because he liked me too." I'm still amazed at my own naiveté.

"So I just listened and smiled and nodded. He finished his drink and I offered him mine and he drank that too. Then he threw both cups out the window. I didn't like that. I started to say something, but all of a sudden he grabbed me and kissed me. Stuck his tongue way into my mouth. I'd never kissed anybody and didn't expect...that. It was...icky. The shock of it, the feel of it, the taste of it." I shudder.

"But again this romantic in me came up with an excuse. He was overcome by passion, I thought. He was nervous and desperate because he liked me so much. Then he grabbed my breasts through my sweater, and it *hurt*—he was rough—but before I could say anything, he reached around me and put my seat back. He was still kissing me, fumbling with his pants and my skirt, and then he climbed over and shoved himself in, and it *hurt*...and then it was just over before I could even figure out what to say."

Angus's arms have tightened around me but he keeps quiet.

"And then he drove me home. I don't remember us talking. I got out and went inside, thinking romance wasn't nearly as nice as it looked in the movies. But I was still sure what happened was a relationship beginning. I thought... I thought somehow that was a starting point and we'd get better from there. I believed he liked me."

It takes me a minute to shake off the shame of that. "But the next day the bullying started. I wasn't invisible anymore. I was a target. My crush didn't want anything to do with me, but everybody else wanted a piece of me. Boys groping me in the halls, taunting me, making horrible faces and filthy gestures. Girls giggling, whispering, saying nasty things just loud enough for me to hear. Anonymous notes in my locker. Dirty graffiti on the boards in my classrooms and in restroom stalls. I don't know why they zeroed in on me. I'm sure other girls at school were used for sex too. But no one had ever noticed me before, so maybe it was just—I was fresh blood."

I can feel Angus breathing, deep and slow like he's trying to calm himself. My sigh riffles his curls. "I tried to ignore it. I thought if I pretended nothing had happened—that none of it was happening—they'd get bored and move on. But it just got worse. It was like they were gunning for some kind of dramatic reaction. They got more and more blatant. I *know* my teachers had to have noticed. I *know* they did. But none of them said a word, to me or to anybody else. It went on for weeks. Anonymous emails. Notes in my locker and on my chair, saying things like, 'Kill yourself, you stupid whore,' and 'Die, slut,' and...worse. They told me how worthless I was, how stupid I was to have thought anybody cool could like somebody like me."

Angus

She pulls back enough to look me in the eye.

I see wariness there, and strength. I hide my rage, willing her to see only love.

"You know, I still can't wrap my head around people being so cruel. As entertainment." She shakes her head, her pretty face bewildered, and my heart splinters in my chest. "Anyway. They broke me, Angus. A month of that and I was this close"—she holds her thumb and forefinger a sliver apart—"to following their suicide suggestions. There was no way to make things better at school. Nobody I could look to for help. The girls I used to sit with at lunch didn't want me around anymore. They were afraid they'd become targets. The teachers were turning a blind eye, and I didn't have any reason to think the administrators would do anything but make the situation worse, because...snitch."

"I couldn't tell my mom because she'd be so disappointed in me. I was so ashamed. She'd wanted me not to make her mistakes with men, and here I'd... And then one day someone drew this hideous caricature on the board—somebody with some talent, because it actually looked like my face—me as a cow with a huge udder and that boy standing behind the cow, having sex with it."

She trails off. I'm fighting to keep quiet and not destroy the world.

"And I was done. I was just done. I broke. I walked out of school. Left everything in my locker, walked away. Went to the restaurant, talked to the manager, got them to put me on full-time to replace somebody who'd quit. My mom was *furious*. She couldn't believe it. After all our plans for a better life for me... I think it felt like a betrayal to her. I couldn't tell her what had happened, so she never understood why I couldn't be in that school one minute longer. I'm sure she thought I'd just gotten lazy. I told her I'd get my GED, but that wouldn't give me the same chance at scholarships."

She shrugs. "I don't blame her. I'd have felt the same way in her position if I didn't know what happened. But I couldn't tell her. She wouldn't have been able to do anything to fix it. And she'd have had to share my shame on top of it. And I was afraid she'd blame me. So I just let her think I was a quitter." She looks away. Falls silent again.

I inhale slowly and let it out on a quiet sigh. Take both of her hands in mine, raise them to my lips. "I wish I could go back and do battle for that girl, Rosie." I press a long kiss to her knuckles.

She nods, gives me a tiny smile. "I know. You would. That's why I trusted you. With the story and…you know." She gestures at our entwined bodies.

My heart feels swollen, bruised for her. "And that rapist asshole made you not want a relationship—sex—for all those years?"

She looks at our hands. "Well, to be fair—and I'm not making excuses for him, because he was definitely an asshole and might have forced me if I'd tried to refuse—I didn't think of it as rape. It all happened so fast, and I never protested or tried to say no, because I was too busy spinning a romance in my head. Years later, I realized it had a lot of elements of things I now consider rape, but at the time…"

She sighs. "But yeah, it did a real number on me. I was too young for sex anyway, really, and there was nothing—absolutely nothing—enjoyable about it. It was textbook 'how to make someone hate sex.' And, you know, even if any part of it had felt okay physically, the experience wrecked my head. If anybody had shown interest in me after that, how could I have trusted them? How could I know they weren't just going to use me too? Especially after the bullies drilled into me just how low a life-form I was, and how nobody could possibly really want *me*, and how stupid I'd been to think differently."

She gives a tiny shrug. "So. I basically retreated. I never—never—assumed anyone might be attracted to me. I assumed they *couldn't* be. I don't know of anybody flirting with me in those years, but if they had, I would have misidentified it."

She takes a deep breath and I brace for a revelation. "And I—this part's hard to explain... I disengaged from my body. It turned something off in me before it had ever been turned on. I believed my body was disgusting. I had these"—she gestures at her beautiful breasts, her soft sweet belly, her bottom that I love to squeeze—"big new unwieldy *parts*. I disgusted myself. Never even tried to make my*self* feel good. Didn't imagine I *could*."

She gives me a smile so bittersweet my chest cracks wide open. "So this, with you, is a gift. I haven't even had *friends* since high school, except for one sweet man who was almost eighty when I met him. I didn't trust anybody enough to let them in." She touches my cheek with a gentle fingertip. "But then I came here and met Sabina, and July, and you. And I trust all of you. There's something about you all that's just...decent."

I take her face in my hands and try to pour the tenderness I'm feeling into our kiss. "Like you, Rosie."

She's smiling when she opens her eyes. "And then came that rainy day where all of a sudden there you were, wet and shirtless... Oh my god." She closes her eyes again, shivers, and pulls me closer. "Thank god for you." Then she cocks her head. "Of course, I haven't seen July or Sabina without their shirts yet..."

Apparently I can growl and laugh at the same time. I follow

it up with a very slow, very thorough demonstration of affection designed to leave her no doubt that I find every bit of her precious.

But I want to go back in time and burn down that whole fucking school. Beat that asshole rapist kid to a bloody pulp, and then do the same to every one of those other little shitheads who tormented Rosie, and every incompetent fucking adult who looked away when she needed help. I'm raging inside, helpless, thinking about what she went through.

My sweet Rosie braved the hell of that school alone, day after day for weeks, more and more depressed, nobody to turn to. Imagining that pushes me to a dark place I haven't been for a long time. I'm sick that I couldn't be there to help when she needed it. I actually want to kill.

But this woman…this Rosie who somehow made it through with her dignity and hungry mind and feisty sense of humor intact, and the courage to build a new life in a new place. Including taking a chance on a relationship with a giant, which must have terrified her. Goddamn. I thought she was amazing before. I had no idea.

This explains a lot. How someone so lovable could've been so alone. Why she never asks for help. And why she's inexperienced with money and might not manage it well. How could you learn to handle something you've never had?

My mind circles back around to her high school tormentors and the fury rises again. Takes me two sets of breathing exercises to calm down.

I'm glad my work for today involves a lot of nail-pounding.

CHAPTER 24

Rose

"ROSIE, KEEP YOUR FINGERS CROSSED. We might have some good news!" Angus hollers out the back door to the pool, where I'm floating in a chair, studying a Spanish workbook.

"Oh yeah? What's that?" I tip my straw hat back so I can see him better.

He comes out to the pool edge. "Robin just got word some people are looking to fund programs serving vets. I think I got something in yesterday's mail from them, but I haven't opened mine yet. She's going to make a few adjustments to our grant proposal and submit it to them."

"That sounds good." I hold my workbook between my teeth and paddle over to the steps. He grabs my hand to pull me closer to the edge. I climb out, toss the workbook aside, and give him a big hug.

"Too early to count chickens, but we're hopeful. That's an improvement over the last few weeks."

"Too early to celebrate?" I rub my cheek against his chest.

"Probably. Don't want to jinx it." He wraps both arms around me and rocks us back and forth, kissing the top of my head.

I jazz up our dinner menu into a not-celebration celebration anyway, but halfway through our meal, he gets a crisis call and leaves to meet somebody at his office. So I scrape my hair back, pin it into a tight little bun, put on a navy and white top that I hope looks vaguely nun-like with navy slacks, and then I go out hunting.

The gas and electric company is closed for the day—sometimes I can find an anxious-looking mom or elderly person there holding one of those ominous, red-edged Disconnection notices—so I go to Ahmed's market again. I load a twelve-pack of Coke into my cart and cruise around, dropping some bills into the open purse of a white-haired woman in house slippers as she peers at her list, lips moving as she pokes at the tiny calculator she's holding.

I pull the "Sir, you dropped this" on the stooped old guy in front of me in the checkout line, handing him another wad of cash, hoping he'll eat something besides the cat food in his cart for dinner for the next couple of weeks.

Before he can protest, I spy the kids. The little one is in desperate need of a bath and a Kleenex. The older one, who has him firmly by the wrist and is towing him to the exit, has two bananas tucked in his waistband.

What kid, if he's shoplifting for a thrill, steals bananas?

I abandon my cart and beat them to the door, blocking their path.

They stare up at me, the older boy's eyes wide and wary.

"I want you to have a better dinner than those bananas," I say as calmly as I can.

The kid's eyes dart down to where his shirt has caught on the fruit. He tenses and I can tell he's about to run. Then he glances at his little brother. He can't outrun me with short stuff in tow.

"Let's get you some more groceries. I'll pay. You can think about whether you need help finding a place to stay. If you do, tell me and I'll help you."

"We have a place," he blurts, fast. "Just no food. Mom's been…at work."

I study him for a sec. "Your refrigerator work, or should we get stuff that doesn't need to be refrigerated?"

"It wuks," says the little one. His brother nods.

Silently we fill a basket. The older one, still skittish, stays between me and the door. Bread, cheese, fruit, peanut butter, packets of tuna, bottles of chocolate milk. From the hot bar, mounds of fried chicken, mac and cheese, green beans, and yams melty with marshmallows. I pay, have the clerk—one of the Ahmed grandsons, I think—double-bag everything, and at the door again I slip the older boy some money and my phone number. "For the next time you need groceries or help, okay?"

I leave before he can get any more nervous.

I'll watch for them from now on.

I'm still awake thinking about them when Angus comes in a little after midnight. I'm ridiculously touched that he bothered to come over so late. I snuggle into his big spoon. "You okay?"

"Yeah. I'm good now." His lips and beard are soft and warm on my shoulder.

"I love you, Angus. Thanks for showing me what this is supposed to be like." How embarrassing. Sappiness is not me.

But he pulls me closer and buries his face in the crook of my neck. "Thanks for giving me a chance, love." His voice is husky.

I turn in his arms. “Hey. I have something to show you, but I might need help with it.”

“Sure, Rosie.” The moonlight shows his tiredness, but he still smiles. “What you need?”

I reach under my pillow and pull out a condom packet.

Angus goes completely still, all except his eyes, glowing in the dim light.

“We can wait if you’re too tired.”

He laughs, the sound rusty like that first time I’d heard it. “Rosie. I’m not *dead*.” His eyes half close as he takes my face in his hands. “I’m never going to be too tired for you.” He kisses me breathless as he undresses us, and then he picks up the packet from where I’ve dropped it, tears it open, and shows me how to pinch the end. How to roll it on.

Then, with his voice rough as sandpaper, he urges me up as he rolls to his back. “Why don’t you take charge this first time, Rosie?” He touches my face so tenderly I could cry. His hands skim over my breasts, down my sides to my hips. He slides a hand between my legs and strokes me softly with his fingertips. Circles softly with his thumb.

And I’m so used to his lovely touches by now that I arch over him, and when he positions himself at my entrance, I sink down on him, inch by thick hot inch, and it feels perfect. He feels perfect. And when, stretched full, I finally bottom out on him, I glance at his face and see his eyes are closed and he’s wearing a tiny smile. And he’s not moving. At all. Anywhere. Not breathing.

“Angus!” I’m not quite in a panic, not really. Well, maybe just a little. “Angus, are you okay?”

His eyes open and find mine. “I’m savoring the feel of you, Rosie. You feel wonderful.”

"Well, don't fucking scare me like that!" I go to thump his chest with the heel of my hand, but his muscles distract me, as usual, and the movement causes him to pulse inside me, which is freaking amazing, and then he starts laughing at my expression, which both pisses me off and makes my entire body tingle and burn at the motion, and I shift a little to see how that feels, and then he groans and grabs my elbows and slides a little way out of me and then back in, and it's so full and perfect and hot that I lean forward and brace myself on his chest, moving in time with him, sliding my body along his, over and over until we're both slick and panting. And then everything speeds up and we are riding each other, in and out, up and up and up...

And Angus is shouting my name and gripping my ass and I am coming like all the heroines in all those books, coming and laughing and crying just a little, and as we're floating back to earth, he gathers me into his arms and hugs me to him like I am the most precious thing in the world, laughter rumbling in his chest, his lips warm on my forehead and nose and ear as he presses kisses there.

I don't understand how I could have gone so many years without this. Without him.

"Tell me about your old man friend."

We've just had a yummy dinner, grilled foil packets of shrimp, corn, sweet onions, black beans, cilantro, and spices. Today Angus finished painting the library mossy green and stained the new shelves around the room. Tomorrow he'll start on the garage, but this evening we're relaxing on the chaise on the patio, face to face in our swimsuits, me in a daze as he strokes me lazily from shoulder to waist, over my bottom and then back up again.

My eyes are half closed. I'm trying not to purr. His question rouses me.

"My old man friend?" I rest my palm on his chest.

"Yeah. You said you only really had one friend in Indiana."

"Mr. Brown." I smile, but it's bittersweet.

"You called your friend Mister?"

"Yeah. He was seventy-eight when I met him a few years ago. It wouldn't have been polite to use his first name."

"How'd you meet him?"

"He was a regular at the diner. You would've liked him, Angus. He was lovely."

"Did he die?" He's still stroking me.

I nod. It still hurts to remember.

"I'm sorry." He presses a kiss to my forehead. "What was he like?"

"Quiet. Thoughtful. He'd owned a bookshop. His wife had died and his kids lived out of state with their families. None of them wanted to take over the shop, so he sold it when he retired. I think he was lonely. I liked waiting on him. One day he came in while I was on break, and I was reading some book about Eleanor Roosevelt, or maybe Maya Angelou? I was in a famous women phase. He sat nearby and asked me if I read a lot. After that, we talked almost every day about books. Sometimes he brought me one he thought I'd enjoy. After a while he asked why I hadn't gone to college. Started encouraging me to go." My eyes mist and I close them for a beat. "He even offered to help."

"Did you let him?" There's a gruff edge in Angus's voice.

I shake my head. "Of course not. But he did get me thinking about school again."

Angus

Of course not. Rosie, accept financial help? Never. "Sounds like a good guy."

"He was. The world seemed colder after he died."

Definitely some tears lurking. I run my thumb along her cheek. "Was that why you left Indiana—because he died?"

"Well, yeah, I guess. Things got harder for me after he died. And there was no reason to stay anymore. So." She lifts her hand to my face and traces my jaw. "And he...left me something. Enough that I had options I never had before. He's why I have this house, actually, and why I can pay you to fix it up for me."

And there it is, an answer to so many of my unasked questions. I follow her lead on the subject change. "What will your next project be after the house is done?"

She hesitates. "I guess...I'm kind of figuring out what I want to do work-wise."

Ahh. Another answer. Mr. Brown's money must be running out. That's okay. I'll be around to help from now on.

"Are you thinking about going back to waitressing?"

Her head shake is firm. "No. I want to do something completely different. I'm trying to figure out what, exactly." She gets up and pulls me to my feet. Leads me over to the pool but my phone rings, ending the conversation.

It's Robin, with such good news I drop the phone and do

a running cannonball into the pool. "Rosie, we got it! They're funding us!"

I grab her and whirl her around till we're both laughing in a pool full of churning water.

"Wonderful!" She braces her hands on my shoulders, beaming.

"I'm gonna take you out Saturday to celebrate." I feather little kisses all over her face. "The Blue Shoes are in town this weekend. You get dressed up, and I'll take you to that new Italian place for dinner, and then we'll go hear the band afterward. Would you like that?"

"Very much." Her smile is as bright as if something great had happened to *her*.

Saturday I'm at my place as usual, meeting with clients. The new guy, Bobby, is fitting in just fine with the morning group. They seem to be doing each other some good. Pain in *my* ass, though, ragging on me to stop smiling all the time, saying it's creepy, asking, "What's her name?" in that damn singsong voice perfected by middle-schoolers.

Frank comes in for his hour, the lines on his face just as deep, his self-loathing just as evident.

I offer him coffee and usher him into the office. "Frank, you ever hear of a thing called moral injury?"

He shakes his head tiredly. Begins to perk up when I describe it to him.

I let him ponder it for a minute when I'm done. "Sound familiar?"

"You're thinking of me having to leave Farzin and his family behind?" He's squinting, nodding slowly.

I shrug. "You tell me. How often have you thought of them since the withdrawal from Afghanistan?"

Farzin was a translator who, Frank had told me, was "like a brother. Saved my ass more times than I can count." Right after he told me the story, he dissolved in tears and helpless rage. "We *promised* them, man. We *promised* if they helped us, we'd take care of them. And then we *left* them. And the Taliban wants to *kill* them."

And Frank hasn't been able to reach Farzin for over a year, and it's eating him alive.

So we talk some more about moral injury and how to treat it, and I give him names of organizations working to fulfill our promises to those translators.

Afterwards I get cleaned up and go to pick up Rose for our seven o'clock reservation. I ring the front doorbell like a real date, bouquet of bold painted daisies in hand. Never heard of them before, but they're bright and beautiful like my woman.

She opens the door and I root to the spot, unable to step in or hand her the flowers. "My god, Rosie."

She's trimmed her hair into something flirty. Got on smoky eye shadow that turns her eyes devilish. She's also wearing a dress. Sleeveless, snug on top, and scooped low enough that I can't look up at her face for a minute. She spins around to show me. "You like it?"

"My god, Rosie."

She stops spinning and frowns at me.

I step in, wrap my free arm around her and dip her backwards. Press my mouth to her neck and then to the bare top curves of her glorious breasts.

"Oh my goodness!" She seems to like gentle suction there. "You've gotta stop that or we'll never leave!"

"Mm. Okay with me," I mumble into her other breast.

"No! This is a celebration. We've got pasta to eat and music to hear." But she weakens when I sweep my tongue inside the low neckline to her nipple. "Oh my! Or not..."

"No, you're right." I can be noble on occasion. Goddamn saintly, on this one. I set her away from me, hand her the flowers. "We'll take this up later. I'll be thinking about it all night. Goddamn." I have to turn away to adjust myself.

"Good." She tugs her dress straight. Heads for the kitchen to put the flowers in water. "These are gorgeous. Thank you!"

I follow. "I've never seen this dress before. Have I ever seen you in a dress?" I trace her shoulder with a shaky fingertip. "This is—you're beautiful."

She deposits the pitcher with the flowers on the dining room table, then leads me outside. "To tell the truth"—she casts a look up at me as she locks the front door behind us—"as far as I remember, this is my first-ever brand-new dress."

"No shit?"

I run my fingers through her soft hair and pull her close on the way down the walk. "Well, you look beautiful." *But let me buy the next one, so you don't have to spend more money.*

The restaurant is great. We split chicken cannelloni and something with scallops, and then make it to the bar just in time to see the band setting up. There's a doll-sized table near the wall. We grab it, order drinks, and settle back, her hand in mine. I'm flooded with peace.

"God, I love you." This comes out of my mouth out of the blue, as we watch David, James, and Rashad tune their instruments.

She turns to me, eyes bright. "I love you too. What brought that on?"

I shrug. "Don't know. Just felt filled up with it." I lean in and brush my mouth over hers. Eyes closed, she kisses me back, then scoots her chair closer so I can wrap an arm around her.

"Hey." She nods at a group seated between us and the stage. "That's the woman in white from the other time. The woman David couldn't take his eyes off of."

"Huh. They must have gotten together." I look at them for the first time. "There's Tisha and Shay. Don't know those other people."

"If I ever meet her, I'm gonna ask her nosy questions about love at first sight."

I hug her closer. "'Course you are."

Lenny wanders over to give Rosie a hard time about some nonsense they joked about last time they saw each other, and to tell me this is a family bar so cool the PDA.

The band's as good as always. Blues, crossover rock. An original love song that's playful and serious. Rosie watches David sing it to the woman at the other table. I watch Rose. What a kick Grandpa and Grandma would get out of her. The evening takes on a perfect golden glow.

And then the band strikes up a song that's like nothing I've ever heard. Chris and James lay down a strong, smoky beat like sex. The guitars join, pushing in and out, and Lenny does something tickly on the keyboards.

Rosie edges closer and I wrap my other arm around her waist.

David's singing about honey and sriracha. Never thought of those in connection with a sexy love song before, but the whole audience seems to be having a physical reaction. Couples pulling together, kissing... When the music ends and the spell finally breaks, Rosie's hand is high on my thigh and mine is creeping toward her breast.

She shakes herself a little, her pretty haircut riffling. "Damn! What was that?"

Then Lenny's explaining into the mic that the band just got a contract to record that song—another original—and that, in fact, we're all part of the first live recording. Lenny waves thanks to a guy sitting behind a bunch of equipment at the back of the bar.

Everybody's clapping and whistling, and Rosie turns her head to look up at me, her eyes trickling over me like warm honey, same as mine on her.

"Rosie..."

"...we've got to go home *now.*" she finishes.

We wave hastily at the band on our way out.

We only get as far as the van before we fall on each other. I pull her around to the back, help her climb in. She's agile, probably doesn't need the boost, but hell, I need to touch her. I shut the doors behind us, toss down some drop cloths, and I'm on her again, sliding my hands up under her skirt, tugging down her silky scrap of panties, finding her with my mouth, drinking her in like *she's* made of honey and sriracha.

She moans and writhes and presses herself against me, but it only seems to make her more frantic. Her hands fist in my hair, my name on her lips as she tugs me up. It takes her only a second to undo my slacks and close her hand around me, and then I'm *right there* and—

"Wait!"

"Wait!"

"Wait!"

"Oh shit!"

We fumble in my wallet for the condom we'd been *this close* to forgetting, and then I'm inside her and we're entwined, bucking together on the floor, not caring if the whole van is shaking.

Afterwards I shift her onto me to get her off the unforgiving floor. Her hair is in tiny damp curls around her forehead and I kiss each one of them. She smiles lazily at me, tickling my neck with her fingers, pretty eyes heavy with sleepiness or contentment or both.

I am the happiest man in the world.

CHAPTER 25

Angus

AND THAT WAS A REALLY close call. In bed later, curled around my sleeping Rosie, I can't stop thinking about how it might have turned out badly. How she might have gotten pregnant and then faced a difficult choice...one that might have made her miserable.

I suck in a deep breath. Press my lips to her bare shoulder. From this angle I can see down her nightgown to her breast, impossibly smooth and creamy in the moonlight, her nipple full and soft and pink. The sight, the vulnerability of her fine skin, chokes me up. I let my breath out silently. It sweeps across her, raising goose bumps along the full curve, puckers her nipple into a tight little bud I ache to take into the shelter of my mouth.

The intimacy of this, her body's immediate response to me, her trust... Tenderness swamps me. I squeeze my eyes shut, tightening my arms around her gently, gently so I won't wake her.

I want to spend every night with this woman for the rest of my life.

"That was a close call last night." We're out on the patio having Sunday lunch.

She doesn't ask what I'm talking about. Must've been on her mind too. "Yeah." She licks a speck of blue cheese dressing from her lip. "What would you have done if I'd gotten pregnant and wanted to have a baby?"

No-brainer. "Learn to be a good daddy. Start a college fund."

"And what would you have done if I'd wanted to use Plan B to make sure I didn't get pregnant?"

Again, no question. "Helped however I could. Made sure we never forgot protection again."

"See?" She looks at me with her heart in her eyes. "*That's* why I love you so much." She leans over and gives me a soft sweet kiss, then sits back down and lays her hand on my arm. Her expression sobers. "Angus, I don't think I'm ever going to want kids. I think...I'm going to find a doctor and talk about more foolproof birth control."

Smart. I nod. Turn my arm to clasp her hand. "Okay. Let me know if you want me to go with you."

"Do you? Want kids?"

I shrug. "I'm okay either way, Rosie. Up to you." *I just want you.*

Rose

Up to you. His matter-of-fact acceptance of a future with me—children or no children—warms me more than the bright sunshine. After thinking about it all morning, I'd figured I should tell him how I felt in case it was a relationship deal-breaker for him. His reaction could not have been more perfect. Angus is the perfect partner for me. The best life companion I could imagine.

Still... "Do you think I'm weird for not wanting kids? Sometimes I wonder if my mom felt the same way."

His brow crinkles. "I bet lots of women don't want kids but get pressured into it. What do you think?"

"Maybe you're right." I poke at a bread crumb with one fingertip. "I don't mind being different, but I don't like wondering whether there's something...missing from me."

"There's not a damn thing missing from you, Rosie. You're one of the most complete people I know." He reaches to tuck my hair behind my ear, his fingers lingering there. "Why do you think your mom might've felt that way?"

"Seemed like motherhood wasn't any fun for her. Maybe it was our circumstances—no money, her having to work so hard all the time. She was tired a lot. Didn't seem to feel much joy, even before she got sick. Maybe she was depressed."

"Maybe." He nods, scanning my face. Even his gaze is gentle. "Was she sick for a long time?"

"She got sick when I was eighteen. Died when I was twenty. Lung cancer."

"Who took care of her?"

"Mostly me. Hospice helped at the end. We lived less than two blocks from the diner, so I'd run home on my breaks, do whatever I could for her as fast as I could, and hurry back to work. It was a real relief when hospice started coming." I tear off a bit of pita bread and nibble it, then decide I'm done eating.

It's hot. Damn hot. We move to the edge of the pool, dangling our feet in the water.

He stares at his toes. "My mom was really young when she had me."

"She was?" He's never talked about this with me.

"Yeah. Sophomore in high school. She wouldn't name my father. We never figured out who he was or why she wouldn't say. Anyway, that's why we lived with my grandparents."

"What was she like?"

"Still a kid herself. In my first memory, we're playing in the yard. Later I remember her arguing with my grandparents, wanting to go out and do the things her friends were doing. But really, I'm never sure what's a real memory and what's just my imagination fleshing out bits and pieces I've heard."

"Is she still alive?" Surely he would've said so earlier if she is.

"No, after high school she worked in a warehouse. There was a forklift accident. Pallet hit her on the side of the head. She died when I was four."

"So your grandparents raised you." At his nod, I ask what that was like.

"Good. They were wonderful people."

I scoop up a handful of pool water and dribble it over our knees. "Tell me about them."

"Hm. Grandma did lots of service stuff—collections for people who'd run into hard times, funeral lunches for families, cleaning the church, stuff like that. She and Grandpa believed in helping people wherever they could." He draws a finger through the water droplets on my leg.

"And your grandpa taught you the skills you use in your work now?"

"Yeah. What's funny—because I know you're talking about construction skills—is that he also taught me skills I use in counseling. How to be patient. Listen. Not judge."

"They sound lovely. I'm glad you had them." I lean my head on his shoulder but it's too hot for cuddling.

He climbs to his feet and helps me up. "I'm damn lucky."

Me too, Big Man. Me too.

CHAPTER 26

Angus

DESPITE MY DESIRE TO DRAG out my time here forever, I finish work on the garage.

Rose decides to host a Before and After party.

We walk the house and property beforehand, looking for more tasks or repairs to do. After I oil a few hinges and touch up some chipped paint, I put my arms around her. "Guess I'm done." I rest my chin on her head so she can't see my sadness. The place looks wonderful—the perfect home. This time here has been the best of my adult life.

"You've made it just what I wanted, Angus. I can't believe it's done. And mine." She hugs my arms to her waist. "I'm happy and sad both."

"Gonna be weird not working here anymore." My words are muffled by her curls. "I won't get to see you as much."

She pulls me into the kitchen and pours us both cold water from the fridge. "What's this going to mean for us?" That's my Rosie, open and direct.

I keep my eyes steady on her face as I take a drink. "What would you like it to mean?"

She meets my gaze. "I'm going to miss seeing you during the day. I really hope you'll still spend your nights with me."

I try not to show my relief. "Me too, Rosie."

She reaches to touch my arm. "What if I clear out a couple of drawers and some closet space so you can keep a few things here? So you won't always have to go to your place between here and work?"

"You sure you're okay with that?"

"Yeah."

"I'd like that, Rose." I take her glass and put it with mine on the counter. Wrap both arms around her. "I'm sure going to miss having you in hollering distance during the day."

We spend a few bittersweet hours upstairs under the bedroom's lazy ceiling fan, then have to hurry to get ready for guests. Sabina and July and Lenny and, at the last minute, Chris, after he drops his kids at his ex's.

Rose has made a wonderful pork and cactus dish with rice and fresh picante and homemade tortillas. She's posted "before" pictures all over the place so everybody can walk around and see how each spot looked when she first bought the house.

Our friends are complimentary.

"Between your ideas and Angus's work, y'all have made this a great place to be," Sabina says over dinner.

July nods. "How's it feel to have the work finally done?"

"Mixed." Rosie's honest, as usual. "I love the way everything turned out, but I'll miss having Angus around every day."

I squeeze her hand under the table.

Then July asks Lenny and Chris how their bandmates are

doing, which leads Rose to ask about David and his girlfriend, which leads to a debate about whether there's such a thing as love at first sight, and whether or not there's only one perfect partner for everyone. Chris goes even quieter than usual. Lenny fills the void. "Lord, I hope not. This is a big planet. I'm gonna need better odds than that."

"I hope not too." July's voice sounds strained. "Those kinds of breakups are awful."

Sabina pushes her arm. "We're talking about perfect pairings. Soul mates. Not the ones that break up!"

July says, "Oh. Right," and changes the subject.

I mention that little bit of weirdness to Rosie later as we get ready for bed.

"Yeah, I noticed that! It was very unlike her. I wonder what she was thinking." She pulls back the covers and climbs in. "I'll try to pay attention, make sure she seems okay next time I see her."

I slide in next to her and wrap my arms around her. "Tonight was fun."

"It was, wasn't it? I need to remember to ask people over more often. Sometimes I forget I like other people besides you."

I can't hold back my grin.

I start work on other people's houses. Best part of my day is still walking through Rosie's door, seeing her face light up, catching her as she launches herself at me.

She finds a doctor she likes and goes on the pill. We have one of her funny little ceremonies to bid goodbye to the condoms, but this time we consummate it properly. Twice.

Later, after supper, she watches me clean up the kitchen. Took a while, but I've finally convinced her I don't need help.

"Guess what came in the mail today? Check this out." She slides a thick envelope toward me.

I dry my hands on a towel and empty the envelope onto the counter. It's her brand-new passport. "Another thing off your refrigerator list!" I smile down at her. "Where you going first?"

"Don't know yet." She's perched on one of the island barstools, swinging her feet. "Guess I'll research that next."

Wonder how much of her answer is due to money constraints. Maybe I can help her with that goal.

She watches me start the dishwasher and wipe down the counters. "You've been lots of places, haven't you?"

I shake my head. "Not really. Mainly the Middle East when I was in the army. Germany a couple of times during that period." I flip off the kitchen lights. "Inside or outside?"

"How's the front porch, 'til the bugs start biting?"

Rose

We settle into my spiffy new rockers. He holds my hand.

It's time to ask. "It was terrible for you, huh? The army."

After a long moment he nods. "Some of it, yeah."

I squeeze his hand. "And the vets you work with now... You do that because you needed help when you got out?"

"Mostly."

We rock side by side. He's looking off down the street, but I think he's seeing something much farther away.

When he speaks, his voice is quiet. "The PTSD was the worst. My physical injuries weren't bad."

"The shrapnel?"

He nods. "Yeah. Another one here." He points to his jaw, but his beard covers the area.

"Can you tell me about it, or would you rather not?"

He breathes in deeply, raises his shoulders and lets them fall. "Near the end of my last deployment, vehicle in front of mine hit an IED. Two of my best buddies were in it. They didn't make it. Everybody in my vehicle had injuries, but we all made it. I got patched up and sent home. Lot of us had problems. Not conducive to family life or holding down jobs. Some of us made it through; others didn't."

We breathe as twilight falls around us. There's a lot in what he didn't say.

"And now you try to provide services you all needed then?"

He nods. I kiss his knuckles. We sit, barely rocking, until mosquitos begin to buzz our ears.

When we go inside, I try to show him, with my lips and hands and body and words, how precious he is to me. How happy I am that he made it.

My birthday's the next week. Usually I just ignore it. Haven't had anyone to celebrate with. So when Angus gets me to meet him for late lunch at July's, and Sabina and July join us, and July's staff brings out a fancy little birthday cake, and they all sing to me—I even catch Miz Ames mouthing the words from across the room—tears pour down my pathetic face. My heart is overfull and achy.

"How did you know?" I wipe my eyes on my napkin, doing my best not to dissolve into embarrassing sobs. How the hell do normal people handle this shit?

Angus puts his arm around me. "Date was on your passport."

Jesus, he noticed that?

As the group breaks up, he slips me a card. It reads: *This entitles you to a weekend in the Canadian or Mexican town of your choice. Let's use that passport.*

I tear up again over his simple signature: *Yours, A.* It's so like him, to say so much with so few words. *Yours.*

He's my real gift.

That night he takes me to dinner and gives me a beautiful pair of dangly earrings with tiny shells and bits of metal and natural stone and sea glass. "They're like you." He touches my earlobe with one finger. "They're pretty, they're real. Interesting. Strong." He takes me home and makes love to me, and then he gathers me to him and holds me while I drift into the sleep of those who feel very safe and unbelievably lucky.

And content, because after months of thinking and reading, I've finally worked out what to do with the money. I want to partner with someone who's an expert in financial matters, set up a charitable organization to turn the money over to, and earn a reasonable salary for finding and funding nonprofits and individuals who need help.

I know next to nothing about the procedures or legalities or decisions involved in any of this, but I know who to ask for recommendations for a good partner. I just need to decide how much to reveal and exactly how to frame my question.

I get my chance one day as July and I are eating together

during her after-lunch lull. "July, I need another recommendation, and I need it to be confidential."

She studies me for a moment. "Okay. What do you need?"

"Somebody who's a financial expert but who is also really serious about doing good. Helping others."

"A professional financial person?"

"Yeah." I abandon my sandwich to give her my full attention.

"You know, it's weird that you ask. I know someone like that—best financial advisor around—and I just recently heard she's wanting to shift toward nonprofit work."

"What can you tell me about her?"

"She's energetic, extremely ethical. Scary smart. Does a lot of volunteer work for the county youth home. I only know that last bit because I've seen her there."

"I'd sure like to talk to her."

July nods. "Lemme see if the rumors are true. If so, I'll text you her number."

I smile at her, full of relief. Finally. "Thanks."

A few hours later, she texts me: Rumors true. Meg Allen and a phone number.

CHAPTER 27

Rose

I CALL THE NUMBER JULY gave me, but someone at Meg's office tells me she's on her honeymoon. I sign up for her first available appointment, hoping Mr. Brown would approve of my plans.

When Angus gets home after work, I sit him down and bring over two plates with meat loaf, mashed potatoes with brown gravy, and green peas. A basket of dinner rolls and two green salads dressed with only tomatoes and croutons and Thousand Island. I've lighted a little candle in the middle of the table.

He observes all this quietly. "This is different. What's up?"

"This was Mr. Brown's favorite meal. I've been thinking of him today. Used to serve him this at least three times a week at the diner. I've made pumpkin pie for dessert."

"Nice way to remember him, Rosie." He takes a bite. "Mm, good meat loaf. What happened to him?"

I study my plate. "He collapsed outside the diner. Heart attack. It was his usual time to come in, so I was watching for him and I saw him fall. I ran out, but he died before help could come." I drag my fork through my mashed potatoes, arranging them in straight starchy lines.

He reaches for my hand. "Did he know you were with him, Rosie?"

I nod. "Yeah. He talked to me a little. I held his head on my lap until the ambulance got there."

"I bet he was happy you were there."

I feel my smile twist into a grimace. "He was worried about me. I was crying. I'm pretty sure he knew he wouldn't make it. When you're dying, you shouldn't have to worry about somebody else."

"You must have been important to him." Angus comes to my side, pulls me up, and envelops me in the kind of hug only he can give. "I'm sorry you lost him, Rosie."

I burrow into his warmth for a long minute, and then I sniffle and wipe my eyes. "Come on, we have to eat while the food is hot. Mr. Brown wasn't picky but he did like it hot."

I meet with Meg Allen on a Monday morning. She's probably my age, but she's got a glow about her that makes her look younger. Newlywed life must agree with her. But there's something else about her...

"Have we met somewhere?" I ask finally, after she's waved me to a comfortable chair.

She settles in a matching chair and examines my face. "I don't think so, but I'm not sure. Maybe we've seen each other but not been introduced?"

"Hmm. Maybe that's it."

"So how can I help?" She clasps her hands loosely on her lap.

"First I need to make sure that everything we talk about is confidential."

"Within certain limits. Confidentiality wouldn't hold up against a court subpoena, but no one in this office would ever discuss your business with anyone else. We wouldn't even confirm that you were our client if someone asked." Her tone is firm.

"Okay. Good." I blow out a breath. "Money stuff has caused me a lot of misery in the past, so I want to keep my personal business as private as possible."

She nods. "Of course."

I've given a lot of thought to what to say next. "Okay, so I'd like to sketch out a proposal, and if you can tell from that that you're not interested, I won't take up any more of your time."

She raises her brows. "Okay."

"I got your name from July Tate after I told her I needed a financial expert who was really committed to doing good. Like, social good. She thought of you. Said you're a financial whiz, very ethical, and that she'd heard you were wanting to move more into nonprofit work."

"I'm wanting to go that way, yes." Meg's brow furrows with what I hope is interest.

"Good." This feels so risky it makes my heart beat faster. "The thing is, I have a lot of money nobody here knows about. A whole lot of money. I don't need much to live on—I have pretty much everything I want already. So I want to set up some kind of philanthropic organization to fund people and projects doing good work. Here in Galway, because this town's been so welcoming to me."

There. It's out. My breath comes easier. "I'm looking for someone who knows how to set up that kind of organization, and who can invest and manage the money so that we can use the interest to fund really worthy projects. I'd like a salary—nothing big—for researching and choosing projects, without anyone knowing it's me doing the deciding. All the rest of the money can go into the organization."

Meg's got an excellent poker face. At my last sentence, though, her eyes widen briefly. "You...would put everything into the charitable organization except your salary?"

"Yeah."

"And you're approaching me to potentially handle the setup, investment, and money management?"

"Yeah."

"I'm definitely interested in hearing more. I'm assuming you know you have to start with a pretty big amount in order to fund projects just from interest earnings, without touching the principal."

I spare a glance down at my comfy cotton slacks and blouse. Not impressive. "I've got eighty million. I just really don't want anyone to know about it."

Her eyes widen again. "Okey-doke. Well, that's a good base." She moves behind her desk, retrieves a legal pad and pen, then resumes her seat. "What kinds of projects are you interested in funding?"

"I've got lots of ideas. Stuff to help older people, for one. I read about a really neat place in Illinois that provides low-cost housing to seniors and foster families, and then brings the seniors together with the families. The seniors become friends and surrogate grandparents and extra support for the foster families, and in return they stay active and connected, and they know they're needed. It sounds very cool and very creative."

I'm talking too fast. I force myself to slow down. "But also maybe projects aimed at returning veterans, survivors of rape or domestic violence, homeless people, low-income people who need affordable medical or dental or childcare services..."

I pause when Meg pinches her own arm, leaving a white mark that quickly turns red. "Um, you still interested?"

"Oh my god, yes." She grins. "Just making sure I wasn't dreaming."

She's a woman after my own heart.

We spend the rest of the hour firing questions back and forth at each other and making notes—I brought a notebook of my own—and then she leads me out to the receptionist's desk and we schedule several planning meetings.

"I'm so happy July gave me your name." I squeeze Meg's hand at the door.

"Me too." Her eyes are shining. "This is exactly what I've been wanting to do."

Angus

When I look back at my pre-Rosie days, my memories are in black and white. No color or warmth in my world. Coming home to Rose, having her smile and take me in her arms, spending the night together talking and laughing, eating, and making love...*that's* living. It's so right I feel like I should have sensed sooner that she was somewhere in the world, so I could've searched and found her earlier.

The realization hits me as I pull in beside the garage: I want to marry her.

When I picture it, day-to-day life wouldn't be much different. But I could free her from the need to find another job. She's had to struggle so hard all her life…I just want her to be able to continue the break Mr. Brown's bit of money gave her. It's the best thing I have to offer her.

'Course she could look for work if she wants, or she could concentrate on school. I don't care, long as she's happy and doesn't have to worry about money. I'm not wealthy, but I can support us. And if she wants to stay in her house, I could sell my place. Put some of the money toward building an office in her garage and give the rest back to her to help make up for all the money she paid me for renovations.

Got some discomfort at the idea of calling her house "ours." Shouldn't bother me, but it does. If the situation were reversed, I wouldn't want her to feel weird about moving in with me. I'll just suck it up, make sure everything stays in her name, and maybe I'll get more comfortable with it over time. Get past the feeling I'm mooching.

Freeing her from money worries will be my contribution.

That's assuming she'd accept my proposal. I *think* she will. We enjoy each other. We talk about everything. She trusted me enough to tell me about the rape and the bullying. I told her about Iraq and the aftermath. With all our secrets out and the way we're so easy together, how could she doubt we'd have a great marriage?

Except for the fact that the house is hers, we have a good balance to our relationship. That's the crucial thing. Balance.

I come in the back door and toss my keys into the basket she keeps on the counter for my stuff. "Hey, Rosie, guess who I'm going to be working with starting Thursday?"

She looks up from dinner preparations, gives me that smile I love. "Who?"

"David Ballard from the Blue Shoes. He married the woman in the white dress! They're building a new house up in the hills." I add my wallet and phone to the basket and come around the island for her hug. Our mouths brush and I nibble the corner of her upper lip. "You going to have me pester him with questions about love at first sight?"

She pulls back, wide-eyed. I see something click in her mind. "Oh my gosh. *That's* who she is!"

"Who?"

"I met someone today and I *knew* she looked familiar, but I couldn't put my finger on it. It was the woman in white! David's new wife. Her name is Meg. They just got back from their honeymoon. My god, you should have seen how she was glowing!"

"That's quite a coincidence." I raise a hand to brush my knuckles over her soft cheek. "You at a good stopping point there?" I nod toward the vegetables she's been chopping.

"Yesss..." Her breath catches as I slip my other hand up under her sweater, ghosting up over her side to her breast, my thumb finding her nipple. Her hands tighten on my back.

"Come upstairs with me. Bet you glow just as bright..." I murmur against her lips.

"How'd you propose to your wife?"

David Ballard and I are towing a trailer with a rented Bobcat up to his property.

He glances over at me. "You thinking about proposing to your lady?"

"Yeah."

"Cool." David grins. He looks relaxed and ridiculously happy. "I was sure Meg was it for me. One day we talked about it kind of casually. The next day I went out and got flowers and fixed her a nice dinner, and when she got home from work, I gave her a ring."

"She like that?"

David smiles a slow, sweet, private smile. "Yeah. It was a really nice night."

I can imagine that with Rosie. "She like the ring you picked?"

"Yeah. Loved it. I got her best friend to take a look at it ahead of time, just to make sure."

"Diamond?"

"Nope. Didn't think Meg seemed like a diamond person, and her friend agreed. Found an emerald that was more her style. She says it's the best ring ever. So. Sorry your girl can only have second best."

I laugh, but he's got me thinking.

I'm a little late the next few nights. Not late enough for Rose to ask where I've been, just enough to give me time to check out the ring selections around town. Rosie doesn't seem like a diamond person either. She needs something unique. Less traditional. Maybe a little funky.

Finally I find what I'm looking for, in the last place in town. It's a plain heavy gold band with a rough-cut heart-shaped ruby embedded in it. I've never seen anything like it. I have the jeweler inscribe it: "R, my heart is yours. A."

I lock the ring in the glove box of the van for now. On my way home from the jewelry store, I make dinner reservations at a French place in Asheville for right after the Mayor's Celebration of Service. Tomorrow I'll make sure my suit still fits, my dress shoes are polished, and that my one dress shirt is still snowy white. Gonna do this thing right. Rosie deserves a lot better than I can give her as it is.

The next morning as I take that first perfect swallow of coffee, I set my plan in motion. "Rosie, will you go to a fancy thing with me next weekend?"

"A fancy thing?" She's in one of my T-shirts, leaning on the island, sipping her Coke through a straw.

All those sexy nighties and she chooses my old T-shirt "because it smells like" me. Warms my heart. Besides, if I squint I can still see her nipples, and if she catches me looking, they harden and give away their exact location, and then... *Focus, dude.* "Mayor's Celebration of Service. Annual town cocktail party for nonprofit and service agency employees and volunteers." I make myself turn away from Rosie and her soft thighs and mesmerizing breasts to fill my thermos. "Dressy thing. Skipped it last year, so I really ought to go this year. Take you out for dinner after...?"

She gives me her sweet smile. "Sure. How dressy?"

I wince. "I'll be breaking out my suit."

Her grin turns pure smart-ass. "Oooh! I'm in for sure."

Saturday morning Rose is already up working on something, a thick stack of paperwork by her side, when I come downstairs on the way to my office to see counseling clients.

I bend to give her a kiss goodbye. “The thing starts at seven tonight, so I’ll be back to get you around six-forty. What’s all this?” I nod at the papers.

A letter from an Indy law firm is on top of the pile. Rose tosses her notebook over it and stretches, completely distracting me. “Meg’s helping me, giving me some money advice. This is some stuff she asked for. Did you know she’s a financial advisor?”

“David’s Meg? Nope, didn’t know that.” I kiss her again, properly this time, before heading out the door.

I don’t know how to feel about Rose seeking out money advice. On one hand, it would be great if she’s talking to Meg about managing whatever she has left of Mr. Brown’s money. On the other hand, the meeting might mean I was right; there’s no money left and she’s in debt over her head. If only she’d *tell* me about her financial problems...

Correspondence from lawyers seems like a bad sign. Maybe she’ll feel better after I pop the question tonight. She’ll know I’ll be there to help. If a creditor has sent her to collections, we can climb out of debt together. Surely she’d let her husband help if she was in trouble? True, she’s really independent. But at least I can be her safety net.

I meet with my morning clients and the afternoon therapy group, and then grab a quick sandwich on my way to the barbershop. Afterwards as I sit in my backyard, tilting my naked face to the sun for a while before I shower and change, I laugh at myself for going overboard for the occasion. But I can’t expect a woman to marry me if she doesn’t even know what I look like.

CHAPTER 28

Rose

THIS WEEK I MEET WITH Meg and her office mates: a lawyer and an accountant. She wastes no time after introducing me. "Okay. First thing, before we talk about setting up the new organization, is taking care of you, Rose."

"I know you said you just want to draw a salary from your work with the org, but it's my professional obligation to make sure that you have full information. We have to plan in case something goes wrong or you want to quit work earlier than expected or you have some kind of health crisis and need long-term care...and we also need to make sure you'll be okay at retirement age." Meg's tone is reasonable and no-nonsense. "You told me your work history, and I know you didn't have any kind of pension plan and didn't earn enough for your Social Security to be a livable amount. So let's protect you first, and then go from there."

The others around the table nod in agreement.

I don't want to use any more of the money for me. The house

and pool are enough. I'll have a salary. I don't need more. Don't want to be greedy.

But I remember the never-ending stress and bills I'd battled while trying to care for Mom, and I picture Angus's face. If something happens to me, he would saddle himself with that. I know he would. I can't put him or anyone else through that.

So I listen to Meg and her colleagues, make notes of all their questions, and list all the things they want from me. Tax returns, info from my money people in Indy, things they want me to think about. Apparently, giving money away big-scale is not as easy as stalking unsuspecting people in a grocery store.

So when I woke up extra early this morning, I came down and got to work, wanting to get this red tape out of the way. And I breathed a sigh of relief at my near-miss after Angus leaves. I shouldn't have been in such a rush. Shouldn't have had all these papers out while he was home.

I'll have to tell him about the money at some point, although it would be wonderful if somehow I could escape that. At the very least, I want to wait until it's transferred to the new organization so I'll be a normal working person with a normal salary by the time I tell him. Then maybe it won't change—read: *wreck*—everything.

I've bought another new dress, this one a slinky dark plum–colored number that bares my arms and upper chest, dips low in back, and hugs my curves almost to my knees. I inspect myself in the mirror and marvel at the degree to which the love of a big, sweet man has increased my confidence. I would *never* have felt comfortable in anything like this before Angus.

I wear it with low heels—there's no event in the world fancy enough to make me wear high heels—and a strand of pearls. Not as fancy as Miz Ames's, but still.

I think I'm ready when Angus rings the doorbell at exactly six forty, but I open the door and promptly stagger sideways into the dining room, groping behind me for a chair, sinking into it.

The impossibly gorgeous giant stranger follows me in, holding a bouquet of bright poppies. "Aw, you look beautiful, Rosie." I know that gruff voice, at least.

"Angus?" When I can stand, I circle him slowly, drinking in his new appearance.

Really, I had no idea just how handsome he is. "My god, Angus." I reach up to touch his clean-shaven face. "My god. You are *such* a beautiful man." His beard and mustache have been hiding a hard square jaw, lovely cheekbones, and a firm chin. The combination of new with beloved features is heart-stopping.

He stands watching me, an amused gleam in those turquoise eyes. I trace a long thin scar, barely visible along the edge of his jaw. "Why would you have hidden this face?" I ask finally.

He grins, nearly causing me to faint, then shrugs and heads into the kitchen for the pitcher I use as a vase. He fills it with water, sticks the poppies in it and comes back to set them on the dining room table. "Maybe I won't now," he says, finally answering my question. "I kind of like this reaction from you. From other people it's a pain in the ass."

"Why?"

"You probably won't believe this, but I am a private man, Rosie. Don't want too much attention. The beard and mustache do a good job of scaring people off."

"Okay, I can't wait another minute. Come let me kiss that

pretty face." I cup my hands around his neck and pull him down to me, learning his smooth cheeks and jaw with my lips. "Mm. Lovely. I could eat you like gingerbread."

His eyes crinkle and his laugh rumbles over me as he sets me away from him. He looks me up and down. "I've got a bit of an appetite too. You look wonderful, Rosie. We'd better get out of here or we'll never leave. C'mon. We've got people to dazzle and hors d'oeuvres to eat."

I lock the door behind us and follow him to the gate, which he holds open for me. He slides his warm palm over my bare back as I pass. I shiver. There's something dazzling about an attentive tall handsome man in a nice-fitting suit. "My god, Angus. I am quite overcome. I totally understand now why people swoon. And I'm feeling territorial. I've never felt territorial about a man before. Would it be bad form for me to deck anybody who ogles you? I don't care if they're saintly volunteers. They look at you too long, they're going down. Also, I feel like I'm cheating on my beloved man because you look so different, and I am definitely going to have sex with you six different ways tonight. Probably before dinner."

"Rosie." He helps me into the van and closes the door, then jogs around and climbs into the driver's seat.

"Hm?"

"You're babbling."

I grin. "You're just embarrassed by praise."

He blushes. *Blushes!* "I'll make the most of your attention later. So. You just plan on sleeping in tomorrow, 'cause you won't be getting any rest tonight."

I settle into my seat and turn so I can enjoy his pretty profile as he drives. "My god, Angus."

He reaches for my hand and holds it all the way to the venue.

July greets us as we walk into the party in the courthouse lobby. “My god, Angus! I’d forgotten how pretty you were in high school. Didn’t we vote you prom queen one year?”

“That was Lenny, smart-ass.” Angus turns to see who’d hailed him from a group near the door.

I’m not surprised to see July here, not with her massive involvement in the community. Meg and David are here too, across the room. I wave to them and then July introduces me to some other folks.

My pretty Angus gets quite a bit of attention. After two women approach, seize his arms, and try to lead him away, he says something to them and makes his way back to my side. “Save me,” he mutters in my ear. “I knew I shouldn’t have let go of you. Dance with me?”

He tugs me over to where a jazz quartet is playing at the base of the stairs leading to the courtroom level with several couples dancing nearby. He pulls me into his arms and we move together to a slow, smooth melody.

I happy-sigh, closing my eyes, my cheek against his warm chest. “This is nice, even though it’s that jazz shit. I didn’t know you could dance. Heck, I didn’t know *I* could dance.”

He tightens his arms around me. “It is nice. Maybe we should do it more often.” He rests his cheek on the top of my head.

“Mm… You smell clean like my man, and you hold me nice like he does, but I still feel like I’m cheating. I think it must be your yummy aftershave.” I nuzzle his chest. “You want to tell me the prom queen story?”

His lips quirk. “Maybe some other time. When Lenny’s around, so I can see you give him a hard time. Right now I just want to hold you.”

I hum agreement and we dance awhile in dreamy silence.

"I love you, Rose," he murmurs into my hair. "I'd dress up and come to this party every year for the rest of my life if you'd be my date. Would you do that?"

His words aren't casual. He isn't flirting.

Warmth courses through me. "Yes." It's that simple. That absolute. We hold on tighter.

How on earth could my life, in a single year, have taken such a turn? How could such a perfect life exist?

I wish Mom could see me, see me happy, with everything I need and want, after all her hardship.

A lot of people would attribute this happiness to the money, but all the money did was free me from day-to-day struggle long enough to find this place. These friends. Angus. Especially Angus. It's been sixteen years since I had any faith this kind of love was possible. And now... I've never felt so safe, so comfortable, so cherished. Life is frighteningly, impossibly good.

Angus

At the party I mingle as long as I can stand. Somewhere south of two minutes. Then I pull Rosie onto the little dance floor and hold her tight. She feels so right in my arms that I consider chucking my plan and dropping to one knee to propose right here and now.

But David and his wife join us, and when the next song ends, Rose introduces me to Meg.

Meg touches Rose's elbow. "I didn't expect to see you here this year. There's someone I want you to meet." She leads Rosie away.

David and I watch them go. Something's nagging at me, but I can't pin it down.

"They seem closer than I would've expected." I'm thinking out loud. Maybe Rosie's feeling grateful for Meg's help with her problems. But that doesn't quite fit...

"How do they even know each other? I would've thought it would be us introducing them." David snags a couple of puffy things from the tray of a passing waiter and hands me one.

I shrug. "I think they just met last week. Meg's giving Rose money advice."

"Huh. I'm surprised Rose was able to get an appointment. Meg's been all wrapped up in a new project. Kind of her dream job."

"What's that?" I ask because it would be rude not to.

"She's been wanting to switch over into nonprofit work. That's where her heart is now." His eyes shine with pride for his wife. "Last week out of the blue a new client shows up—filthy rich—wanting her help to give away money. I've never seen her so excited. Anyway, I thought that's all she'd been doing lately." He shrugs. "Must've found a way to squeeze Rose in."

Across the room, Meg and Rose are with the mayor. There's something I'm missing...something I should be seeing. Makes me nervous. Don't know why. *I didn't expect to see you here this year*, Meg had said. What did that mean? Why would I even notice such a little thing?

"Angus!" Robin bustles across the room, waving her arm at me. "Damn, Angus, you clean up good. You two look like GQ models over here. It was all I could do to get up the nerve to come talk to you."

David snickers.

I roll my eyes. "Robin..."

She cuts me off. "The funds came through from Lorne and Crossley. We're good to go on hiring. Let's find us a military sexual assault counselor." She beams up at me.

I beam back. "That's great! We'd better start interviewing, then. Damn, that'll be a relief."

Robin doesn't stick around. She sees someone else she needs to talk to and hustles off.

Rose and Meg are heading back our way. I automatically smile and then it hits me. *Mr. Brown left me something. New client—filthy rich. Lorne and Crossley*...the name of the law firm on the paperwork Rose had this morning. An Indianapolis firm. The firm that contacted us out of the blue weeks ago with questions about our work with veterans. The firm that claimed to have a wealthy anonymous patron looking to fund such projects, right after I told Rose about our grant falling through. Right after she'd asked me questions about Robin.

I actually stagger back a step, eyeing the women. Could—I can barely complete the thought. What if Meg isn't helping Rose because Rose has too *little* money but because she has too *much*? That would explain how Rose got in to see Meg. It would explain Rose's need to learn more about money management. It would explain why Meg said she "didn't expect to see" Rose at this event "this year" instead of just plain "didn't expect to see you here." It would explain the weird financial phone call I overheard, and why Rose told me she's okay money-wise, even after paying for her house, renovations, the furniture, the pool, and way too damn much of our food.

Shit, she doesn't need my help.

She doesn't need me at all.

It's fucking hilarious how much she doesn't need me. Except it's not funny at all. But she's probably gotten a good laugh out of it. God knows Rose has a great sense of humor.

And if I'm right, she hasn't felt the need to share even a tidbit with me about a pretty-fucking-important part of her life. Maybe because me not knowing is so damn amusing. While I've been worried about how to get her to let me help pay for goddamn groceries and patio furniture and new dresses, she's been funding my grants behind my back. Fucking hilarious.

"You look a little green, Angus. You all right?" David keeps his voice low. "You proposing tonight?"

"Uh...not sure." I feel like I've been kicked in the balls. Here I'd been planning to ride in like a hero on a white horse with my little ruby ring and save my Rosie-in-distress. There's no distress. She doesn't need me. Not even to talk to about important things.

I don't know this woman at all.

I'm a goddamn fool. Why didn't she tell me? Why had I thought—? I've been trying my best to keep even with her on the scoreboard, never even realizing her side of the board needs room for a whole lot more zeros.

David slaps me gently on the back as the women reach us. My eyes are fastened on Rose. I can't seem to open my mouth.

She tucks her arm through mine. "What time's our reservation? You getting hungry?"

It takes all my effort to answer, and it comes out rough. Raw. "We could go now."

I let her say our goodbyes. I can barely meet David's sympathetic eyes. Shit, if only proposing was the biggest thing on my mind.

My world—my future—is breaking apart under my feet as we walk to the van.

"You're awfully quiet." Rose slides her arm around me under my suit jacket. "Is my tall dark handsome stranger the silent type? Ooh, he doesn't happen to have a sexy accent, does he?"

I can't answer, can't make myself put my arm around her. I unlock the van and help her in, conscious of the ring ticking like a time bomb in the glove box.

She leans away and peers at me. "Angus?" Her voice is hesitant.

I walk around and climb into the driver's seat but I don't start the engine. "Rose." The parking lot is full but it feels like we're the only people for miles. "Is there something important you haven't told me?"

She freezes. Fuck.

"About?" she asks finally.

Jesus Christ. How many fucking secrets does she have?

Can't breathe. My throat and eyes are stinging. I drop my head, shake it once to clear it, swallow hard, and start the van. Instead of heading to Asheville, I drive straight to her house and pull up out front. I don't turn off the engine.

"I can't do this tonight." My throat is full of broken glass. "I'll watch 'til you're inside."

Her brown eyes go huge with alarm. "Angus—"

I shake my head fast to stop her. "Go. I'll watch you 'til you're inside."

"No, Angus—" She's pleading now, her hand on my arm.

I flinch. "*Rosie! I can't!*" I've never raised my voice at her. Never rejected her touch. Haven't had my voice break like this since I was thirteen. "Go," I say more softly. "Please go."

At first it seems like she might not get out, but after a long moment she does. She leans back in and, in a tiny shaky voice, says, “Angus...I don’t know what’s wrong but come home as soon as you can.” She shuts the van door and goes through her gate and up the walk onto the porch. Looks back again from the front door. When I don’t move, she goes inside.

I drive away.

CHAPTER 29

Rose

I WATCH FROM THE DARK front hall, gripping the doorknob, until I can't see the van anymore. Then my knees give out and I slide down the wall to the floor, a giant lump of fear and panic burning in my throat. What the fuck just happened? What's wrong?

He was fine when Meg and I walked away.

But now our perfect evening has taken some kind of terrible turn and I don't know why.

But I have a suspicion.

Still on the floor, I scrabble in my little evening bag for my phone and dial Meg, my hands shaking.

"Hey. What's up, Rose?"

There are sounds of music and voices and laughter in the background. Meg and David must still be at the mayor's event, with their world intact.

"Meg, did you tell anyone about the money? About me and the money?" My voice sounds hoarse, almost frantic.

"No!" Meg sounds shocked. "Rose, you okay?"

"Not even David?"

Meg lowers her voice. "No, not even David. He knows I have my dream opportunity, but he doesn't have any idea it's connected to you."

"Could anybody at the office have said anything to anybody?"

"It's a strict rule we've followed for years. I can't imagine anyone breaking it. I'll double-check, but I'm ninety-nine percent sure they wouldn't have. Rose, are you okay? What's happened?" Meg's voice vibrates with intensity and concern.

"Angus is really upset about something but he wouldn't say what. We were supposed to go to dinner but instead he just brought me home. He asked if there was anything I wanted to tell him, and when I said, 'About what?' he just...shut down and wouldn't talk to me. He made me come inside and then he drove off. I don't know what happened. I don't know what else it could be if it's not the money. *Fuck*."

"So even Angus didn't know about the money?"

"No, Meg. You're the first Galway person I told." *I will not cry. I will not cry.* "I swear he was fine at the party." More than fine. He'd been downright romantic, hinting again at our future, letting me know he wanted me in it with him. "Until he wasn't. I think maybe something happened when we walked away to talk to the mayor. Did you see him talking to anybody then?"

"I wasn't paying any attention. David was with him, but I don't know who else. Let me check, okay? You want some company? I can come over..."

"No." I'm suddenly exhausted. Emotional whiplash. "I'm just going to sit here and rethink my life. And hope he comes home and talks to me. But thanks."

As I pull the phone from my ear, I hear Meg say to David, "Honey, I need you to tell me everything that happened after Rose and I left you and Angus..."

I end the call and stare into the dark dining room. The poppies Angus brought me not two hours ago—two freaking hours—are silhouetted against the orangish glow of the streetlight, their stems looking too fragile to support those big, lovely blossoms.

How could this perfect, enchanted evening have turned into such a shit show? Is this about the money? If so, how much does Angus know, and how did he learn it?

And where is my big, sweet, terribly upset man now?

He doesn't come back. My calls go straight to voicemail. When I can't stand being on the hall floor any longer, I drag myself upstairs and strip, letting my clothes lie where they land. In the bathroom I brush my teeth and wash off my makeup and stare into the mirror, trying to see myself clearly.

Am I a terrible person?

He has to have found out about the money. That's the only secret I've kept from him.

How would he feel, learning about the money from someone else? Would he think I hadn't trusted him?

Would he be right?

What would he think about the money itself? What must he be thinking of me? Is this fixable? Did my chickenshit response to his question in the van break us?

Are we that easily breakable?

I can't quite get into his mindset. He probably can't get into mine either. He'd try, I know, but because I never told him about the money, he doesn't know what happened when people found out about it before. He wouldn't understand the panic that swamps me whenever I imagine telling anyone here.

Am I rationalizing? Making excuses?

My face stares back at me, blank, bereft, eyes like black holes.

Eventually I drop onto our bed, facedown, my arm stretching across cold empty sheets where his big warm body is supposed to be. After a long time, I fall asleep, only to be awakened by a nightmare. I can't remember it, but it's bad enough to send me running to the bathroom with dry heaves. It's almost dawn when I finally crawl back into the cold bed, still alone.

I can't get warm.

A few hours later, the doorbell rings. I jerk awake, reaching for my phone. No calls. I plug it in to charge. The doorbell rings again, and I grab my robe and shoot down the stairs, hoping against hope it's Angus following his sometimes-odd-but-always-honorable rules about doors and locks, and respecting my privacy and property.

It's not. It's Meg. She's brought still-warm croissants and two big icy Cokes.

I smile half-heartedly, stepping back and holding the door open, gesturing her into the living room. "I'm just gonna go put on some clothes. I'll be right back."

She's curled in one of the big armchairs when I come back down in jeans and a bulky sweater. "What a lovely, comfy home you have, Rose."

I look around, seeing the good bones of the house and all the painstaking work Angus put into it. "Thanks." I duck my head to poke in the bakery bag, so she won't see my near-tears, and drop onto the sofa.

She gets down to business. "I'm sorry to barge in on you like this. I had to make sure you were okay. Have you heard from Angus?"

I shake my head.

"I've talked to everybody from the office, and no one's breathed a word about you or the money to anyone. I also talked to David about everything that happened between the time I took you to meet the mayor and when we rejoined the guys. I think Angus must have had some kind of realization somewhere in there." She tells me what David said about his conversation with Angus and Angus's conversation with Robin.

"Shit."

"I'm so sorry."

"It's not your fault. I should probably have told him before. Shit."

"Why didn't you?" Meg tilts her head. "Tell me to mind my own business if you want."

I wave that aside. "I was afraid to tell anybody because last time I did, people, like, swarmed me. I ended up having to leave my hometown and everything I'd ever known. I thought the same thing would happen if I told anybody here. I really don't want to leave Galway."

I stare down at my croissant. "But I can see it was really stupid to lump Angus in with 'anybody.' He wouldn't have been like those other people. I was just...operating off fear rather than thinking it through."

She nods. Takes a croissant from the bag, pulls off a flaky layer and pops it into her mouth. Takes her time chewing and swallowing. "David told me something else. I wasn't sure whether I should say anything, but I'm thinking you should know. In case it helps in some way. I don't see how it could hurt."

I lean forward. "What is it?"

"David thinks Angus was planning to propose last night. He'd bought a ring for you."

I'm stunned. I don't know whether to laugh hysterically or cry or run back upstairs for a few more dry heaves. "Oh." *Fuck*. It's inconceivable, how bad I've screwed everything up. *Fuck*. I slump back on the sofa, concentrating on forcing air into my lungs, doing my best not to cry.

"Listen, you want to get out of here for a while?" Meg slides to the edge of her chair. "We could take a walk, go for a drive..."

"Naw, thanks. I want to stick around in case—" I wave my hand.

She nods. "Want company?"

I give her a wobbly smile. "No, but thank you. I need to be able to cuss and scream without worrying I'll scare somebody."

She rises to her feet, sympathy in her eyes. "Call me if you need anything, okay?"

"Yeah. Thanks." I walk her to the door. We hug and then I'm alone again.

Angus

My attention's not on my driving when I leave Rose's. I end up in the higher hills above town, turning off onto David's property, following the curving unpaved track past the area where we're laying the foundation, and on across a natural clearing to the edge of the drop-off, startling a doe and half-grown fawn. I turn off the engine. Gradually the night noises resume around me. Away down the dark hillside, the lights of Galway glow.

I can't wrap my mind around all the ways I've been wrong.

This relationship has become my life. I thought it was all honesty and openness. I thought it was balanced, with both of us giving and taking. I had something to contribute—something I was *burning* to give, I was so sure it would help—rather than taking and taking until I suck the life out of somebody else.

I thought I knew her. Thought she was this down-to-earth scrappy little fighter who wouldn't let anything defeat her. Man, I was going to jump right in so she'd have somebody fighting at her side for a change. Somebody to have her back so she could rest.

I don't even know how to picture "filthy rich" Rose. Rose with major secrets. Rose who wouldn't give up those secrets even when the man who loved her asked her about them outright.

Something terrible washes over me, burning my skin, my eyelids, my gut. Embarrassment, for ever thinking she needed me. Shame, for thinking maybe I'd finally caught up on that scoreboard in the sky. For thinking I might've earned something so perfect.

Clearly Rose doesn't think I have anything valuable enough to offer in exchange for trust or honesty.

I've never felt more wrong, more foolish. More useless.

It's almost dark Sunday evening when I go back to her place. I ring the front bell. She holds the door wide, but I can't go in. "I need to stay out here. But I need to know the truth, Rose." My voice sounds scratchy. Haven't used it since I left her.

She steps out toward the rockers, but I sit on the top step. After a minute she settles a few inches away. Must be able to tell I can't handle her touch right now. I rest my elbows on my knees, focus on my clasped hands.

She doesn't make me ask again. Her voice is quiet but certain. "My name is Alice Rose Barnes. I've got about eighty million dollars. From the lottery."

Holy fuck. I didn't even know her real *name*? And eighty mi—that's—I can't even imagine that much money. It takes all my self-control to stay quiet. I turn just enough to keep an eye on this stranger beside me.

"I didn't do anything to earn it. The day Mr. Brown died, he was carrying a little bag from the gas station a couple of blocks away. He kept pushing it at me, saying, 'For you. Just you.' When he should have been, you know, trying to breathe. Finally I took it so he'd quit worrying about it. I stuck it in my pocket and forgot about it. Found it that night when I got home. Looked in the bag, found a box of peppermints and a lottery ticket. Mr. Brown loved his peppermints."

Her smile is sad. "The lottery ticket—he bought one every week. He used his wife's birthday and his birthday or something romantic like that. I don't know. I never played the lottery. I just kept his ticket on my dresser because...it was Mr. Brown's gift to me."

She fiddles with a loose thread on the cuff of her sweater. "I got fired a few days later. My boss was a jerk—the son of the guy Mom and I had worked for when I was in high school—and he would not quit harping about me running outside to be with Mr. Brown without clocking out first. Kept saying over and over that he wasn't going to pay me for that time. As if that mattered. At first I was numb and ignored him, but after about his tenth asshole comment, I cussed him out in front of most of the employees and a half-full dining room."

She sighs. "I didn't even care. Didn't care about work, didn't care about bills...just didn't care. I went back to my little apartment and crawled into bed and didn't get up for three days except to use the bathroom. Finally I was so hungry and so thirsty and so sick of lying there, I got up and fixed myself a cheese sandwich. I turned on the TV and the local news was on."

Her clasped hands are a tight ball in her lap. "The newscaster said a winning lottery ticket had been sold locally and no one had claimed the prize. I almost didn't check Mr. Brown's ticket against the numbers, but I needed an excuse to get up and move around, so I got the ticket and...it was the winner. I couldn't believe it. I kept double-checking to be sure. I went online to see what a person is supposed to do if they have a winning ticket, and I tried to follow all the suggestions about how to safely claim the prize."

Temperature's dropping. She shivers. Rather than interrupt, I take off my jacket and drop it around her shoulders. Her eyes dart to mine and she looks like she might cry. I steel myself against caring.

"Thanks." She pulls the jacket tight around her and rubs her cheek along the collar until she catches me looking. "Anyway, I hired lawyers in Indianapolis to help me claim the prize. They helped me find a financial advisor too. Mr. Brown had said, 'For you. Just you,' but he had kids and grandkids, so I had the lawyers send them a few million dollars in Mr. Brown's name. Let them think it was part of his estate."

"As soon as people found out I'd won, all hell broke loose. Day and night, people at the door, sometimes pounding on it. It was scary. I was afraid they'd break in. People outside the apartment building yelling stuff at me, people on the phone begging me for stuff and then cussing me out when I didn't want to talk to them. Strangers, workmates who never bothered with me before, my neighbors and landlord and asshole former boss, people I'd waited on for years who had never left a decent tip... Everybody was my new best friend and everybody wanted something from me. Even some of the people who'd tormented me in high school—every single relationship I had, changed."

Her knuckles are white where she's gripping the edges of the jacket. I make a tiny move toward her and then stop myself.

"I couldn't go outside, couldn't even open my blinds, couldn't answer the phone or the door. I felt trapped and hounded, like everybody in the world wanted to use me. You know, like my only *real* friend had died and everybody else was fake, maybe dangerous. A couple of weeks of that and I couldn't stand any more. There was no reason for me to stay in Indianapolis. No friends or family, no job, nothing. None of my relationships were close, and they'd all twisted with news of the money. So one night I snuck out with a change of clothes and a few other things. Hopped on a bus toward St. Louis, got off early, and bought Lillian and changed direction and... eventually ended up here. I was looking for someplace that felt like home. This is it."

She's hunched over her knees, her hands between her sock feet on the porch stairs.

I ache to curve my arm around her, but I can't.

"I like it here so much—the town, Sabina, July, this house, you, especially you—and I didn't want to lose that. I was afraid if anybody found out about the money, it'd mess everything up and I'd have to leave." She shifts to look at me, her eyes enormous. "I don't want to leave, Angus."

She shivers again. "I pretty clearly don't need eighty million dollars. Nobody does. I found Meg and I'm working with her to give it away to good causes without letting anybody know it's from me. So I can keep my privacy and not have to give up my life here."

I don't make a sound, don't move, my outsides frozen like my insides.

CHAPTER 30

Rose

WHEN HE FINALLY SPEAKS, HIS voice is a croak. That and his aloofness and his handsome, beardless face turn him into a cold stranger. "So you thought I'd—what'd you think I'd do if you told me?"

I shake my head. "I didn't know. I was too scared to even think it through. I just really, really hoped no one would ever find out, so my life here wouldn't be wrecked like in Indiana."

We sit in the chilly night in silence, not touching.

Eventually I speak again since he's clearly not going to. "I'm sorry I didn't tell you sooner. I see now I shouldn't have worried about you. You'd never act like all those other people did. I'm sorry, Angus."

I turn my face toward downtown, careful not to blink, to keep the tears from falling.

He clears his throat, then clears it again. "This has really thrown me, Rose. I don't know what to say or do or think about it."

Rose. Not Rosie. Something in my chest cracks.

"Does it change how you feel about me?" I hate that my words come out tiny and weak.

He sighs. Drops his head, scrubs his hands through his hair. "It changes everything. Changes how I feel about you, how I feel about us." His voice gets softer, more vulnerable. "How I feel about me."

Tears streak down my cheeks. I press my face to the jacket sleeve to let it soak up the moisture. I will. Not. Sob. He's the one who needs comfort. "Can I—can I hug you?" I force the words past the lump blocking my throat.

"No. Can't handle that." He climbs slowly to his feet and fishes something out of his jeans pocket, pressing it into my hand without touching my skin. It's his keys to my back door and gate. This time he won't take them back when I push them at him. "No, Rose. I need some time to think." He shakes his head and moves down to the sidewalk. "I don't know what to do."

Come inside with me, where you belong. But I can't rush him and I'm not going to beg. I shrug off his jacket and hold it out.

He takes it from me, swallows, nods, and then he's gone, through the gate and into his van before I can draw my next shaky breath.

"Don't go," I whisper to the empty street. "Come back."

It's a long time before I let the cold drive me inside.

I spend the next week trying to make myself care about my schoolwork, keeping up in my classes but just barely. My concentration's shot. Sometimes I have to read things three times before they make sense.

I check in with Jerry and Lydia. Their excitement and enthusiasm for their new job, touching as it is, exhausts me. I smile and say, "Good! Great!" and escape as soon as I can.

Angus still has clothes at my house, and a toothbrush and a sci-fi paperback, but that's it. He could easily walk away from that. He hasn't called or come over since the night on the porch. Maybe he doesn't plan to ever see me again. The thought makes me want to throw up. Makes me want to curl up in a ball to hold myself together.

I avoid almost everyone because I can't bear the thought of having to talk about Angus. I'm not sure even how to describe the situation. Have we broken up for good?

Even if I felt up to talking about him, how could I tell Sabina or July without also telling them about the money? I'm determined not to talk about it with anyone else until I can speak of it in the past tense. So I work, in meeting after joyless meeting with Meg and her colleagues to get the Galway Brown Foundation, as it will be called, set up so I can sign the money over. Start supporting myself, earning a paycheck again.

The first few nights Angus is gone, I sleep holding his pillow, breathing in his scent. Finally, though, that faint trace of him disappears and I have to wash the sheets. I consider moving my stuff to the guest room and sleeping in there to block memories, but some stubborn part of me won't allow that. Instead, I go to the home store and buy new bedding: a thick color-wash quilt, cotton blankets, and soft flannel sheets in warm colors. I cry as I put them on the bed, but I sleep a little better that night.

I rarely cook. It's too hard to be in the kitchen where I spent so much time with Angus. Besides, nothing has any flavor, so why go to all that effort for one person?

I give up on my Spanish self-study. I can't concentrate well enough to make any progress anyway. And I'm just too tired. I know that's a sign of depression. If I don't start feeling better soon, I should probably find a therapist—somebody who's paid to listen to me, who I don't have to see outside of counseling sessions. Someone ethically bound to keep my secret.

Angus

David and I sit at the edge of the drop-off, looking over the hills. He's just shoved one of the thick sandwiches he'd brought from home at me. "Here. You're not eating enough. You okay?"

"Not really." I flick at a dark speck on my bread.

"Proposal didn't go well?"

"Didn't get that far." I toss aside a pinch of crust. "Turns out Rose was keeping a secret. Changes things."

"Wanna talk about it?"

Dude's ridiculously open. Probably never needed therapy in his life.

"Can't. Her secret, not mine. But I can't get past it, so…"

"It's *your* decision to be apart?"

I glance over at him, then back at my sandwich. "Yeah."

"You're not doing something right, man." He shakes his head. "You're not supposed to look like shit when the breakup's *your* idea."

I do look like shit. My beard and mustache are at an itchy, mangy-looking regrowth stage. Got circles under my eyes.

Pretty sure I've lost weight. I forget to eat. Not sleeping well. Keep having wild dreams and waking up pissed and sad and ashamed. If I don't clean up my act, I'll scare off my clients. They're already starting to look at me funny. Therapists aren't supposed to look like they can't take care of themselves.

I hate going home at night. I hate that the house is never full of that warm somebody-loves-living-here feeling. Hate going to sleep and waking up without Rose warm and soft in my arms. Hate not having her to smile at me and talk with me and make me laugh. Hate not being able to look at her and touch her and make love with her.

Hate feeling like I've been sharing all that with a stranger who's playacting.

I can't get a feel for her now. Have I ever even met the person she really is? She seemed so genuine when I was with her, more than anybody I've known. I *loved* the woman I thought she was. Loved everything about her, even when I'd thought she had a spending problem and a lot of debt. But now...who *is* this rich Alice Rose Barnes? Who *is* this person who snuck around and met with people secretly without letting the guy she was practically living with know anything about what she was doing? How does *that* woman's mind work? What was she thinking when she was with me?

And even if she isn't some stranger—even if she's who I thought she was—how could I go back to a relationship with her now? I sure as hell can't propose like I'd wanted. She said she'd been afraid if anyone found out about the money, all her relationships would change. I can just imagine the way she'd look at me if, right after finding out she's rich, I show up with an engagement ring.

The idea makes me want to puke my guts out.

Marriage had seemed like the next logical step before I found out about the money. If we can't take that step, what's left? Especially now that I know how little she needs anything I can offer. I can't go back and live off her. Let her keep feeding me and paying the water and light bills while I hang around like a big, hairy, useless sugar baby.

Why in the hell was she even with me? I was good at fixing up her house, but she paid me, and that's done. The sex was amazing, she'd probably agree with that. But all she has to compare me with is a teenage rapist. For all she knows, I'm the second-worst sex partner in the world.

While I was thinking we were falling in love and building a great, honest, equal relationship that would last a lifetime, she was thinking…what? What's she really like, and what could she have possibly wanted with me? Was I, like, part of some working-class lover fantasy?

Naw, that doesn't really sound like Rose. Not the Rose I thought I knew. And she was working class herself until recently. Still, she sure must've gotten a kick out of me offering to help her with bills. Trying to stock the fridge.

Not sure why I feel so ashamed every time I think of that.

I try really hard to stop thinking about it.

CHAPTER 31

Rose

FINALLY, TWO WEEKS AFTER ANGUS left me, Meg and I complete the foundation setup and I'm able to sign over the money. Hallelujah, I'm a normal person again. Job, broken heart, and all.

My primary income will be from my new salary as an employee of the foundation—in other words, I'm no longer a rich woman—but Meg and her colleagues made sure I'm well prepared for retirement at whatever age I wish, and also for health problems or old age.

To the outside world, I'll just be an office worker for the foundation. Unless I tell someone different, no one will know that the money was mine at one point, or that I still have power over who benefits from it.

I blow eighty million pounds of stress from my lungs the day I walk out of Meg's office after signing the paperwork. I suck in some fresh air, take out my phone, and invite Sabina and July to Sunday dinner. I buy the ingredients from Ahmed's, watching for those two little boys, but they're nowhere in sight.

Sunday as I prepare the meal, I try not to dwell on how big a part Angus played in my previous entertaining efforts, but his presence lurks in every corner. I keep expecting his arms to slide around me from behind. His tickly beard and warm mouth to settle on my neck. I try not to let my sudden tears oversalt the dinner.

My friends bring wine, lots of wine, which they crack open as I put the finishing touches on our crepes and mixed greens.

"You always have a dinner theme, Rose." Sabina looks up, bright blue eyes expectant, from the wine July has just poured. "What is it tonight?"

"Hm." I rub my chin with the back of my sauce spoon hand. "Optimistically I guess I'd call it a 'help me celebrate my new job' dinner. Realistically I should probably call it a 'come clean' or 'update on changes' dinner."

Sabina's brows rise. July pauses with her wineglass halfway to her lips.

"Go on," they say together.

I finish fixing the plates, hand them each one, and lead the way into the dining room where we settle at the big round table. "It's a good news/bad news situation."

"This is delicious, by the way, before you tell us," July says, and Sabina nods, eyes closing momentarily as she chews.

"There's plenty more if we want it. Nutella crepes for dessert."

I've got their full attention. Best just to dive in.

"The bad news," I have to fight back sudden teariness, "is that Angus and I appear to no longer be together."

Sabina makes a soft sound of concern and her eyes mist.

July breaks the long silence that follows. "Appear?"

"Yeah, I think it's because I didn't come clean with him soon enough on something related to the job stuff. You two are my best friends, and I didn't want to make the same mistake with you that I made with him, so I need to tell you some things."

We eat, drink wine, refill our glasses, have seconds on the crepes, open a new bottle, and demolish dessert while I tell them about Mr. Brown and the money and the foundation and my new job. When I finish, they're full of questions.

Sabina goes first. "For outer appearances, you have a grunt office job, but really you get to direct the funding? So you can keep your privacy and people don't descend on you like vultures?"

I nod. "Basically, yeah."

"Cool."

We all touch glasses, then lean back from our Nutella-smeared plates.

"Wanna go in the other room? Leave those here." I wave at the plates but take my glass and a half-full wine bottle.

We settle into the comfier seating of the living room.

"So," July starts, and Sabina finishes for her, "what's the deal with Angus?"

I shake my head. "I'm not sure but I think me not telling him about the money hurt him bad. I don't know if it's fixable. I mean, I don't know if I'll ever even see him again." I describe the Mayor's Celebration of Service night.

When I finish, there's silence.

July goes into the kitchen and comes back with a new bottle of wine and the corkscrew. She removes the cork, refills our glasses, and then sinks back into her seat. "And you haven't seen or heard from him since that weekend?"

"Not a peep."

"Wow, that stinks." Sabina looks as sad as I feel. "Rose, I'm so sorry, sweetie."

July nods, looking more tired than I've ever seen her, a furrow in her forehead. "Love stinks." Beneath her words is something vehement. Despairing, almost, although I've never heard her mention a relationship, past or present.

Sabina has turned to look at her too. "July?" we say together, but July shakes her head and waves us off.

"That's a story for another time." And I will get it out of her one of these days, but now she sets her jaw stubbornly. "Go on, Rose. You were gonna say…?"

I let out a half laugh, half sob. "Meg's David thinks Angus was planning to propose to me that night. Said he'd bought a ring. So. When I screw up, I really screw up."

"Oh my god." Sabina drops her head onto the chair back, tears in her voice too.

July heaves a huge sigh. "I love the man, but I'm gonna have to kill him."

"No." I rub my aching forehead. "Don't be hard on him. He must have been really hurt. Or he can't deal with the idea of the money. Something." I watch the wine swirl in my glass. "I just wish he'd come back and talk to me. Let me know what he's thinking and whether this…separation…is forever." I have to stop talking then. Tears clog my throat. I lower the glass to my lap so I can look down.

"What do you want us to say if we see him?" Sabina asks, sounding every bit of her age.

I shrug. "I doubt there's anything you can do about the relationship damage, but there's no sense pretending you don't know what's going on."

"You know, you remove one letter and *Angus* becomes *anus*," July muses.

Sabina and I burst out laughing.

"Stop!" I'm horrified at myself for laughing.

"No more wine for you!" Sabina orders but then promptly refills July's glass.

We sit in silence for a few minutes, drinking and thinking.

"Well." July points at me. "I can certainly understand now why you didn't need my paltry wages the day you helped at the restaurant."

Sabina hoots. "Yeah, and you must've wanted to laugh when I asked if you were sure you could afford to stay at the B and B."

"I believe I did smile in the privacy of my room, yeah."

It feels good to laugh with them.

"Thank you so much for listening and not judging me. You two make Galway a real home for me." I don't try to hide the tears this time.

"Rose, you are very easy to love." Sabina leans over to take my hand. "I'm glad you found your way to us."

"And I've gotta say how cool it is that you gave that money up to be used for philanthropy. Geez, woman, how many people would do that? And so casually, like 'Pfft—eighty mil? I'll give it away.'" July drains the last swallow from her wineglass and stands. "Thank you for not building some kind of eccentric neon castle at the outskirts of town and turning Galway into a sideshow."

I snort. "That would have been my second choice of what to do with the money, yeah."

They help me carry everything to the kitchen and rinse and load the dishes into the dishwasher.

"I guess you don't send leftovers home with a restaurateur and the owner of a B and B renowned for its yummy food, huh?" I dig in a cabinet for appropriately sized containers.

"Nope. Especially after you feed them so well they'll never need to eat again." Sabina pats her belly. "I'd love your recipes from tonight." Casual, as if the money revelation meant nothing to her. Inconsequential to our relationship.

"Okay." I hug them, promising to call if I need anything, and see them off on their walk back to the square. Without them, the house is way too quiet again.

God, I miss Angus. If he were here, we'd be talking about how fun the evening was. We'd squabble over cleanup duties. We'd go upstairs and get ready for bed, and he'd reach for me and… I shiver and let out a long sigh. God, I miss Angus.

I do one more walk-through of the downstairs, checking the locks, and then turn off all the lights and go up to my cold quiet bed. Tomorrow's a big day: my first official day as an employee of the Galway Brown Foundation, in a tiny modest office suite in the same building as Meg's group. When word gets out and the foundation gets busy, we'll hire a receptionist, but for now it will just be me, to keep administrative costs at rock bottom.

I'm so glad to have somewhere to go and something to do.

Angus

Sundays now are endless and god-awful quiet. I don't know how many more of them I can take alone in this silent little house. I try to sleep in but wake up early anyway, so I go work out—the smart-asses at the gym say they've changed their minds; they'd like creepy smiling Angus back—and then out to breakfast, and then invent errands to do on my way home. I cut the grass and tidy up the house, but then end up standing in the middle of the living room looking around, desperate for something—anything—that needs attention.

Fuck it. I have to try to talk to Rose. Don't know what to do, don't know what to say, but I have to know whether she's the woman I thought I knew.

I drive to her house, figuring I'll park out front and ring the bell. Maybe she'll be sitting down to dinner, ask me to eat with her...

But even on her well-lit family-friendly street, her house is visible from a block away, glowing warm in the night. It looks like every light on the ground floor is on. Is she having a party? I slow and cruise by instead of parking. Don't recognize the cars out front. The curtains are still open, and I can see wine bottles and dishes on the dining room table and people moving around in the living room. *Fuck*.

Well, what had I expected, that she'd sit waiting alone for me, not knowing whether I'd ever come back? I already knew she didn't need me. *Fuck*.

Last time I felt this alone, I was a newly divorced guy with PTSD.

I can't make myself drive home. I go to Lenny and Chris's. Watch the tail end of a football game with them. Couldn't tell you who was playing.

God, I miss my Rosie. It's more than just not wanting to be alone. That never bothered me for long. But now I've got a new hole inside that's her exact size and shape.

Next day's appropriately gray and rainy. David and I can't

work in this weather, which is good because Robin and I have an interview with our last candidate for the military sexual assault counselor position. We spend the first part of the morning with her and the rest of the morning deliberating over which candidate we want. By noon we've decided, called with a verbal offer, and emailed the finalist the paperwork for her signatures. I'm relieved, even though I'm afraid the money came from Rose. Haven't mentioned that to Robin.

She sighs and leans back from her desk, smiling. "Productive morning!"

"Yep. Glad that's taken care of. Buy you lunch?"

She glances at the clock. "I've just got time to walk over to July's real quick, but I won't be able to stay long. Will that bother you?"

Not as much as spending more time alone. "Nope. Let's go."

True to her word, Robin wolfs down her food as soon as it's brought to the table. She offers to treat, and when I decline, she says a quick thanks and goodbye and leaves on the run for her next appointment. I stay, eating slowly, ordering coffee and then dessert and then more coffee, not wanting to leave the warmth of July's, despite sour-faced Miz Ames glaring daggers at me from across the dining room.

What other errand can I run to keep from going home?

"Hey." July slips into the booth across from me, sandwich in one hand and iced tea in the other. The lunch crowd has thinned out while I sat here stalling.

Uh-oh. This could be good, in that July is good company, or bad, in that July is Rose's friend too and probably not thrilled with me right now. Unless Rose keeps secrets from her too.

"Hey." My response is a beat late.

She eyes me as she takes a bite of her sandwich. "I had planned to come over here and rip you a new one for breaking my friend's heart, but you look like shit. Your heart broken too?"

Okay then.

I gaze into my coffee mug. "Maybe." Rose's own secrets are hurting her too, huh?

"The fuck you doing, Angus?" July's voice is soft.

I meet her eyes. "You know what happened?"

"About the money and your apparent breakup? Yeah. She told me and Sabina yesterday."

So that's who was at Rose's last night. "Why'd she keep it secret from me? Goddamn, I was wrong about *every*thing." Comes out fast, harsh.

July chews and swallows. "Such as?"

I spread my hands. "Everything! Our closeness. Her feelings. Who she is. The future. What I have to offer her."

"Who do you think she is, Angus?"

"I don't *know*, July. I just know... I didn't think we had any big secrets. I thought she trusted me like I trusted her. I wouldn't have kept something like that from her. So...she isn't who I thought. I don't know the person she really is."

July sets her sandwich back on her plate. "I'm trying to understand your reaction." She sips her tea. "Sabina and I just found out last night, and neither of us is the least bit upset that she didn't tell us before. Why do you think that is?"

My disbelief has got to be all over my face. "You and Sabina weren't in her bed every night, July. You didn't hold her and spend every day thinking of ways to make life easier for her, showing her she could trust you. You didn't tell her all your secrets. You didn't have a stupid fucking engagement ring locked in the fucking glove box of your stupid fucking work van. You didn't have to figure the mystery out by yourself and then, when you asked her about it, have her play dumb and make you wonder how many other goddamn secrets there are that you're gonna have to figure out by yourself 'cause *she's* sure not gonna share." More words than I've ever spoken at one time, flowing and burning like lava from my chest.

July thinks about that for a few minutes. "Okay. You've got some good points. I think she screwed up not telling you, or not telling you sooner." She picks up her sandwich and takes another bite. "But I think you're screwing up too."

I sigh. Hang my head, weary to the bone. "Possible. How?"

She stops chewing and swallows. "I think you're imagining she had some other motive than fear for not telling you. I think it's messing with your head, making you feel like she's been some stranger putting on an act."

"Why do you say that?"

"Angus, you know more about her history than I do, and even I can tell she hasn't had an easy life, hasn't had much reason to trust people. What she's done here in Galway is sort of...blossom. I think close relationships are new to her. We mean a lot to her. *You* mean a lot to her. She had it in her head that if she told anybody—*any*body—about the money, it would mess up her whole life and all these new relationships. She's not evil. She's not a schemer. She was afraid. Maybe afraid of being alone again. Having to start all over from scratch again somewhere new when she really loves it here with all of *us*."

I watch July finish her lunch. She's got faint circles under her eyes. "You doing okay yourself?"

She looks up, studies me, says, "Do you remember, in high school, J—?" then stops and shakes her head. "Never mind. I'm fine. Just old ghosts in my head lately."

I want to ask more, but I don't.

Finally she stands and picks up her dishes. "As for who Rose is, last night she was the exact same Rose she's always been. Sweet. Warm. Funny. Humble. Open about her feelings for us." July scoops up the check the waitress had left for me. "This is on me." I don't even protest—neither does my scoreboard, which has probably decided I'm a lost cause—and she moves away. Then she pauses, turns, and comes back.

"Does the thought of her being so rich bother you because you're not?"

I meet her gaze. "Some." I hold up a hand. "I know it shouldn't, okay? The reverse wouldn't bother me."

"Yeah. That's some sexist bullshit you've got going on there." July nods at her own words. "Anyway, it's not a problem anymore. She signed it all away."

"What do you mean?"

"She and Meg Allen set up a charitable org. Put everything into it. She's not rich anymore. She's going to get a normal salary for doing research for the foundation. *She* didn't want to be rich any more than you wanted her to be." July walks away again and this time doesn't come back.

Across the room, Miz Ames gets up from her booth, curls her lip at me, and sweeps out with her nose in the air. Don't know what that woman's problem is. Really don't care.

I'm a million years old. I pull myself to my feet, drop a twenty on the table, and step out into the rain. Don't know what to think about all this. What if July's right about Rose and

Rose *is* who I'd thought she was? And I've put us both through this because I underestimated her fear level or hadn't allowed her to make human mistakes? *Fuck*.

My grandpa would have done a whole lot more listening and a whole lot more accepting. A whole lot less running. And my grandma...would've given the money away too.

Without consciously thinking about it, I drive to Rose's house. I'm through the gate and up on the porch ringing the doorbell before I even realize I'm out of the van. I wait. Knock. Ring again. Nobody answers.

I could call her cell...but I fucking hate phones. I don't want to hear her voice without being able to see her face, look into her eyes. *Definitely* not texting. Way too impersonal. *Fuck*.

I turn back into the rain.

CHAPTER 32

Rose

I'VE NEVER HAD AN OFFICE job and therefore never had an office. Even though the foundation's space is tiny and modest—just my office barely wider than my desk, an equally small reception area, and a conference room beside a miniscule powder room—I love it.

I also love the distraction it provides. Things are not fun in my head right now.

At some point I should probably professionalize my wardrobe. Today, though, I'm in jeans and a T-shirt, because no one knows about us yet, I've been here since six, and I'm painting.

Don't know the building policy on painting, but I heard somewhere it's easier to ask for forgiveness than permission. So Saturday I bought supplies. Today I let myself in, move our simple furniture away from the walls, and paint. Faded denim blue for the reception area, conference room, and bathroom. My own office has a big window, so I go with a burnt orange in there. Both colors look good with the slate-gray carpeting, but I might keep an eye out for a bright area rug for reception.

If Angus were here—if he still liked me—he'd say, "Lookin' good, Rosie."

If I hadn't been such a coward.

But I had been.

By two thirty, I'm cleaning my brushes and rollers. Water-based paint dries fast, and I'm starving and have some office shopping to do. It's a relief to know I can still feel purposeful. And hungry.

I don't have to avoid July's anymore, so I head that way. Miz Ames is nowhere in sight, thank god. I can't handle her attitude today. But Sonya hands me a note when she brings my food. At my raised brows, she shrugs. "Miz Ames was in earlier. She asked me to give you that next time I see you. She said, and I quote, 'Tell her I can't sit around waiting for her forever.'"

Oh, lord. I am so not up for this. I almost tear it up without reading it, but if I'm going to live in this town and frequent this establishment, I need to be forewarned about what Pearl's up to.

I peel it open and then have to read it three times to make sure I'm not imagining things.

In narrow, spidery handwriting it says, *Rose Barnes, don't you let anyone steal your spark. You're too fat and too sassy, but that spark is special. Don't you let some big overgrown oaf put it out.*

Well. Okay then.

I'm sure my lunch is delicious as always, but I'm so bemused I don't notice.

Afterwards I hit the artists' co-op on the other side of the town square for office wall decor: prints and photos of Galway and the lake and surrounding mountains. My favorite is an eastern bluebird, a little blue and orange ball of feathers, fat, sassy, and full of sparks. I'll name it Pearl. Hang it over my desk.

From a home store, I buy funky metal and glass lamps and those bulbs that simulate natural light. At Target I find cleaning goods, green plants, and magazines for the waiting room, coffee and Coke for the conference room, and basic office supplies. A big glass jar full of Tootsie Pops for the reception desk, and a triangle-patterned rug, off-white with faded stained-glass colors.

By five thirty I'm back at the office, pushing furniture into place, arranging my purchases, and admiring my handiwork. There's a bone-deep satisfaction to setting up this new space. Tomorrow I'll unpack the computer and teach myself how to use the office software Meg and her colleagues recommended. It's a relief to be out of the house where everything reminds me of Angus and his absence. Maybe I'll do my schoolwork here in the evenings.

Meg comes to check on me the next morning. "This looks great!" She turns in a slow circle. "You've given it a whole different feel. Very welcoming."

Excellent. Just what I was going for. "Thanks. Want a Coke? I've got some in the fridge in the conference room."

"No thanks, I'm already having trouble sitting still." She tries all the seats, one by one.

"Oh yeah? What's up?"

She sinks into one of the client chairs in my office. "Wow, these are roomy and comfy. I should replace ours upstairs. You know David and I just got married, right?"

"Yeah..."

"Well, we've been trying to get approved to foster three kids we know from the youth home. The paperwork came through, so we can finally take them home with us."

"Oh my gosh, that's wonderful!" I may not want children, but my heart swells to think of Meg and David taking home three lucky little ones.

"Rose, they're the most wonderful kids..." She stares off into space, dreamy. "Siblings. Old enough that they were in danger of being split up or not adopted at all. We just love them."

"I bet you two will be amazing parents." I can picture it. She and David have great energy and warmth. "I'm so happy for you all."

She gives me a blinding smile. "We asked the kids what they want to do for Memorial Day weekend. We thought maybe they'd say Disney World or the beach or something, but they said they want to go camping! We checked the weather report and it's supposed to be nice. So David and I went and got a family tent and some more sleeping bags last night. God, we're so thrilled." She shimmies in excitement.

I squeeze her hand. "I love how happy you are. What a great family you'll be!"

"Actually, that was all a long lead-up to a question I have for you. What are your plans for the weekend?"

I'd forgotten about the holiday. I've got no plans. Nobody to cook for, nobody to talk to, nobody besides me to make noise in that whole house. July's going to her parents' condo in Florida. Sabina said I should come over, but she's booked solid the whole week and I'm not going to impose. I've got no plans at all. "Nothing special." I aim for a casual tone. "I'll just take it easy. Float around the pool. Do some reading. Relax."

"I want you to come with us." Meg's voice is firm. "You can use our little tent. We'll set it all up for you and you'll have some privacy and be perfectly snug. We'll cook over the fire—I'm telling you, no food ever tasted so good as David's camp cooking!—and roast marshmallows, and David will play his guitar for us… We'll play cards, and you can bring your books and go off by yourself whenever you like."

She touches my arm. "Please come. It would mean a lot to me."

Damn, that's sweet. "You all don't need me butting in on your first family holiday together. I'm practically a stranger to David, and I don't know the kids at all."

"You and I are going to get really close over the coming months, Rose. Let's go ahead and spend a holiday together. David and I are building our family and the kids could use another good aunt." She seems completely sincere, her eyes clear, her voice warm.

I'm surprised at just how interested I am. I've never camped and never expected to be an aunt, but neither sounds unpleasant. "Okay." Apparently loneliness makes me easy. "On one condition."

Meg beams. "Anything."

"I'll bake desserts and breads for the weekend."

"That sounds fabulous, Rose. Oh, this will be fun!" She practically skips out of the office.

I sit smiling after her for a long time.

What a relief, not to have to spend those days alone.

What will Angus be doing? I wish he could come with me. I hope he has somewhere to go and somebody to be with for the holiday. Lenny or somebody. Not another woman. I'm not that generous. I just don't want him to be alone.

Call me, Angus. My first prayer in…forever.

That night I run into Lenny at the grocery. He's frowning, staring at the cold beer selection, package of hot dogs in one hand, rubbing his head with the other.

I move to stand beside him. "Are we pissed at the ales or the lagers?"

He jumps. "Oh, hey, Rose. I was just wondering which goes with hot dogs." He sighs. "I'm so sick of hot dogs."

"Been a while since you've had a decent meal?"

"Yeah. Can't remember the last one. Yeah, I can—It was at your house."

I sigh too. "I don't cook much anymore. Wanna go try that new barbecue place? Beats eating hot dogs alone."

Half an hour later we're sitting in a no-frills, concrete-floored barbecue joint, eating pulled pork and coleslaw and onion rings at a picnic table covered with red-checkered plastic, sampling all the barbecue sauces and arguing over which is best.

"Our grumpy friend showed up out of the blue last week," Lenny says around a mouthful of cornbread.

"Yeah?" I try not to appear desperate for news.

"He sat facing the TV while Chris and I watched the game, but I bet he couldn't have told you a single play afterwards. Or the score. Or who was playing. Or, you know, which sport."

"Yeah?" I have got to come up with a better response.

"You know, we played football together in high school, me and Angus and James and Rashad."

I peer at an onion ring before taking a bite. "I believe Angus mentioned that."

"He probably could've gotten a free ride to college if he'd

wanted. He was good enough and big enough and a natural leader." Lenny digs a pickle out from under his meat. "He was team captain junior and senior years. Really unusual for a junior to be voted captain."

I stop feigning casualness. "Really? But you all picked Angus?"

He nods. "Yep. He was the clear choice."

I toy with my onion ring. "Why?"

He jabs a forkful of slaw. "First year, most of us freshmen on the team are scrawny, terrified, afraid to open our mouths 'cause we don't really want to be noticed, right? We're just in survival mode, trying to get through the drills and not get killed. Not embarrass ourselves. So this one day the first week, we come into the locker room after practice, and the biggest meanest senior on the team has one of the freshmen cornered in the shower, picking on him and screaming at him, just for fun. Just to terrify him. Guy's known to be a real asshole, so it's nothing unusual for him. But the freshman's about to wet himself, he's so scared. Senior reaches out and grabs him by the balls, and that's it. Next thing I know Angus is over there in the senior's face, telling him to cut that shit out."

Yeah, I can totally see Angus doing that.

"The senior can't believe a lowly freshmen would talk to him like that. Angus is already pretty tall—six foot, maybe?—but hasn't filled out yet, so the senior has about fifty pounds on him. The senior drops that other kid and turns on Angus. Another senior grabs Angus and holds him and the first one starts hitting him. Angus jerks loose and gets a few good shots in at both of them, but he's definitely losing. Then somebody hollers that the coaches are coming and everybody pretends like nothing happened. Angus goes into the shower and washes off the blood so nobody gets in trouble. Afterwards all the freshmen are like, 'Dude, they coulda killed you. Why'd you do that?' Angus looks surprised. Says, 'Why didn't you?' Next day he's all bruised and sore, but he doesn't gripe about it. Same senior corners another kid in the shower and damned if Angus doesn't get up in his face again. The senior turns around real slow with this smirk, and his asshole friend steps up beside him...and then James steps up next to Angus, and Rashad and me and the other freshmen are right with them this time. The senior acts disgusted, like he's too good to bother with a bunch of freshmen, but the hazing ended that day, 'cause of Angus."

When Lenny shakes himself out of the memory, I'm mopping my eyes with a paper towel from the dowel in the middle of the table.

"Shit, Rose, I'm trying to make you feel good about him, not make you cry!"

"I fucked up, Lenny." I sniffle and wipe my nose. "He's the best man I'm ever going to know, and I fucked up."

"What'd you do, Rosie?"

Rosie. It's all I can do not to wail.

"I...kept a secret from him because I was scared it would mess up our relationship. He figured it out, and I think he's hurt that I didn't tell him." I can barely meet his eye. "I had...some money he didn't know about. It seemed to kind of freak him out when he found out. I'm not sure whether it was the money that did it or me keeping it secret. Maybe both." I shrug, helpless. "I don't have it anymore, but it's too late. I hurt him and he's gone."

Lenny frowns down at the onion ring he's dragging through a lake of ketchup. "Did you know Angus is kind of a scorekeeper?"

Without even thinking about it, I say, "No, he's not. He's the least selfish person I know."

Lenny nods. "He's a backwards scorekeeper. He's not interested in whether other people are doing their share. He's busy trying to make sure *he* does more than his share. Always trying to put more good into the world to make up for stuff he thinks he's done wrong."

Yeah, I can see that. I nod.

Lenny's not done. "He ever tell you about his grandparents?"

"Some. They sound like wonderful people."

"They were the best. I think they fed half the football team two or three times a week. You have any idea how much a high school football team can eat? And they weren't wealthy by any means. His grandma always pretended she was asking us over 'cause we were friends and teammates of Angus, but somehow it was always the kids who didn't have enough food at home. I was one of them. Wasn't unusual for them to have two or three extra kids crashing on their couch or floor either, whenever things got ugly at home for us."

His smile is small and bittersweet. "I think Angus's family saved some lives. I know for a fact they gave us a better example of how to act than we got from our own families. Angus's grandma would hear about somebody needing help, and she'd do whatever—buy whatever, give away whatever—to get them that help, and Angus's grandpa would just quietly pick up an extra job or two to pay for it. Never occurred to either one of them to do anything any different. That's who shaped Angus."

I'm unable to speak.

"Rosie, I don't think Angus is comfortable when he's not

sure he's doing his share. Is there any way he might've thought that you were doing more—or giving more—than he was?"

"What? No!" But—shit. The grant money. Angus would have no way of returning that favor. I sigh. "Yeah, maybe."

Lenny nods. "That'd make him pretty miserable."

We talk about lighter things as we finish dinner. I tease him about being prom queen.

"On account of my glorious hair," he says, patting his orange frizz. I laugh.

He gives me a one-armed hug as we part ways. "Rosie, if ever anybody deserved to be happy, it's Angus. I've never seen him as happy as he was with you. I hope y'all work this out."

I stand beside Lillian, watching Lenny cross the lot to his car.

I hadn't planned to go after Angus to make him talk to me. I don't want to chase somebody who doesn't want me.

But so help me, if that man is staying away because of some stupid imaginary score on some stupid imaginary scorecard, he's going to hear from me about it.

If he hasn't come around by Memorial Day, I'm going to hunt his ass down.

CHAPTER 33

Angus

I'M SO GRATEFUL FOR DAVID'S Memorial Day weekend invite I almost break down and cry like a big old baby. My alternatives were to stay home alone—the idea of one more second of that makes me want to puke—or fly to Vegas with Lenny and Chris. And I hate glitter and noise. And crowds. And losing money.

My only regret, as I help David put up tents, is that I wasn't able to catch Rose at home this week. Stopped by several times but she was never there. Maybe she's on a trip somewhere? Maybe using that passport without me. Goddammit.

But I hope she's doing *some*thing fun this weekend. Hate to think of her all alone.

David and Meg's kids are pretty cool. The littlest one, Melly, comes over and looks up at me, squinting against the bright sky. "Are you a giant?"

"Naw, just tall."

"What can you see from up there?"

"Wanna see? I'll bend down. You can climb up on my shoulders. When I stand back up, you'll be even taller than me."

"Yeah! I'll be taller than Text and Julian and Ruby too!"

"Yep."

So we do, and when I stand back up, Melly squeals. "Hey!" she yells at her big brother and sister. "Hey, you little people! Look at me! I can see everything!"

In a minute, the other kids are hopping around us and David's asking whether she can see their house in town. Wheels crunch on gravel behind us. Meg pulls up about ten yards away in a spiffy Subaru SUV. I barely have time to register that someone's with her before Melly clamors to be let down so she can "go see Herc." I duck my head and lift her down.

"Who're Text and Herc?" I ask David as the kids surround the car. The oldest, Julian, moves a little stiffly but seems just as excited as his sisters.

"Nicknames for me and Meg. Long story." David moves toward the SUV.

I follow but pull up short. That's Rose stepping out of the passenger side.

What is it people say? *All the feelz*? I'm blasted with them. Relief, hurt, happiness, uncertainty, excitement, nervousness... But anger is missing.

Rose glances my way and her eyes widen. My own feelings are mirrored on her face.

My turncoat body carries me to her. I stop a few feet away.

Her hair's a little longer. Faint circles under her eyes, but otherwise she looks like my Rosie, in jeans and a giant—is that *my* T-shirt? Yep. Woman's richer than god and she's wearing my castoffs.

"Hi." The word sticks on the way out of my mouth.

"Hi."

"You're a busy lady."

She doesn't answer, just raises her brows.

"I've...stopped by a few times. Could never catch you at home."

Her eyes flicker away and I can't read her expression. "I wish I had known you were coming," she says finally. "I'd have been there."

"So you're...so they invited... Are you staying the weekend?"

"Yeah. You?" Her fingers toy with the too-long hem of that shirt.

I nod. "Explains the tent mystery."

"There's a tent mystery?"

I wave toward the small tents about fifty feet away. "We put up my tent and that other one near the fire pit, but then the kids wanted us to put the big family tent up here inside the foundation for their new house. I wondered what the extra was for." I duck my head. "Figured maybe it was a honeymooners' getaway tent, but then why would David put it right by mine?"

She frowns. "We've been set up?"

"Big time." Our tents are within arm's reach of each other. Be torture to listen to her slow night breathing and not be able to touch her.

"Well." She stares at her sneakers. "This is potentially awkward."

Takes me a minute to decide on an answer. "Potentially. But I'm happy to see you."

She flashes me a glance and a tiny soft smile. "Me too."

We separate then, to help unload the car, distributing sleeping bags and pillows and lanterns among the tents. Set up a folding food table and camp chairs and a grill between the cars and the fire pit. The coolers and food stay in the cars, safe from bears.

"That's you, Rose." Meg points to the small tent closest to the fire pit.

Everyone stows their personal stuff in the appropriate tents.

Then Rose brings out homemade cinnamon rolls, still warm, smelling like heaven, and they're a huge hit. We descend on them like locusts, even though it's afternoon and we'll be eating our main meal soon.

Then the kids explore the clearing while we adults prepare the big meal. I gather firewood and kindling and lay a fire. Meg peels and cuts potatoes, and Rose chops peppers and onions to be cooked with the potatoes in foil packets. David rigs up a system to rotisserie a couple of chickens on a spit. We call the kids back for the ceremonial lighting of the fire, and while the food cooks, we play gin rummy at the table. Ruby and Melly and Rose have never played before, so there's a lot of explanation and laughter and G-rated trash talk.

Rose and I don't touch or talk or even sit next to each other during the game, but I'm aware of her every move. Her laughter. Her hair brushing soft on her shoulders. The curve of one pink cheek as she smiles. Her hands quick and graceful with the cards.

Part of me is enjoying this day. Another part wants to skip ahead several hours, in hopes we'll get a chance to talk alone. I don't expect much. Be enough just to get past this stage of not knowing where we stand.

Meal's a success. Meg sets out a cold salad made with broccoli and carrots and raisins, and Rose passes around fresh baguettes and butter.

She seems surprised at my homemade guacamole. I brought drinks too. Earn myself a wobbly smile from her when I hand her a Coke still icy from the cooler and whisper, "If I'd known you were going to be here, I'd even have brought you a straw."

After the main part of the meal, Meg and Rose and I relax while David plays freeze tag with the kids. Rose's eyes follow the boy, who moves with slight hesitance and stiffness. "Meg, did you tell me Julian's recovering from some kind of accident?"

Meg nods. "Yeah, he was hit by a car. He was in a coma and had some broken bones. Both legs and one arm. He's only been out of his casts for about a month. Making great progress though. The doctors say he'll recover completely."

Rose shakes her head. "Kids' healing powers are amazing."

She watches Julian feint away, laughing as David tries to tag him. "He seems like a really nice boy. Will it make him achy to sleep outside this weekend?"

"To tell the truth, we're not sure, but he wanted to try. We brought him an air mattress and a good sleeping bag, so I *think* between that and his age he'll be okay." Meg eyes her new family with a misty smile.

Pretty sure Rose notices. Her eyes mist a little too.

She's baked more amazing stuff. After freeze tag she brings out apple pie to go with melty ice cream from a metal thermos. We demolish it. Then half of us clean and bear-proof the campsite, washing dishes and packing away all traces of food and trash, while the rest of us use the last hour of daylight to stock up on firewood and kindling for tonight and tomorrow. After dark, we roast marshmallows and make s'mores. Brush our teeth using a jug of water Meg and David brought for washing up.

Rose is clearly nervous about having to relieve herself in the woods, but she's a hell of a good sport. She's smiling as we settle in around the fire. It's getting chilly. If things were still good between us, she'd be cuddling up to me, letting me warm her. Now she grabs a sweatshirt from her tent. Sits with her back against a big smooth rock. I'm a few feet away, trying not to pay too much obvious attention to her. Ruby—the middle child—is on her other side staring into the flames, mesmerized.

"Have you ever been camping before, Ruby?" Rose asks.

Ruby regards her seriously. "No, this is my first time."

"Mine too."

"Really?"

"Yep. What's your favorite thing about it so far?"

Ruby frowns in thought. "Well, I like the food. And the fire. And the smells of everything. And playing games. But mostly I guess I like being here with everybody."

Rose nods. "Yeah, I get that. Everything else is good, but the people make it great." She catches me nodding as she turns her face back to the fire.

Meg and David talk about tomorrow—weather forecast, the menu, games we can play, a hike around the property boundaries—and then Meg says, "Babe. You know you're not going to get out of playing for us, right?"

David squeezes her knee, gives her a kiss, and fetches his guitar case from the car. "Y'all have to sing too. What do you want me to play?"

The kids watch his every move as he tunes the guitar. They mainly know songs they learned at school. Couple of folk songs, a patriotic song. Rosie's mouth moves—yeah, of course I'm watching that—but I can't hear her voice.

David teaches us a round and everybody tries to keep it going through four full verses, but it's absolute chaos and laughter by the third. Little Melly requests a Christmas song. Then David plays a lullaby, his voice mellow and low, and it works magic. The kids cuddle up to Meg and to each other, their eyelids drooping. A few soft songs later and all three of them are sound asleep.

David puts the guitar away and comes back to pick up Ruby. Meg takes Melly and follows him, and then David returns for Julian. "Meg and I are going to turn in too. Pretty sure the kids'll wake us up at the crack of dawn. So, good night. Angus, you'll take care of the fire before you go to sleep?"

"Mm-hm."

"'Night. Please tell Meg good night from me." Rose gestures to include me and the small tents. "And that we see what you all did here."

David grins like the lucky man he is and helps Julian back to the big tent.

Rose fidgets, watching them go. Tucks her knees up, pulls the sweatshirt down over them, locks her fingers around them.

I break our silence. "This was a nice day."

She meets my eye. Nods.

"You want to talk?"

"Yeah." She doesn't look happy that her voice comes out quavery. "You haven't told me what you're most upset about. I'm still really sorry though."

A log snaps and I focus on the flames. "I keep having this dream. We're at your house and it's morning. I kiss you goodbye and go off to work, and after I leave, you close the door and press a hidden latch. Opens up a secret part of the house. Everything in it is white, modern, not like the rest of the house. You spend the day in there doing mysterious stuff I've never seen you do. Never even knew you could do."

She shifts and I turn to face her. "In there, you're a different person than you are in the rest of the house with me. Right before I get back from work, you come out into the regular part of the house and close away the secret part. You smile and kiss me hello and act like the Rose I know. And in the dream, I don't know anything about the secret rooms. I'm just this big, ignorant, oblivious fool who doesn't know who I'm living with or what's going on under my own nose. I'm feeling good because I've brought you a little flower, and I don't know there's a whole greenhouse garden in the secret part of the house."

Her brow furrows, she's listening so hard. She's beautiful in the firelight, her eyes dark, her skin glowing. The space between us seems wrong, an impossible mistake.

Her forehead wrinkles. "Angus, you know pretty much everything I did. I called the money people in Indianapolis once a week. I met with Meg. Gave away little bits here and there when I saw someone who needed something. That's all. Nothing else I did was any different than what you knew about. School, cooking, sometimes lunch with Sabina or July. Did you want a list of my activities? You don't seem like a control freak."

I shake my head fast. "No. Nah. Of course not. I think the dream was about me worrying that if you kept secrets, you must be somebody different than I thought. Somebody fooling me. A stranger."

Always before when she's acted angry with me, it's been

just that. Playacting. But now she's genuinely pissed. Hands clenched, sparks in her eyes. "That's bullshit, Angus." Her words are hard as bullets. "I may have failed to enumerate my assets, but I *never. Once.* Lied to you about who I am."

I don't know what to do with a truly angry Rose. I think she's right—she is who I thought she was, basically, but this new side of her is an unknown quantity. "I'm beginning to see that. I was just hurt you didn't trust me enough to tell me."

Her face crumples, her outrage draining away. "I was a chicken. I underestimated you. Lumped you in with the people in Indy. I'm sorry."

Woman can't hold a grudge to save her life. She's only a few feet away. I could scoop her up and pull her onto my lap, comfort her. No sense both of us feeling bad.

I shake my head instead. "It hurts, yeah, but I can see why you'd worry. Turned out bad for you last time. I get that. But I hope you know now you could have trusted me."

She sighs. Hunches further over her knees. Gives a tiny nod.

I shift, uncomfortable on this cold hard ground. "I'd be lying if I said you being rich and me just having an average income didn't bother me. July said, 'That's some sexist bullshit you've got going on there.' She's right. I know. I don't think it's all sexism though."

I hold her gaze. "It's the main thing that's still bothering me. In my head we had a certain kind of relationship and I knew my role. Knew what I had to offer. I felt...valuable. But when I found out about the money, it meant my ideas about our relationship were skewed. And that meant my role was different, but I didn't know how. Didn't have a single idea what rich Alice Rose Barnes needed. No way of knowing whether it was anything I could give. I didn't feel valuable anymore; I felt... stupid." My words scrape like gravel. "Unnecessary. Ridiculous for ever thinking you might need me."

Her dark eyes widen. "Oh, Angus. I am so sorry. I had no idea. I am so sorry I made you feel that way. That is not how I see you at all."

I scrub a hand through my hair. "You didn't *make* me. But yeah, that's the part I'm still struggling with."

CHAPTER 34

Angus

IT'S A RELIEF TO FINALLY get all that out, even though I don't know what'll come of saying it. How it could make anything better. In the firelight she doesn't *look* like a stranger. She looks like my Rosie.

That sweatshirt she's wearing is soft from many washings, and she's always sweet and cuddly in it. *Come over here. Sit with me. Hold me. Let me hold you.* But she doesn't.

It takes her a minute to speak, and when she does, her voice shakes. "Can I help? What can I do? Can I…? How can I help you see how valuable you are to me?"

The idea makes my brain squirm. "Rose, even if you tried to tell me, I don't know that I could really…feel it. I don't trust my own judgment anymore. Everything I thought was so wrong."

She leans forward, reaching out and then pulling back her hand without touching me. "What was wrong exactly? What had you thought?"

I huff a laugh. "I thought you were having money problems.

Thought as soon as you trusted me enough to tell me, I could help you out."

She sits back and looks at me oddly. "But...money never had anything to do with anything I wanted from you. I told you more than once I didn't need money. Didn't you believe me?"

I wave that off. "I thought that was you being stubborn. You're independent. I thought you didn't think you should ask for help."

She frowns. "You were fine with the idea that I was in money trouble?"

"Yeah." I shrug. "I can help with something like that."

"But once you figured out I was rich, you weren't fine? You weren't relieved to learn I wasn't having trouble after all?"

Well, hell, when she puts it like that... I frown too.

"What the fuck, Angus? You need me to need saving? Is that what we were about for you? A white hat opportunity? You only want me when I'm the little fat chick who's bad with money and needs to learn to like sex? What the actual fuck, Angus."

Little fat chick? Sex? What do those have to do with anything? "Rose, what are you talking about?"

Her turn to wave me off. "Never mind. Do you or do you not prefer me when you think I'm broken in some way? Is that why you think I wanted you—because I needed you to fix me?"

I spread my hands, at sea. "Broken? Rosie, no. I was never sure *what* you needed from me. Money was the one thing I thought I'd finally identified. My way to contribute. Otherwise...I was practically living in your house. I'd taken a paycheck from you for weeks. You were cooking for me and buying groceries and I just..."

I'm talking fast, trying to make her understand. "And when I figured out you'd funded our grant... One more thing I owed you for, only I would never even have known about it, so I could never have paid it back. I have trouble seeing what I added to the picture."

She gapes at me. "Oh my god, Angus. You gave me so much that was worth more than those things. Do you *really* not know that?"

She raises a hand to stop me when I try to answer. Drops her face, shakes her head. "Think about this, then. What exactly have I contributed to *your* life? That grant? I was funding a worthwhile project—something I wanted to see done too—and trying to keep my privacy at the same time. *Not* trying to chalk up some kind of relationship IOU. Yeah, you were at my house a lot, but not because you were sponging off me. You've got that nice little house of your own. You were with me because I wanted you there. Yeah, you got a paycheck for your skilled labor, most of it before we were together. I benefited. Yeah, I cooked for us, because it was something I wanted to learn anyway, and because it's a whole lot more fun to cook for more than one person. I was thrilled whenever you agreed to share something I made. And in return you did all the cleanup, *and* you bought a ton of groceries."

She pins me with a look. "So, if you weren't adding anything valuable to our relationship, then I wasn't either. Is that how you feel? I don't even get it, Angus. How can such a smart, sensitive person like you not see how much more important stuff we had?"

Tears clog her voice as she pushes to her feet. "Were we just about money and buildings and food to you? Do you really have no fucking idea how bleak my life used to be, and how much being with you changed that?"

With that quiet parting shot, she steps wide around me, as if touching me would kill her. She tears open her tent flap and climbs in, the sound of the zipper's metal teeth biting the air as she jerks it closed behind her.

Well. That went well.

I stare at the fire, dumbfounded. It's an eternity before I can finally make my way to my own tent. Everything is now so fucked up I don't even know how to think about it.

Shit. The campfire.

I turn back to take care of it and find I've got a perfect view of Rose's silhouette against the backdrop of the flames.

She can't know that from this angle her tent walls are practically transparent. She probably thinks she has privacy. She's cross-legged, elbows on her knees and head in her hands. Motionless. I'm frozen too, watching. What is she thinking? What does she need? After that hellish conversation, I should probably know, but I've got no clue.

Finally she straightens. Swipes her fingers across her cheeks. I imagine I can hear her sigh. She opens her sleeping bag, unzips her jeans, and raises her bottom to slide them down and off her legs.

Angus, turn the fuck around. I'm a damn pervert for looking and for growing hard, but I can't move.

She slips off her sweatshirt. Pulls my T-shirt over her head. When she reaches behind her back and unhooks and removes her bra, I see the outline of her full breast against the flames, see her nipple peak in the cool air of the tent.

A decent man wouldn't stand here staring. But we've established what kind of man I am.

She shifts, sliding into the sleeping bag, and lies back against her pillow, arms bent over her face.

Every fiber of me wants to go to her, take her in my arms, and comfort her. To lift her hands and hold them while I kiss her sweet face.

Somewhere in my brain, a memory rises and speaks in Rosie's low, no-nonsense voice. *I believed my body was disgusting. I disgusted myself. Never even tried to make myself feel good. Didn't imagine I could... So this, with you, is a gift...* And another time, when I was just holding her: *Thank you for showing me what this is supposed to be like.* She's said she trusts me with her body and her feelings. Told me she loves me a million different times, a million different ways. I remember her shy, wordless invitation when she gave the keys back to me the day of our first kiss. All the days and nights we made love, laughing at the same time. The way it feels to work beside her, to bicker and squabble over music and food without ever losing affection or humor. To talk to her and learn another little piece of her past, the stories that make Rose Rosie. Lazy Sundays we spent together doing exactly and only what we both felt like doing. Eighty million precious moments having nothing to do with money or with trying to earn anything—having only to do with enjoying and caring for each other. She's never asked for more than that.

Maybe that really *is* all she needs.

And... I can do that. I *want* to do that.

And so when Rose rolls to her side, curls up, draws the sleeping bag over her head, and begins to shake, I do.

Rose

I didn't think anyone could hear me crying, but there's movement outside my tent.

"Rosie." Angus, his whisper sounding broken.

He called me Rosie.

I choke out a watery, "Yeah?"

"Can I come in?"

Why not. Might as well give the big jerk the rest of my heart, to go with the chunk he already has. "Yeah."

He unzips the flap and eases himself in, re-zipping behind him and finding me in the dark. He draws me into the magnet of his arms. "Shh," he whispers into my hair as I press my wet face to his throat. "I'm sorry, Rosie. I didn't mean to underestimate what we have, what we give each other. I'm sorry."

He clasps me tighter and rocks me. "The hole in my life since we broke up doesn't have a goddamn thing to do with money. It's…not seeing your smile when I come in at the end of the day. Not having your arms around me. Not having you to talk to me or make me laugh."

"I know." I whisper it into his neck. "Love you."

He buries his face in my hair. "I love you too."

And shameless floozy that I am, I need instant consummation of our reconciliation.

When I tug impatiently at his sweatshirt and the buttons of his flannel shirt and the zipper of his jeans so I can reach his warm skin, he gasps, "Rosie, are you still on the pill?" and when I answer, "I hadn't given up on you yet," he surges into me, the hot hard slide of him filling me. And as we cling and rock together in perfect reunion, I know *he* knows he matters to me in ways money never will.

Afterward, entwined with him, his hands locked at the small of my back, I trace his features in the dark. "Angus. I need to tell you how you make my life better."

He opens his mouth to speak but I press a finger to his lips.

"I don't think it would be easy for a normal person to picture just how alone I was before I came to Galway. The people I worked with raced home as soon as they got off work, because they had families or boyfriends or parties or school. My apartment neighbors were always changing and always busy trying to make ends meet. I was on okay terms with everybody, but we didn't socialize. Except for Mr. Brown, I didn't have a single soul I considered a friend."

He wraps his hand around mine and holds it.

I brush my foot over his shin. "I would work and go to the library and read, and that was it. I had fantasies about things I'd do if I had a 'real life,' but it was enough of a challenge just to pay the bills. I never actually did any of those things. I just read about them. I couldn't even afford a cat, so sometimes I left the TV on for hours, just to hear voices."

He cups my head and kisses my temple. I trace his ear with one finger and he shivers.

"So then all the stuff with Mr. Brown and the money happens, and I leave Indiana looking for someplace to start over. Maybe start on that 'real life' I'd imagined but never really believed in. And one day when I need help in a snowstorm, I meet this big wild-looking man. He's damn cranky and he doesn't like me, but he helps me anyway."

His lips curve up under my fingers. No self-respecting cranky man should smile so easily.

"I find Sabina's B and B, and she's kind and wonderful and she gives me a room that feels like a lovely cocoon. I go to town to get a warmer coat and I discover July's, and that feels like another lovely haven. And I start spending time in those two places, and all of a sudden, I have friends. I have a home. And then I start to feel like you and I are friends too."

I wrap one of his curls around my finger. "And then, after more than fifteen years of my body being, like, asleep, you woke me up. Angus, you were the first person I ever felt any kind of desire for. The first person I ever voluntarily kissed or touched. That experience in high school stunted me—forever, I thought—but you replaced it. You gave me this whole new experience of my body and relationships, and it was built around caring and pleasure and love rather than...using somebody."

I splay my hand over his heart to feel the strong, reassuring beat there. "I hope you hear what I'm saying, Angus. I'd lost all hope of any kind of intimacy when I was sixteen. Sixteen. I thought if I lived to be ninety-six, the last eighty years of my life would be spent alone, with no one to touch and no one who would want to be with me. You opened up a whole big part of life I'd thought was closed off to me forever. And it turns out I really, really love this when you're in it with me. In my whole life, I'd never felt so safe or so loved or so...hopeful."

His arms tighten around me and his mouth finds mine. His cheeks are damp. It's a long time before he speaks. His voice is gruff when he does.

"You're such a natural at this stuff I forget it's new to you." He rubs his forehead against mine. "Last couple of years I was married, I was trying so hard to survive I didn't have anything to offer anybody else. I was this—husk of a person. My poor wife, she tried to fill me back up, but I stayed empty. I had nothing to give."

"Thing is, that wasn't a new feeling for me." His voice softens in my ear. "I have a memory of my mom yelling at my grandma, 'I didn't even *want* a kid! He's ruining my life!' I don't know if that really happened, but it's clear in my head that I wasn't good for her. And what good was I to my army buddies? And then, when I came back wrecked, I'm pretty sure the worry took a couple of years off my grandparents' lives. So I'm always, like, afraid I'm using up more good than I put into the world."

He closes his eyes for a long moment. "After Sandy left, I didn't even try for any kind of relationship deeper than sex. Couple of years of that and I was so used to being alone I didn't even seek sex very often. When I pictured the future, there was never a partner for me in it. Couldn't shake that feeling I didn't have anything to offer."

"With you, I can see different now. But I guess the belief I was empty had rooted pretty deep." He rubs one knuckle along my cheek. "Guess I...played up the hairy giant image to keep people away. And then here you come, all sassy and funny and sexy, refusing to be scared off, and...you got to me, Rosie."

He kisses me again, the big muscles of his shoulders and arms bunching as he rises over me in the dark tent, entering me, thrusting deep and slow, gripping my hips as I rise to meet him, my hands on the strong column of his neck, my eyes on his as we move together, our heartbeats and breath mingling.

Later he goes to put out the fire and comes back with his sleeping bag so we can lie with one under us and one over. He gathers me close and holds me until morning.

I never imagined a tent could feel so much like a home.

CHAPTER 35

Rose

IT'S NOT QUITE FULL LIGHT. From nearby I hear birds and, across the clearing, the occasional child's voice. Very carefully so as not to wake Angus, I turn in his arms to watch him sleep. His spiky lashes flutter against his cheek as he dreams. I'm thinking about pressing my mouth to his when his eyes open. Clear turquoise, focusing on my face and then warming, crinkling at the edges. He smiles. "Rosie." His voice is soft.

"This is the best thing ever, Angus. Waking up next to you." I kiss him then. Tender kisses. A statement of my joy.

He smooths his hands down over my back and pulls me closer. "That one of the kids I hear?" he rumbles.

"At least one." If he keeps kissing me, my bones will turn completely liquid.

"And we're naked in here together."

"Yup."

"We gonna scandalize anybody?"

"Well, probably, if we go out there like this. Especially you."

“Me? Why me?”

“Well, I can’t help but notice that you are hard.” I nudge him very gently with my knee. “Like, Mommy-why-does-their-tent-have-an-extra-pole hard.”

He snorts. “Yeah, I had noticed that too.”

I ease over on top of him, careful not to touch the sides of the tent. “I can’t let you go out like that. Child welfare is at stake.” I’m whispering, wrapping my hand around him and taking him into my body.

“Ohh…” he breathes, his sigh echoing mine. “You think we can do this without rocking the tent?” His eyes telegraph how much he wants me to say yes.

“Let’s try.”

Later, he watches, his eyes at half mast, a lazy smile on his lips as I wrestle a wet wipe out of the package. “Rosie, I think you’re part dolphin. Or maybe otter. You’re not supposed to be able to move like that. I think you should get your spine checked. For science.”

“You think I need to get that fixed?” I root around for my bra.

“God no. Leave everything just the way it is. It’s the best thing ever. You’re right, waking up together is the best thing ever.” He watches me dress, his fingertips brushing each section of my skin gently just before I cover it.

“Yeah, about that ‘best thing ever.’ I’ve changed my mind.”

“You saying it’s *not* waking up with me?” His frown is ferocious but fleeting as Smug Angus makes an appearance. “Oh. You mean what we just did?”

“Sorry, that was great, but no.” I lean over to give him a quick kiss. “It’s indoor plumbing. These wet wipe thingies just don’t cut it.”

"Well, hell," he mutters, sitting up and reaching for his own clothes. "Get my broken heart repaired and then re-broken again in the space of eight hours."

"I'm sorry." I wrap my arms around him. "You're a really close second."

He topples me into his lap. Spends several minutes kissing me and tickling me and insisting I admit that the best thing is, in fact, waking up next to him.

"Alright! Alright!" I half-yell, laughing, unzipping the tent, and staggering out. "I give! It's you."

Meg and David and the kids are puttering around putting food on the table and building a new fire. "Are you arguing with that tall man?" Melly asks.

I straighten my sweatshirt, ignoring Meg and David's enormous grins, and aim for dignity. "We are having a disagreement, yes."

"What about?" Ruby asks.

I wait hopefully for David or Meg to tell the kid to mind her own business, but they just look at me too, their eyebrows raised in unholy interest.

"About what the best thing in the world is." I sound like a grumbly child myself.

"Surprise! It's me!" Angus leaps from the tent.

Meg's eyes go wide. David bursts out laughing at this totally un-Angus-like behavior.

"Indoor plumbing," I cough.

"What's that, Rosie?" Angus swaggers toward me with mock menace. Who *is* this guy?

I dash around to the other side of the table to escape him. "You're tied with indoor plumbing, you big bully!"

Now Meg and David's entire family is laughing.

Angus nods thoughtfully, pausing to look over the food. He pulls off a piece of leftover cinnamon roll and pops it into his mouth. "I can live with that."

"I think sweet rolls are the best thing," Melly says.

Julian shakes his head. "No, bacon."

Meg and David don't weigh in, but their arms steal around each other. They lean together, smiling at their kids and, I suspect, counting their blessings.

Angus

It's a great day.

After a hot breakfast—bacon and eggs and leftover cinnamon rolls—we all tromp around the property, locating the boundary markers. David and Meg show Rose and the kids the planned layout of the house and where each child's room will be. Takes them awhile to come down from their excitement.

A few cutthroat games of gin rummy, then we eat lunch. All through the day I find myself reaching for Rosie, to hold her hand, touch her hair, brush against her, and she's always right there reaching for me. Something deep inside me relaxes a little more with each contact.

After lunch cleanup, we sprawl around the fire. The kids stare glassy eyed into the flames, and David and Meg murmur quietly beside them, arms around each other. Rose cuddles up to me, her hand on my bent knee.

She tugs my earlobe. "Angus," she whispers, "do you have your heart set on staying all weekend?"

"Why, Rosie?" I brush a kiss to her temple.

"I would kill for my shower right now."

"Are you asking me to take you home?"

"Only if you don't mind staying there with me. If you want to stay here, I will too. I'll just stink. A lot."

My laughter stirs her hair. "You *do* love me, don't you?"

She kisses me. "I do."

I climb to my feet and pull her up beside me. "Ruby. Julian. Melly. Y'all think you can keep your folks out of trouble if Rosie and I leave you in charge here?"

Julian rouses himself from his campfire stupor. "Are y'all leaving?"

"Rosie's going on again about indoor plumbing. I'm pretty sure if I get her to her shower within the next hour or so, I've got a good chance at fresh hot cinnamon rolls in the morning."

The kids are in total sympathy with that.

I dismantle my tent and load it and my stuff into the van while Rose packs her things and rolls up the sleeping bags. She brought her baked goods in aluminum foil pans, so we leave all that with Meg and David and just take a bag of trash for disposal at home. When everything's packed, Rose gives Meg a big hug. "Thank you so much, for everything."

Meg hugs her back, winking at me over Rosie's shoulder. "David and I were afraid we might've had a hand in breaking something. We wanted to see if we could help fix it."

"You did good. I'll never forget this." Rose squeezes her again.

David stays quiet but lays a hand on my shoulder before raising it in a wave.

It feels comfortable and, at the same time, new to have Rosie in the seat beside me for the drive home. Like we've gone through a fire and come out the other side unsure what we'll find.

"How you doing, Rosie?" I take her hand as we turn onto the main road.

"Good. How do you feel?" She turns in her seat to face me.

I glance over, dead serious. "I feel like I'm going home."

"Will you stay with me?"

I don't ask whether she means for me to stay the day, stay overnight, stay for a lifetime… I just nod. "Yeah."

At her house, I pull up at the garage so we can dump the trash. As we cross the backyard to the house, my tight muscles loosen more. I step inside behind her, flip the locks shut, and wrap my arms around her shoulders.

She leans back against me with a big sigh. "There it is."

"What?"

"Home. It hasn't felt like that much lately." She kisses my forearm. "I am going to use the facilities and then take the world's longest steamiest shower."

I join her in the shower, working shampoo into her hair, soaping every bit of her, kissing each part as I turn her under the spray. She returns the favor. A few more kisses, and then I wrap her in a big towel and carry her to the bed.

"I didn't believe anybody really did this," she says, looking up at me from my arms. "Sure didn't think anybody would do it with me."

I grin down at her, and then notice the bright quilt and sheets. "You've changed things."

"The others felt too lonely without you." She touches my face as I lay her down. "I'll put them back on if you want."

"They don't matter, Rosie. Just you." I follow her down.

EPILOGUE

Six months later

ANGUS IS DOING THAT THING again. The one that makes me lose my mind.

It's the night before Thanksgiving, we've got somewhere upwards of twenty people coming for dinner tomorrow, and he's "helping" in the kitchen. Wearing a Henley. With the sleeves pushed up. As he sorts and washes and chops vegetables.

How. The Fuck. Am I supposed to get anything done with all that sinewy flexing of tendons and muscles and whatnot?

I set down my knife and fold my hands on the countertop. "Angus."

"Hm? Hey, I've been thinking about July, wondering what's up with her. We should pay extra attention to her tomorrow, see if she seems all right." He frowns down at the potato he's holding, turning it over and over so that his forearms…

Oh, for the love of god. We can talk about July later. "Angus!"

His head comes up, his Caribbean eyes widening at my tone. "You okay, Rosie?"

"Remember a couple of months ago when we were standing in this very kitchen and I officially asked you to move in with me, and without a word you took off out the back door like a shot?"

His brow crinkles. "You make it sound terrible."

"Like. A. Shot, Angus..."

"Rosie, I was back in thirty seconds."

"...leaving me feeling abandoned and alone..."

"With a *ring*, Rosie. I was back in thirty seconds *with a ring*." He puts down his own knife and steps into my space, crowding me against the kitchen island.

I push on, despite my understandable breathlessness. "Do you remember what happened next?"

He picks me up like it's nothing, carries me around to the other side of the island, and sets me down in a clear space between serving dishes. "Hell, yeah. Not every day a man goes down on his knee to propose." He lowers his forehead to mine and scowls. Ferocious.

I shiver with—well, not fear.

He growls that growl that makes my insides flip over and melt. "It's also not every day a man gets knocked on his ass by his future wife in the middle of the kitchen."

I trail my thumbs along the warm skin at the edges of the button placket of his Henley. "It was more of a tackle, Angus. I would never hit you. And I had a purpose. Do you remember?"

His frown clears and a dimple appears in his right cheek. "I remember. Is that what this is about?" He nudges my knees apart and steps in closer, his hands cradling my hips.

"Yeah. I'm gonna need us to do that again."

"Right here?" His voice has dropped to gravel pit register.

I skim my hands down his chest. Hook my fingers in his belt loops. "Yeah."

"Right now?" He nuzzles my forehead, a tiny smile on his lips.

"Yeah." I kiss that smile, and I keep kissing him as he picks me back up and lowers us both to the floor.

"Marry me, Rosie," he murmurs, sliding his magic hands into my clothing, making it miraculously disappear.

"I did." It comes out on a gasp as his mouth finds my throat.

"Marry me, Rosie." He unfastens his jeans and slides into me as I wrap myself around him.

"Okay," I say on a long breath that sounds like a prayer.

"Marry me, Rosie," he says afterward, as we lie in each other's arms on the kitchen floor.

"I did, you big sweetie, and no matter how many times you ask, my answer's always going to be yes." I press a kiss to his shoulder and breathe in his scent. My favorite scent.

He takes my hand and traces my ruby heart ring and its companion, the plain gold band that matches the one on his finger. "No regrets?"

"Never." I speak that truth with everything in me.

"And no regrets about giving up the money?"

"Nope. Got my dream life right here. Don't need any more."

He wraps both arms around me and hugs me tight. "Sometimes you remind me of my grandma, Rosie."

Not going to admit it, but that's the nicest thing anyone has ever said to me. I clear my throat. "She and your grandpa spend a lot of time rolling around naked on the kitchen floor?"

Angus snatches his arms back and levers away, squeezing

his eyes shut, hands over his ears. “Hell, Rosie. Don’t say things like that!”

I sit up and reach for my shirt, laughing. “There you go, abandoning me again.”

He sits up and reaches for me. “Never, Rosie. Never.”

Read on for an excerpt of *Just the Way You Are*, the next book in the exciting small town of Galway, NC, featuring July's story—the big, strong woman who carries the world on her shoulders, and gives herself away taking care of everyone else…

CHAPTER 1

"YOU'RE A GOOD SON, JOE. I just...really wanted grandkids."

Okay. I guess we're done reading. I shove in the bookmark and set aside her battered copy of *Wuthering Heights*. Not that I mind—Heathcliff's an ass, which probably explains my mom's attraction to him—but I'm tired of this particular conversation.

Her voice isn't as thready or dreamy as when she's just cranked up the meds, though.

"You okay, Ma?"

She lifts one hand an inch off the bed. Waves it dismissively. "Why didn't you ever settle down?"

"Restless, I guess." Not entirely true until recently. I've been in Fort Collins for ten years, long enough to make a success of the restaurant and open a second in Loveland. Long enough for Dad to die and Mom to get sick.

She shakes her head, grimacing, her face grayer, her papery wrinkles deeper than last week. Deeper than yesterday. "No, no. In a relationship. There something you want to tell me?"

She means am I gay. We both know where she got *that* idea. Dad was fixated on it.

"Still not gay, Ma."

Her eyes open, pierce me. "Would you tell me if you were, Joey? Honestly. It's okay."

"Yeah, I would."

"Then why? Girls always liked you."

I shrug and look away. "Haven't found anybody I want that with."

"In a few years you'll be forty and I won't be around. I don't want you to be alone, Joe." She scratches at the sheet with a fingernail like she does when she's worried, and I pick up her hand.

"Better alone than in a bad relationship, Ma." That may be a little too much truth, given her choices.

Her grip weakens. "Hasn't there ever been anybody, though?"

I look into her watery eyes. "Not for twenty years, Ma. And I was wrong about her."

Her voice drops so low I can barely hear her. "You mean that girl in North Carolina."

I jerk my head in a nod. July. Girl as warm as her name.

Well, until she wasn't.

But suddenly I'm back at Galway Lake and her smile is shining down on me and the sun is making the water and the paler strands of her hair sparkle and I'm hit in the gut again with a rush of want and lust and yearning so strong it almost knocks me out of my chair.

Twenty fucking years and it's still that strong.

Last time I looked her up online it seemed she'd gotten her

dream. Opened a restaurant on the old town square. Filled it with loyal townies and tourists who give rave reviews. No pictures on the website of July herself, but the place and the menu look great.

I promised to help her try out recipes for that menu, back when we were kids and the restaurant was just a gleam in her eye. Guess she didn't need me.

I couldn't find her on social media except for the restaurant's Facebook page. Couldn't find a personal phone number for her, but her address is the same as the restaurant, and her last name hasn't changed.

Not that any of this matters. I'm not going to contact her. I'll never see her again. It's not like she'd remember me anyway.

Mom makes a tiny sound and when I look, her face is streaming with tears.

"Ma, what's wrong? What hurts?" I twist around, praying to see the Hospice worker Frances in the kitchen, but she's gone on her break. I'm half out of my chair, fumbling in my pocket for my phone, when Mom speaks again.

"'S'okay." She gestures to the tissues on the bedside table.

I pluck a bunch of them and dab at her face, her fragile state a terrifying reality in a way it wasn't a few minutes ago.

She takes the tissues and squeezes them into a ball, gripping them like she needs to hold onto something. "Honey." Her voice is a rasp. "Go in my closet. Top shelf. Back left. Shoebox."

"Sure, Ma. Be right back."

The sweet powdery scent of her perfume hits me when I pull open the closet door and I get a glimpse into the not-too-distant future when I'll be doing this again to clean out her things. Something heavy and burning rises in my throat. I choke it down.

Her shoes are lined neatly on the floor beneath her hanging clothes. The box at the back of the top shelf is nearly hidden behind a pile of scarves—handy for covering bruises—and gloves. I pull it down. The label shows a pair of tan dress shoes, size seven, but the box feels too heavy for that.

I take it to her fast in case it's my last-ever chance to help. Settle it gently between her hands.

She shakes her head. "For you." Her voice is heavy. Dread? Exhaustion? Both?

What terrible piece of our past is she dredging up now? Family photos? Dad's wallet? Locks of his hair? Fine, but I'm burning those motherfuckers as soon as she's not around to know.

I sink back into my chair and, at her nod, slide the box onto my knee and ease the lid off, bracing for anything.

Envelopes. Tightly-packed, the once-white paper yellowing. Shit. I'd do almost anything for her, but if she expects me to read love letters to or from my dad, I'm gonna have to draw the line. That wouldn't disappoint her as much as not having grandkids, right?

Ma gestures at the box. "Go on. Look at them."

I sigh. Work my fingers into the mass of envelopes to close around the first one. Ease it out. "Ma, I don't—"

The envelope comes free and her dread becomes mine.

July Tate. 210 Mockingbird Circle. Galway, North Carolina.

The handwriting is mine.

The envelope is unopened. Unpostmarked.

I reach back into the box and pull out another envelope. And another, and another. All the same plain white stationery I'd used when I was sixteen and found myself in Germany against my will.

I count them. One hundred never-sent, never-received, never-read letters in all.

Things I thought I knew—things I'd resigned myself to, beliefs I'd used to chart the course of more than half my life—crumble and smear around me like fresh ash, singeing me.

The eyes I raise to her are murderous, and Ma flinches. She's seen that face too many times, though never on me.

"I'm sorry, Joey," she whispers, and the tears start again.

I rise with the box, cramming the envelopes in every which way, and bolt out of the room. It's the only not-terrible thing I can do.

I throw it on my dresser like it's poisonous. Strip off my jeans and yank on running gear. As soon as Frances gets back from break, I'm out the door and headed for the Poudre trail, Evanescence and my own blood pounding in my ears.

My letters—all those letters—never went out.

July never got my letters.

ACKNOWLEDGMENTS

Love and thanks to all the friends and family who have offered me support and encouragement.

Mary Morris is hands down the world's best critique partner, cheerleader and kick-in-the-pants-when-you-need-it friend. I try to return the favor but damn, those are some big shoes to fill.

At some point a writer has to unclench her fingers and hand her manuscript to others for feedback. My brave, helpful readers have included Pam Jennings, Cathy Miller, Sue Morgan, Carol Loar, Paula Huffman, Casey Jennings, Amy Wasp, and Marlene Riggs. Thank you all for your time and your excellent suggestions!

I'm so happy to have Sara Megibow and KT Literary in my corner and to be working with Deb Werksman, Jocelyn Travis, Rachel Gilmer and Susie Benton of Sourcebooks and Aimee Alker. Sara and Deb, thanks for all your suggestions that made Angus and Rose's story better.

Most people underestimate the difficulty of writing a romance novel. For me, it has taken a lot of practice, a lot of learning, and a lot of help. Thanks to my "teachers" including contest judges, workshop presenters and fellow writers' group members; Cassiel Knight and Heather Howland, who saw promise in earlier versions of this story; and authors Laura Drake, Preslaysa Williams, Suzanne Brockmann, and Elysia Whisler who helped (whether they knew it or not) in various ways at various times.

Love to readers and booksellers (special shout out to Malaprops Books in Asheville), libraries and librarians everywhere (especially the Boiling Springs branch of Spartanburg CPL–I was the woman working by the window who checked out romance novels by the armful).

And finally, to everyone doing anti-bullying, anti-poverty, or PTSD counseling work, thank you for all you do to make the world a better place.

ABOUT THE AUTHOR

Laura Moher is a former associate professor of sociology at the University of South Carolina Upstate in Spartanburg, South Carolina. Her head is full of stories of flawed people who come together to make each other—and their world—a better place. She has deep roots in the South, having grown up in the Louisville, Kentucky, area before moving to the western Carolinas where she taught for eleven years. She has also lived in Colorado and Illinois and is now happily settled near her son in Minnesota.